Prophecy Revealed
Clarima Syd Jones
Jan Toomer

Reality Undefined Publishing LLC

This book is dedicated to my Grams.

Look, Grams! We did it!

Contents

Chapter One

"The World Paranormal Organization was created to certify and legitimize those with abilities. The WPO also offers training for those who need assistance in controlling and maintaining their ability or abilities."
~ Mrs. Witherabbott, United States Head Director of the WPO.

Clari

A man shoved his angry face into hers and rapid fired questions, "Who are you? Where did you come from? What's your name?"

Stupefied, Clari barely registered that the angry man wore military-grade uniform emblazoned in large red script "World Paranormal Organization, HIGH SECURITY TEAM Peace Officer". She squeezed her eyes tightly and then blinked rapidly trying to focus on the bloodshot eyes not inches from her own, but all she managed to focus on was the gun pointed towards her.

She moved her head to try to survey the room to make sense of her surroundings, but too many bodies blocked her view and all the noise around her made it difficult to concentrate.

"Speak! What is your name and occupation!" the officer demanded.

"Clari. My name is Clarima Syd Jones. I'm a registered energy reader and investigator."

"Do you know where you are?" he barked.

Clari's face squinched as she tried to recall everything that just happened. "I knew where I was before something attacked me."

"Stand aside, officer. I'll see to this." A matronly woman who stood five feet five in her motherly two-inch heel pumps, wearing a wool blend skirt and matching jacket, her gray hair pulled back in a severe bun walked up to the WPO Peace Officer. She looked at Clari, "Do you know who I am?"

"Mrs. Witherabbott, the United States Head Director of the WPO?" was Clari's wavering reply.

"Indeed. Can you tell me where we are?"

"I was in El Paso at the annual World Paranormal Organization conference. I was listening to you as you presented the state of WPO's funding. That's when I felt something negative nearby." Clari tried again to scan the room only to find she was surrounded by a mob of onlookers eager to observe the drama unfolding in front of them. Clari adjusted her gaze and realized she was a ragged mess and was still clutching a handful of bloody black feathers still attached to a dead Grigori. Just beyond the dead Grigori's black feathered talons stood a huge semi-transparent snarling wolf that appeared to be guarding Clari.

The realization of what all had just transpired caused Clari to retch and scuttle backwards to get away from her dead attacker; the attacker that she killed.

Mrs. Witherabbott picked up a discarded microphone and using the Voice of God, commanded the crowd of gawkers, "SILENCE. LEAVE US."

As the large crowd began to disperse, Mrs. Witherabbott inspected the crime scene littering the conference space where only moments before she was giving her mundane annual account of WPO's annual spending.

Mrs. Witherabbott looked down at the dead Grigori and gasped. "Serafina?"

Clari was pretty sure that Mrs. Witherabbott was unaware she had spoken out loud.

The WPO Director's eyes turned steel blue as she regarded Clari, and then commanded the Peace Officers, "Take her away."

Clari's five foot two-inch frame was dwarfed by the officers, each one with a firm grasp of her upper arms. So, fists clenched, she had no choice but to with them.

Wolf, now fully physical, growled, he eyes glowing red, * Protect *

* Peace, Wolf. I'll go with them. Stay close, but unseen please *

Wolf whined as he watched Clari being escorted away. Only when she was out of sight did he turn and lope from the conference hall.

The conference attendees loitered in the lobby and as Clari was paraded past them she heard their hushed comments, "What is she?"

"What just happened? What did she do?"

"What was that thing laying on the floor?"

"What a freak!"

"A Level X, I bet!"

Oh, crap, Clari thought. I've lived through a cursed dagger, a cursed dragon, survived attacks from other dimensional beasts and an attack from a human-Grigori with abilities. So why am I so terrified of the WPO?

The Peace Officers showed Clari to her room, which was technically a cell since she was locked in with officers posted outside the door.

Clari paced the room enough times to know that it was eight strides across and twelve strides in length. The room contained a small bed, a grey metal chair and a small desk attached to the wall. A tiny alcove without a door was a toilet and miniscule sink with a small sliver of bar soap.

The door clanked open and a guard handed Clari a towel and washcloth.

As she reached for the dingy linens her tightly fisted hands uncurled and Clari gagged as she watched as the bloodied black feathers gently wafted down to the ground as though unbothered by what was going on around them.

The walls were painted a pasty off-white color, the same color as a person's face right before they barf and Clari thought she might do at any minute.

She hardly recognized herself as she looked into the warbled polished metal mirror. Her hair, usually a bouncy auburn bob, testified she had been through a battle. Her fingers could not make it through the maze of pulp and tangles, until her fingers reached patches of where hair should've been.

After a disappointing sponge bath, Clari attempted to run water over her head but the sink proved too small and her head hurt too much, so she used the small washcloth to little avail. She sponged away as much of the dirt and blood on her clothes as she could and then tried to take inventory in the miserable excuse of a mirror. *Do my eyes look haunted, or is that the look of being terrified?*

Sometime later an officer, well, guard really, entered to place a tray of food on the small table.

"Thank you. Do you know what's going on?" Clari asked him.

The guard shook his head, gave her a sad smile, and left.

Feeling numb, Clari stood in the middle of her room.

The next morning the door opened and two guards entered carrying two folding chairs. They set up the chairs to face Clari's bed and then slipped out of the room.

Mrs. Witherabbott and another woman stepped inside with recording equipment, including a camera. Mrs. Witherabbott looked as nondescript as when she had silenced the people at the conference.

The other woman was the WPO's Legal Department Representative, introduced as Miss Spencer. She wore black pants with a white silk blouse. Strands of red hair escaped her tired French braid.

Even after the sponge bath, Clari felt grungy and was hyper-aware of her physical appearance. She ran her hands down her shirt in another attempt to smooth away the wrinkles and her anxiety.

Mrs. Witherabbott began questioning Clari, "What happened when you came through into the conference room last night?" Mrs. Witherabbott raised her right hand, "No, a better question to start with would be, 'How did you know about the Grigori and explain to us how you orchestrated this catastrophe?'"

Clari sighed, "I suppose it began back when J.R. informed me that someone from the Grigori satellite office was asking him to find me. That was the first time I ever heard of the Grigori."

"And what did J.R. tell you about the Grigori, Clarima?"

Clari explained, "He said that the Grigori are shape-shifters and they have offices all over the globe. They are raised to seek and destroy anyone who shows any signs of abilities that, according to the Grigori, could mean that their targeted individual or individuals might have some awakened trace of Nephilim blood in them. They are trained to hunt and kill what the Grigori deem as Nephilim, or the many-generations-removed peripheral offspring of the fallen angels and humans. The Nephilim are supposedly the sons and daughters of the fallen angels who bred with humans."

Keeping her voice neutral, and monotone, Mrs. Witherabbott replied, "I know what the Nephilim are. So when and where did you meet this

Grigori that you killed?" Mrs. Witherabbott asked. There was no emotion when she asked Clari this question.

"I first met her in a dream. Well, I thought it was a dream. A large black feathered female attacked me in the dream; she called me an 'abomination' and said that I needed to die. But, it was dream walking – or maybe dimensional walking – so I came back from the dream safely but with scratches, dirt and blood. And then, at the conference, I Felt that very same energy signature near me. I was talking with some women at the table when I felt the sting of a whip lash, though I couldn't see the whip, or who was holding it. I energetically reached out and grabbed a hold of the same feathered being that I later learned was a Grigori and somehow we both ended up in the Dragon Realm. I tried hard to evade her. I don't have any fighting skills – but she would not stop attacking me. Something in me snapped. I defended myself as best as I could and then we ended up back here at the conference."

Mrs. Witherabbott pressed, "What about the creature – that rather large wolf that has been seen at your side? Do you own it?"

Clari shook her head, "No, I don't own him. Wolf first showed up at the Beast War out at Mystery Ranch and protected me. It appears that he has since adopted me into his 'pack'. He shows up now and again. I call him 'Wolf'," Clari offered. "I don't have much more information than that concerning Wolf."

"And where is Wolf now?"

"I don't know. He comes and goes as he pleases," Clari informed her.

Hour after hour, Witherabbott and Spencer asked questions and often repeated questions or reframed a question, and kept after Clari until she was beyond exhausted.

After Mrs. Witherabbott announced that they were done for now, Clari asked if she could go home now. "No, Miss Jones. You are currently Level

M. And you may recall, Level M means your certification is suspended pending an investigation. But more importantly, you are also being held for the death of the Italian WPO Director, Serafina Angelucci."

Clari gasped. "The human-Grigori was a WPO Director?"

No one answered her question. Miss Spencer turned off the camera and picked it up. Witherabbott stood up. "We are making arrangements for clean clothing for you. A female officer will then escort you to the showers."

Mrs. Witherabbott knocked on the door to tell the guards that she was finished. Two guards held the door as the women exited, then collected the chairs. The door clicked shut behind them with a finality.

Clari's shoulders sagged.

That had been two days ago.

Morris

Morris' tall frame bolted upright, his green eyes wild and his brown hair stood on end as it had done when he'd his hand on the Van de Graaff static generator back in his high school science class. He bellowed, "Clari!" The monitor sounded an alarm while Morris struggled to get the wires off of him.

Sebastian's blue eyes laser-focused on Morris and his usual silky voice hardened as he addressed Morris, "Morris, stop!", but Sebastian's words went unheard.

Another voice boomed, "Stand down, Detective Morris! That's an order!"

Morris froze. His unfocused eyes moved towards the man that barked the order. His boss, Lieutenant Avery, sported a frown that fit well with his grey almost buzz cut and no-nonsense attitude.

Sebastian moved closer. He put both hands, palm down, on the edge of Morris bed so he could lean into Morris' field of vision. "Morris, you have to calm down or the nurses will sedate you again." No sooner had he uttered those words when the nurses ran through the door. Sebastian continued, "You are in the hospital, Morris. You had a heart attack six days ago. Do you remember?"

As Morris turned his head, his eyes began to focus and then zeroed in on his sometimes friend, sometimes competitor. Morris noted Sebastian's usual laid back calm, collected demeanor was now marred by the look of worry in Sebastian's blue eyes. Morris had never seen Sebastian ruffled before.

"Breathe slowly, Morris," Sebastian encouraged. The nurses stood still and let Sebastian continue to work with Morris to calm him. The heart monitor slowly returned to a normal, safe rhythm.

One nurse admonished Sebastian and Lieutenant Avery, "Whatever you two did, stop it, or I'll have you kicked out of here permanently."

Lieutenant Avery scrubbed his buzz cut and half growled at the nurse. "He woke himself up that way. We had nothing to do with it."

"Yeah, well, if he sets the alarms off again with you two in here, you'll both be banned." She turned and both nurses left the room.

Morris leaned forward and grabbed Sebastian's shirt front. "Something's happened to Clari! We have to help her!"

Sebastian gently removed Morris' hands from his neatly pressed linen shirt and placed them back on the bed. He spoke to Morris while smoothing out the newly acquired wrinkles. "Clari is fine. Well, at least she is safe. But she is safe, Morris, so quit panicking please or they'll sedate you again."

"What do you mean 'again'? Morris' voice sounded scratchy and unused.

"Shortly before we were notified of Clari's incident, you went wonky and your heart rate was off the charts. The doctors immobilized you by inducing deep sedation coma to keep you safe. If you can't keep calm, they'll put you under again. Do you understand, Morris?"

Morris nodded.

Lt. Avery chimed in, "Clari's being detained by the local WPO."

Morris' eyebrows rose as he studied the two most unlikely people to be in his room, especially at the same time. "What has she done now?"

Clari

Fresh clothing and a chance to shower raised Clari's mood a lot, but she was still confined while she waited for the investigation to conclude, if it ever would. But there was nothing to do but sit and wait. She sat on the edge of the bed, leaned over and put her head in her hands.

A puff of dog breath nearly overwhelmed her. She lifted her head and smiled. "Hello, Wolf."

Wolf greeted her with not quite a bark or grunt, but something in between, like a "biff".

Clari smiled. "What brings you here?"

* Go now? * He sounded hopeful.

"Stay. I need to wait for them to decide on what to do with me."

* Alphas? *

"Yes. Well, sort of. It's part of this dimension's rules. I have to wait."

Wolf snorted, unconvinced.

Clari responded with a hollow laugh. "I agree, Wolf."

* Hunger? *

"They feed me here. Full."

She imagined Wolf's demeanor was informing her that he didn't under-stand her ways, but would honor them. He sat and waited with Clari.

Morris

Sebastian explained, "She's not been arrested. She was detained by the WPO Peace Officers pending an investigation."

Lieutenant Avery explained. "There are some...well...gray areas here, so it is still being handled by the WPO. Our police will be called in if they decide it was murder."

The monitor beeps began to speed up again.

"Calm down Henry Morris, or we'll get kicked out and you won't hear what's going on," Sebastian reasoned. He turned to Avery. "Perhaps you are needed at the station? I'll stay with Morris and fill him in the best I can."

Avery's shoulders dropped. "Right. Okay. Are you okay with that, De-tective?"

"Yes, sir."

Clearly out of his comfort zone, Avery looked relieved to go back to work. "Right. I'll check on you later. Take the time needed to heal right, Morris."

"Yes, sir."

Avery stole a quick glance at his watch and then turned to leave for the police station.

Morris turned his attention to back Sebastian. "Talk."

"Boy, you and Clari sure have gotten bossy," Sebastian complained.

"Now," Morris ground out through gritted teeth.

Sebastian let out a dramatic sigh before he began. "In a nutshell, Clari was at the International WPO Conference in El Paso when the Grigori-woman attacked Clari from another realm, causing Clari some physical damage." Sebastian held up a hand, "She's fine. From what J.R. was able to piece together, Clari responded by grabbing the Grigori-woman and Pulling them both into the Dragon Realm. Clari then turned into a dragon, stopped time, snapped the ten foot tall Grigori-woman's neck – in front of J.R.'s clan — then Pulled the Grigori-woman's dead body with her back to the conference room. That's when all heck broke loose. It was also the first time they had to sedate you. You woke up in a total panic apparently the same day Clari-Belle was detained. She's been detained for two days now."

Morris' mouth dropped open, "Clari disappeared, killed the Grigori, and then reappeared with the dead Grigori? In front of the International WPO conference members?"

"Yes, Morris."

"Uh, oh."

Sebastian agreed. "Yeah. Uh, oh."

Morris had an intense day and a half filled with his cardio rehabilitation to learn the exercises that he had to continue at home. His cardio physical therapy appointments were scheduled. He was instructed on lifestyle changes including eating healthier and managing his stress. And on the end of the second day, Morris was released from the hospital. But, as per his doctor's instructions, he was convalescing at home and had to continue his cardio rehab at the local cardio rehab center.

At home, Morris usually found comfort with his heavy leather furniture and his fifty inch television in his living room. Not now though. Restlessness and frustration ate at him. He was stuck at home while Clari was still being held at the local WPO offices waiting for a decision.

Sebastian told Morris that as soon as Sebastian knew anything, he'd call Morris. But Morris itched to do something. Like a petulant boy sent to his room, Morris paced the living room and then plopped down on his couch. He scrubbed his scalp. *Dang. I need a haircut.* Convalescing was not something he did gracefully. He needed a challenge. He craved something to work on.

The phone rang. Morris, excited to see Sebastian's name pop up, answered, "Morris."

"They're done with their interviews and discussions and are preparing to notify Clari of their decision. I'll call when I have more information."

"Thanks, Sebastian."

Sebastian chuckled to himself, but to Morris he drawled, "Short and to the point. Bye, Morris."

Clari

The door opened and a WPO Officer stood at the threshold. "Miss Jones? Director Witherabbott and the WPO Council request your presence." He stepped sideways as he motioned her to exit her room.

As if I had a choice, she thought.

She was escorted to a conference room. The WPO's conference room put the police department's conference room to shame. It smelled of freshly oiled wood. The leather chairs that lined both the conference table and the side wall were inviting and promised comfort. The furniture and plush carpet, under normal circumstances, would demand appreciation. But these weren't normal circumstances.

Only one seat remained available at the table and the officer indicated that she should sit there.

Seven strangers filled the other seats. Mrs. Witherabbott sat at head of the table, opposite of Clari.

Witherabbott addressed Clari. "Clarima Syd Jones, you've been detained pending an investigation and awaiting a ruling as to whether or not you should be allowed to remain a Level IV certified Energy Reader and representative of the World Paranormal Organization. You have also been under investigation to determine your involvement with the death of the WPO's Italian Director Serafina Angelucci. Do you understand, Miss Jones?"

Clari's voice shook, "Yes, Ma'am."

Witherabbott marginally relaxed. "You have put us into a rather delicate situation." She paused to glance at the other council members. She focused back on Clari. "On the matter of the death of Director Serafina Angelucci, charges have been dismissed."

Clari's eyebrows shot up. Witherabbott's warning glance relayed to Clari to keep her mouth shut.

Witherabbott continued. "However, on the matter of your WPO involvement, there are some omissions as to your abilities. The council members have made a decision that your certification will remain suspended until I can determine your current level."

Clari couldn't hold back any longer. "But I don't want to be a Level X and die."

Stunned at Clari's outburst, everyone started talking at the same time. Witherabbott raised her hand and the room quieted. She looked at Clari and demanded, "What are you talking about?"

Clari's fingers fidgeted with the hem of her shirt underneath the table. "Level X is anyone with unknown abilities, or dangerous abilities, and then is never heard from again. So that means you killed them, right?"

The council members all began talking to one another again. Witherabbott motioned for them to quiet down. "Miss Jones, where did you get an idea like that?"

"I had friends who had some pretty awesome abilities if you ask me, and then they were taken away. We heard they had been labeled X and they were never heard from again."

Puzzled, Witherabbott asked, "Are there others who believe that about Level X's as well?"

"Well, yeah."

Witherabbott pulled out her cell phone. "It's Witherabbott. I need you to come up to conference room C. Yes, right now. Thank you." She set her cell on the table and turned her attention to the other council members. "Unless anyone here wants to add to what has already been covered, I think we can adjourn. I'll stay and finish up with Miss Jones."

The council members stood and filed out of the conference room. Witherabbott waved Clari closer. "Why don't you move down towards me so that we can talk without this long table between us?"

Apprehensive, but curious, Clari moved down to sit to the right of Witherabbott. Once Clari settled, Witherabbott told her, "I have someone coming shortly that I would like you to meet."

Clari asked, "Why were the charges dismissed for the Grigori?"

Witherabbott's blue eyes hardened as she answered. "Miss Jones, we did a thorough investigation into your life as well as the incident involving the former Italian Director. We spoke to the Dragon Council, to those who witnessed the incident, and the people in your life. You acted in self-defense. And, we were not pleased at all to discover Ms. Angelucci's...shall we say, after-hours activities.

"We're concerned though, with the abilities you'd hidden from us. We're also confused as to why you hadn't informed us about the threats you'd been receiving. Though now hearing about your — and apparently others — belief about our organization's Level X's, I understand a bit more as to why you hadn't approached us. I hope to remedy this."

A soft knock on the conference room door interrupted them. The door opened and a young woman stepped into the room.

"Ah, Sandra. Thank you for joining us. Sandra, this is Clarima Jones."

Sandra was in her early twenties with a small thin build with waist length dirty blonde hair which she had pulled back into a loose ponytail. Her blue eyes regarded Clari warmly. "Hi, Clarima. It's nice to meet you."

Clari smiled.

"Please come join us, Sandra. I would like you to tell Miss Jones what level you are and what it is you do at WPO."

Sandra sat opposite of Clari. "I'm Level X, and have been for four years now. My ability allows me to know, a little in advance, where, when and how strong natural disasters will strike."

"Wow." Clari wasn't sure if she had spoken out loud.

Sandra shared, "This has actually been helpful in prepping, or clearing an area before the disaster strikes."

Witherabbott added, "Not to mention saving hundreds, if not more, of lives. Sandra, will you explain — in your own words — what Level X means?"

"Sure. Level X's are those abilities that aren't very common. We work to refine them and, like in my case, use them to aid or help others."

Clari wasn't reassured. "You obviously hadn't been killed. Why aren't any Level X's ever heard from again? Why do they disappear?"

Sandra's laughter was melodious. "No, we aren't killed. And, it is the individual's choice to go back or not. But Clarima, how many want to go back and be a freak's freak? I know we really aren't freaks, but Level X's stand out even amongst our own. It really is our choice. WPO does not confine or hide us.

"They work hard to help anyone to learn their abilities, but it's up to each of us to ultimately decide what we will do with our lives and skills."

Witherabbott smiled. "Thank you, Sandra. Miss Jones, do you have any more questions for Sandra before she leaves?"

"Not for Sandra. Thank you, Sandra."

After Sandra left, Witherabbott focused her attention back on Clari. "You were sensitive enough on entry to hide some of your abilities from us. I'm guessing you're probably a Level X, right?"

Clari refused to answer, still afraid to expose all she was able to do ability-wise.

"It is okay, Miss Jones. I really do want to help you, and want to help protect you." Witherabbott picked up her phone again. "Please show our guests in. Thank you."

The conference room door opened again. Three men walked in. Clari was in awe of the power these three men – dragons – radiated. Their combined power felt as though it was too large to be contained in the room. She also noticed that a smoky scent entered the room with them. *I never noticed the smoke smell with J.R. I wonder if the smoke scent is telling of their age or power.* Clari Felt their energy ripple across her skin.

J.R. walked in behind them. His blonde, almost white hair, olive skin, silver eyes and expensive men's wear gave Clari some comfort.

Clari turned to Witherabbott for an explanation.

Witherabbott beamed proudly. "Miss Jones, I'd like to formally introduce you to three representatives of the Dragon Council. The venerable Samson, Rathebone and Reginald. And I am sure you remember J.R.?"

After nodding to the Dragon Council members and J.R., she turned her attention back to Witherabbott.

As soon as the Dragon Council members and J.R. sat, Witherabbott explained, "During our investigation we spoke with all four of the gentlemen seated here. I realize that you don't personally know the Dragon Council members, but they are very aware of you. And J.R. was invaluable during this investigation.

"Should you take me up on our offer to help you learn your abilities, the Dragon Council has offered to help you with your dragon aspect. If you accept, J.R. will oversee your training."

Samson addressed Clari. "I speak for the Council when I say that we would be honored for you to allow us to help refine your dragon, Miss Jones." His gaze swept passed the other three men and returned to Clari. "Please contact J.R. when you have made your decision. If there is nothing else?" The men stood. "Good day, Mrs. Witherabbott. Miss Jones."

"Thank you, Samson. Gentlemen. Oh, and please send in the young man that is waiting outside. Thank you."

The "young man" that entered was none other than Sebastian with his shocking blue eyes, smiled and finger-waved as he crossed the room with the grace of a panther. Clari stood and Sebastian gave her a warm hug. Clari's head reached mid-chest of his tall slender body. Sebastian released Clari and moved towards the director. "Mrs. Witherabbott, a delight."

Witherabbott blushed. "Sebastian, thank you for joining us. Please sit." Witherabbott turned to Clari and smiled. "Another pleasant person I met during the human-Grigori investigation. Sebastian was helpful in providing us with his investigation details. He has become well versed in the human-Grigori phenomenon.

"Again, if you accept my offer of training, Sebastian will tutor you on the history, and hopefully you two can come up with a list of 'tells' of a human-Grigori, such as what is common trait, habit or something that can help us to identify if someone is a Grigori. This training will also include the different abilities this group has been known to exhibit over the years. From there, we can map out a training program for you with our weapons master and our combat master.

"Thank you, Sebastian. We'll coordinate with you, should Miss Jones accept."

Sebastian exited, leaving Witherabbott and Clari alone once again.

Clari was defensive and nervous. "Are there any more people from my life that you wish to parade in front of me?"

Witherabbott's eyebrows rose. "I fear that you've misunderstood my intention, Miss Jones. I am trying to show you that I support, as your friends do, in aiding you.

"And, I am pretty sure that the dragon aspect and what the Grigori incident brought out of you pale in comparison to not only what else you can do — but what you've not even yet discovered about yourself.

"I am excited for you, Miss Clarima Jones, and hope you'll allow me, and the others, to be part of this discovery phase in your life. The decision is yours, of course. Please think about it and let me know.

"Now, unless you have any more questions, here is my business card with my private number and business numbers." Witherabbott handed the card to Clari. "Please feel free to call me should any questions arise or when you've made your decision. And we should be able to begin your re-certification review next week.

"I am sure you are anxious to get back home. There is a driver waiting right outside the door to take you home." Witherabbott stood. "Good day, Miss Jones."

Clari stepped out of the conference room and closed the door behind her. She found Sebastian waiting in the hallway.

"I'm your driver today, Belle. Ready to go home?"

Clari's shoulders and head dropped as she followed him out of the building.

He remained quiet on the drive home, which suited her just fine. She was anxious and lost in her own jumbled thoughts. The incident with the Grigori had exposed her to the world. Some of her most protected secrets had been ripped wide open. She felt raw and cornered.

Sebastian pulled into her driveway, shut the engine off and sat in silence.

She hadn't even realized they'd arrived. Sebastian cleared his throat. She pivoted her head towards with him. When their eyes connected, Sebastian spoke softly. "We're at your house, Belle. I'm going to stay with you for a while. Let's get inside now."

He unfolded his tall and lithe body from the car, walked around to the passenger door and saw that she hadn't moved. He opened her door and offered her his hand. She accepted it, stepped out of the car and glanced up at his face. Clari felt numb and disconnected. Sebastian draped his arm around her shoulder and gently guided her into the house.

Ensconced on the couch with a large glass of pomegranate juice in hand, she still hadn't uttered a word since they had left WPO.

Some distant part of her brain registered that Sebastian was in the house and that she had heard the doorbell. She also recognized that she heard two men talking softly in the background. Exhausted and in shut-down mode, she leaned back, closed her eyes and began to drift towards a light sleep.

She dreamt that she was playing a game of solitaire. *How odd,* she thought in the dream as she stared at the lonely king on the board, *he is nothing until the others join him.* And she slid into a deep sleep.

Chapter Two

The Heart Center ~ The Heart Center is the seat of Love. It is the center for compassion and empathy; love of self and others.

Morris

When he had reached Clari's house, Morris was greeted by a very concerned Sebastian.

"Morris, come in. I think she's asleep on the couch. She's not spoken since I drove her back here."

As they moved to the kitchen table, Sebastian thanked Morris for coming.

Morris' eyes flashed. "I'm glad to do something — you know, besides going nuts for not being there for her. Between worrying about her and not being able to work yet, I've been a bit stir crazy."

"Are you going back to work this week?"

Clenching his fists, Morris shook his head. "No. It's frustrating. I'm supposed to sit around until it's time for me to go for my follow-up appointment. After that, I'll probably be on desk duty for who knows how long until I'm cleared for field work again." Morris shifted in his seat. "Sebastian, um...thank you for, uh, taking care of Clari, and for including me."

Sebastian waved away Morris' discomfort. "No worries, Morris. I respect the fact that we both care for her."

Morris frowned. "I couldn't believe that Clari went ahead with her business anniversary party. I was so angry when Clari used herself as bait to lure out her would-be killer."

"So was I," Sebastian commiserated.

Morris continued, "And then Maria tried to kill Clari at the party, but thankfully you saved her life. You know the police are searching for you, Sebastian. Well, you and your sister, Maria. Both the Lieutenant and I should've brought you in."

Sebastian studied his manicure. "Perhaps we will get to that after we help Clari get back on her feet again."

Morris smiled. "Yeah. Perhaps."

"Now, about Clari, Morris...the WPO dropped the charges against her. They ruled it self-defense." Sebastian went on to describe the people that he saw going into the conference room and finished the story with him bringing her home.

"Thanks for coming, Morris. Since you're staying with her tonight, Morris, I'll go over to Josie's and fill her in. I guess we'll talk tomorrow after you've spent some time with her and get a bead on how she is doing."

Morris grunted his agreement. He walked Sebastian to the door and locked it behind him.

Morris woke up with a start. He couldn't recall where he was. He'd fallen asleep on the recliner while watching Clari as she slept on the couch. Clari got up sometime in the middle of the night and walked towards her bedroom as though she was sleepwalking. Morris heard the door open, and close again.

It took him a while to fall back asleep. He wondered how people got on with their lives when they worried about those close to them, all the time.

Clari

Clari's heart raced as she tried to figure out what woke her. She remembered hearing a loud pop. She opened her Other-Sight and Saw her. Well, "her" was a bit of a stretch...or more of a guess. Clari wasn't really sure how to tell the sex of a skeleton. She was a Reader, not a forensic anthropologist — she just Sensed the skeleton was a female.

She realized a few things while she watched the skeleton as it stood by her bedroom door. First, it was inside Clari's protected space and that could only mean one thing.

* Guys? * Clari asked her Team, * Did you allow her through to me? *

* Affirmative *

Great.

The skeleton joined in on the conversation. * Help find me * she pleaded to Clari.

The second thing Clari realized that though she'd been able to See since she was a wee one and had never, in all of her years, been visited by, or Seen, a skeleton.

And lastly, she Saw that this skeleton was red. Clari ran her hands over her face and asked, "Why are you red?"

* Find me *

She Felt the urgency of the skeleton's plea. The skeleton blinked out, but the energy and her words hung in the air.

She sighed and put up her Other-Sight "Do Not Disturb" energy sign and eventually fell back to sleep.

With the start of a new day and the late-night visitation by a red skeleton put behind her, Clari woke and stretched out and thought how nice it was to be in her own bed again. She reviewed the last few days of having no control; being at the mercy of both the WPO by being held and interrogated by the them and also at the mercy of being attacked by a killer Grigori-woman. Clari felt depressed, very much exposed, and she wasn't quite sure what to do about it. So, one foot in front of the other, she got up and busied herself with her morning routine.

After getting dressed, she aimed straight for the caffeine center in the kitchen. The coffee machine was programmed to have her coffee brewed and ready for her. The carafe was one cup short. Clari had Felt Morris' energy in her house. She turned her phone on and placed it on the counter. Her favorite snarky coffee cup was gone, so she opted for a plain earthenware coffee mug instead.

She filled her coffee mug and blew on it in route to the table where she noticed other signs that Morris was in her house. The recently read newspaper sat next to her missing coffee cup that read: *One lab accident away from being a supervillain.* She heard the guest shower running and a deep voice singing. She couldn't hear the words, but her guess was some country song.

While she mulled over the reasons Morris was in her house, apparently arriving last night, she saw a familiar shimmer in her living room. She watched as a red skeleton waveringly materialized. She remembered the late night visit.

This time the red skeleton held up a cream colored satin-finished evening clutch. Clari froze, coffee cup halted halfway between the counter and her mouth. The red skeleton abruptly disappeared.

She put down her coffee mug. "I don't have a clue to what's going on," she muttered.

Clari was working on breakfast when her peripheral vision noticed movement over by her phone. She saw a fine mist that appeared to be drifting with a purpose, like it was searching for something. Knowing there was nothing she could do until the mist materialized more to make contact she focused back on making breakfast while she waited for Morris to make an appearance.

Engrossed in cooking, she started when her phone chirped. *That's new. My phone doesn't chirp.* Clari wiped her hands and picked up her phone. Her screen showed, "0100100001101001".

Clari felt uneasy. "What...what is this?" She shook her head, put her phone back down and went back to cooking.

"Good morning." Morris' stomach also greeted her by growling loudly.

Clari chuckled. "Morning. Breakfast is ready. Help yourself."

Clari asked Morris, as they filled their plates, "So, I'm guessing Sebastian let you in last night?"

"Yes."

Clari searched Morris' face. His brown hair, that looked red in the sun, was scruffy as usual. His face was paler than normal but a big improvement from the day he was admitted to the hospital. Clari frowned. "Shouldn't you be at home recuperating? Not that I don't like having you're here, but I think I should be caring for you, not vice versa."

"Sebastian was concerned for you. He asked if I'd stay the night to make sure you were okay." Morris scrubbed his face, trying to rub away his frustration. "Clari, we have no idea what you went through. Sebastian told me that you hadn't uttered a word from the time you left the conference room. He thought you checked out. Are you okay? Will you share with me, or Sebastian or Josie...somebody...what happened and how you are doing?"

"I would rather put the whole thing behind me and get on with my life and my work."

Morris sat down across from her. "Seriously?"

Clari's crossed her arms over her chest.

Morris' green eyes hardened. "You're thinking of just going back to work as though this last week had never happened?" He persisted.

She remained stone-faced as she answered. "Yes."

"You can't just continue on like nothing happened. Think about it. Your fears of being 'found out' came true. Your secrets were exposed to the head of the WPO." Clari's mouth dropped open. "Yes, Clari, I've been paying attention to what you've been saying and what you haven't said." He smiled. "I am a detective, remember? Oh, and let's not forget, you killed that Grigori-woman-thing.

"Clari, whenever an officer kills someone — no matter the reason — he is suspended pending an investigation, just like you were following the death of the Grigori-woman.

"The officer also has to go to counseling and can't return for duty until the counselor is satisfied that the officer is fit for duty.

"You skipped the healing process, the whole healing process, Clari. You aren't fit for duty. You need to see a counselor who can help you deal with killing someone. You need help in dealing with all that has transpired. You'll be no help to anyone until you help yourself. And I guarantee you that you will have a meltdown which could possibly lead to, directly or indirectly, causing harm to yourself or others."

Morris' words rattled her. Wordlessly, she stood up and went to her bedroom.

She stretched out on her bed, closed her eyes and began to take slow deep cleansing breaths.

Once calmed, she turned her attention to meditating and was instantly standing before her non-physical guide, Solamba.

Solamba, her lifelong guide and teacher on the energetic realm, always wore a long light blue course-looking robe and reed sandals on his feet. Growing up, Solamba nurtured Clari's compassion and empathy, and soothed her when life seemed to overwhelm her.

She raced into his etheric arms and sobbed. She could feel waves of love, acceptance and encouragement coming from him.

When Clari finished crying, she took in the surroundings to see where they were. It was the garden she often visualized when she was a child. It was her safe place.

When the ridiculing became too much, or she had gone into empathy overload absorbing too much negative energy from another person, she would retreat to her room, close her eyes and enter a meditative state. She always ended up at her favorite garden. Sweet smelling white flowers twined over carved stone columns that surrounded a bubbling fountain. Small birds sang as they flew across the tiled paths, beckoning her to some and sit in the shaded arbor and Feel the peace wash over her like snuggling with a comforting blanket. Even as an adult, she continued to use this same visualization to center herself or when she wanted to sit and talk with one of her guides.

She spoke to Solamba. "I don't understand what is happening to me, Solamba. I've not cried since my father was buried. Now I cry over everything. Not to mention this stuff with the Grigori-woman and the WPO. Please help me. Explain what's going on."

Solamba brought her to a bench in her garden. Both sat and Solamba asked, "Do you remember when Morris had a heart attack and we visited one another while you sat by him in the hospital?"

"Yes."

"I told you that we were 'cleaning out the old so that the new can come in'. You are surely aware by now that sometimes releasing the old can be a painful process. Humans are reluctant to release stuff, even if it's bad for them, because it's familiar."

Clari frowned. "But I haven't gotten rid of anything."

"Are you so sure about that?"

"I can't think of anything, Solamba. Am I missing something?"

'How did you feel right before you left WPO's conference room?"

"Angry. I also felt cornered and exposed."

"Why?"

"Because I had exposed myself to the WPO. My secrets were all laid out, nice and neat."

Solamba sagely nodded.

She didn't get it.

He explained, "You lost the secrets you harbored. The ones that kept you from being the real you when you were around others. It was dead weight. It kept you from moving forward and continuing on your path. You're now free to be the real Clarima, all the time. No more secrets. No more hiding.

"As for crying, this is the closest you've let anyone near you, emotionally, in a very long time. The heart center is opening and working to regain balance."

Clari didn't care if she sounded whiny. "I don't like it. I feel like I've no control over my life anymore. I worked so hard to protect myself. I learned it wasn't safe to trust anyone after my dad died. And WPO, to me, shouldn't have access to all that I can do. I didn't want to be some sort of science experiment for someone or have that institution turn against me, or worse, like label me Level 'X'."

Solamba laughed. "And there's the crux. You're many parts. You have a physical body in this lifetime. But, Clari, you are a soul. Your soul knows exactly what it's doing and it does have control.

"You cry because you are not alone and it brings joy to your heart.

"You cry because, with your heart center opening, you've become more empathic. So, you've become more aware of others' pain, loss, grief as well as their joys.

"You cry because you're tired of always feeling like you had to be the strong one.

"Isn't it wonderful to have so many people who care for you and are willing to help you?

"Isn't it great that you needn't feel as though you are carrying the weight of the whole world on your shoulders?

"Isn't it beautiful to not have to be the strong one all the time?"

As Clari opened her eyes, she realized the tears she cried in her meditation were running down her face. It was time to face her future — the one without her formerly closely guarded secrets.

She dried her face and headed back into the living room. Clari found Morris reading. He put his book down and eyed Clari tenderly as she sat on the couch across from him.

"I'm sorry, Morris."

Morris gave her a tight smile, but offered nothing.

"I think you may be right, Morris. I've never killed anyone before – well, except mosquitoes. I really don't like mosquitoes, they really…"

Morris cleared his throat.

"Oh, sorry. Anyway, I thought I could just move one with my life, but I guess it doesn't work that way."

Morris stood and moved closer. "No, Clari, it doesn't work that way. What changed your mind?"

Clari twisted the hem of her shirt. "You. You did, Morris."

Morris jerked back a bit. "Me?"

"Yes, Morris."

"Didn't you go to your room to talk to your Team?"

"I did."

"Then your Team helped you understand that you need guidance after killing someone, right?"

"No, Morris. I mean, I did talk with a Team member, but we didn't discuss me taking a life. You're the one that made me understand. I'll talk to Mrs. Witherabbott and see if she can refer me to a counselor. And thank you, Morris."

Morris sat and took her hand in his. "You're welcome, Clari. I'm here for you, you know that, right?"

Clari felt a gentle smile emerge as she gently squeezed Morris' hand. "Yeah, I know. Thanks."

"So do you want to tell me what happened? I know what Sebastian told me, but neither of us was there."

Clari shared the events leading up to her detainment at the WPO. "They held me in what they called a 'room', but it was really a type of holding cell. I was so scared, Morris. I had no one to talk to – except when Witherabbott questioned me with the WPO lawyer present. I felt so alone. Oh, and Wolf showed up. He wanted me to leave, but I told him I had to wait."

Morris chuckled. "I wonder what the story is with Wolf. Why can he pop in and out? And how come we all can see him, but we can't see your Team? Do you know?"

"Nope. He just showed up at the ranch during the Beast War or battle, or whatever we call it, and claimed I was part of his pack. I'd never seen him before that, though he pops in now and again. For someone to be able to do that, they have to be a Dimensional Walker. It's like when I physically go to the Dragon Realm. I pop out of here and end up over there. Same thing, well except for I don't think Wolf is from here – our dimension."

"Guides, or members of my Team, do not have a physical body; they're on an energetic realm."

Morris nodded.

"So change of topic, Morris. How are you doing? You had a heart attack. I was only there when you were initially hospitalized. Are you okay? Are you back to work? What did the doctors say?"

"Well, it seems from what Sebastian told me, that I became agitated around the time you were detained, so much so that they kept me sedated for quite a while so my heart could stabilize. The doctor mentioned that he was worried I'd do more damage because I became stressed and panicky. In other words, the doctors induced a medical coma to keep me from damaging my heart more, so I was zonked and missed all of what you went through."

"I was kind of surprised that you could Sense or Feel me, Morris."

"Why is that?"

"Because I spent my childhood building protections so others wouldn't notice me, or Sense or Feel me. I did this to protect myself. I must really like and trust you to allow that connection." Clari look down as she fiddled with her shirt hem. Her hand froze and she looked up and into Morris' eyes.

"What?"

"Well, uh, for that to happen, you also have to trust me."

Without missing a beat, replied, "I do."

Clari beamed at him as her stomach did a little excited flip.

"I'm sorry, Clari," Morris said softly.

Clari frowned. "Sorry for what? You didn't do anything."

"I'm sorry I wasn't there for you."

Clari waved a dismissive hand. "Pah. You couldn't have done anything anyway. I'm sorry I wasn't around for you." Clari muttered, "Stupid Grigori-thing. I sure hope it's all over with now."

Morris stood and offered Clari his hand.

Confused, Clari looked up at him.

"I'd like to give you a hug, Clari. I think we could both use one, eh?"

Clari's face softened as she took his hand again and stood up. Morris opened his arms and she walked into his embrace. *Morris smells and feels like home.*

Clari met Josie at Stephanie's, their favorite restaurant, for some very much needed girl time. Clari was always in awe of her friend. Josie was so beautiful and never noticed the effect she had when she walked into a room

As Josie munched on a carrot her deep brown eyes sought Clari's. "So you are really seeing a counselor?"

"Yeah. I'm glad Morris talked to me about it. I'd never taken a life before. It really does change something inside of you. The therapist is great."

"How did you find her?"

"From Mrs. Witherabbott at WPO. I asked her about therapists who work with Readers."

"Why a therapist who works with Readers?"

"Because in the distant past — though I'm not sure about today — if I told a traditional therapist that I could See and Hear dead people, I would be labeled at least as delusional. Not to mention the other stuff I do. I also don't want have to go through proving myself yet again. We do all that during the WPO certification process."

Josie giggled. "Seriously. That was some intense testing when we tested at WPO for our certification. I'm so glad it's over."

"Not for me. I have to go through it again."

Josie crossed her arms. "Well, petrified posies! All of them again?"

"Petrified what?" Clari shook her head to clear it. "What?"

Josie grinned. "Petrified posies. I figured everyone was tired of me saying, 'Holy moly'. I'm trying new material."

Clari scrutinized Josie as she questioned Josie's sanity. "Okay. Anyway, Mrs. Witherabbott wants to see if my listed abilities are more fine-tuned now, or not. Afterwards, we start with the testing for the newer abilities."

"How are you taking this?" Josie tapped her fingernail on her tooth as she waited for Clari's response.

She shrugged. "I don't think I have a choice in this matter. If I want to keep my WPO certification, I have to play by their rules. But it sucks. I don't have any privacy in that part of my life anymore."

Josie's head bobbed. "I get it. But, on the other side of that coin, Sebastian told me that they're willing to guide and instruct you as well as maybe delve in to see what else you can do. And you have other mentors lined up to help you with other aspects as well. That totally rocks."

"Oh, I forgot to tell you, Josie. Stevie Stiles from our local radio station reached out to me and invited me to come on her show for an interview about the paranormal aspect of what I do."

"That's so cool, Clari! Are you excited?"

"Yes and no. I'm really nervous."

"Why are you nervous?"

"The thought that I'm talking to people that I can't see makes me nervous."

Josie cracked up. "Seriously? You're talking to people that we can't see all the time! This should be easy for you.

Clari shrugged. "Yeah, I guess so. Okay, enough shop talk. It's time for us to let down our hair and have our time."

"I'll agree to that," Josie grinned.

Clari's phone chirped halting their conversation.

"Sounds like you got a new notification sound. What's that tone called?" Josie asked as Clari pulled her phone out.

"I don't know. I didn't set anything new." Clari's eyebrows knit together as she tried to read the new message.

"What's wrong, Clari?"

"I'm not sure, Josie. This is the second message like this. Here, look." Clari handed Josie her phone.

"Looks like binary." Josie read it out loud, "01101000 01101001. What in the cagey capybara does this mean?" Josie handed the phone back.

Clari giggled, "Capybara? Really?"

Josie waggled her eyebrows, "Got to keep you on your toes."

Clari rolled her eyes. "As for my phone, I haven't a clue. I didn't think of it being code thought. I'll look into it later." Clari put her phone away, picked up her fork, "How's work going?" she asked Josie right before she skewered a fried mushroom and put it into her mouth.

"Same old stuff," Josie said, unwinding some of her hair that got caught up in her fork. She tucked the hair behind her ear. "I like what I'm doing, but still don't like the management." Josie went on to describe work as they ate lunch.

Chapter Three

Energy Signature ~ An Energy Signature is the energetic frequency of a being or item and is unique to each individual and item.

Clari

Clari reached up and touched the back of her head, touching the scar. Though she still enjoyed her classic rock music, she didn't have the courage yet to crank it up like she used to before that day...the day that Sebastian's sister, Maria, shot her.

Clari thought back to that day. She had the music turned up so loud it rattled the windows. Clari always did that, past tense, when she cleaned at home. Well, up that fateful day.

Initially, no one knew who had tried to kill Clari, but by the third attempt, it was confirmed that Sebastian's sister, Maria was the culprit. That was also the day that Sebastian's vampiric overlay showed itself. Clari learned that most everyone had a paranormal overlay or energy signature of their ancestral paranormal past, like Lieutenant had wolf shifter in his ancestral past, so he shared some energetic aspects of those beings of old, such as the alpha personality and getting cranky when the full moon came around.

It was also the same day that both Sebastian and Maria disappeared.

Sebastian came back. Maria didn't, and Clari wasn't sure she was ready to find out what happened to Maria.

Lost in the memories, Clari was in the kitchen repotting a plant. Absent-mindedly, she glanced up and gazed out of the sliding glass door, then back down to her plant. She watched her hands as they worked the soil around the pot. She reveled in the feel of the soil and energy from the plant.

She stopped with her hands still in the soil. Her brain was trying to tell her something. *The door.* Something outside didn't belong.

She brushed the dirt off of her hands and walked over to the sliding glass doors that overlooked her backyard. Well, since she lived out the boonies in the desert, she was actually peering over the expanse of the desert between her and "civilization".

Clari noticed something very large, bright red and orange was sprawled out across the desert ground out beyond her property.

What the…? She thought.

Dusting off her hands, she grabbed her phone, ID and keys and got into her SUV. It was four-wheeling time.

Self-driving cars, or automated cars that the majority of people used, were supposed to be safer, but Clari felt that human drivers, while not perfect, could maneuver the roads and traffic all while taking into account the human aspects, such as intuition which plays a big part in driving and anticipating a human's propensity to spontaneity on the road.

Clari read articles about how way back, when the automated tech began, there were almost four-hundred crashes in less than a year, not to mention the un-manned vehicles that caused all sorts of problems, such as causing more accidents by driving the wrong way down a highway. Nope, she'll do the driving, thank you. Not only that, Clari loved the feel of driving her SUV herself. She felt connected with the vehicle, as though it were an extension of her. That and her appreciation for the classic vehicles she picked up from her dad before he died.

She raced further out into the desert flats towards the unknown large red and orange thing. As she neared it she realized it was downed hot air balloon. The basket was severely splintered and was no longer connected to the balloon silks. A downed balloon probably meant at least one person was on the ground.

As the SUV rocked to a dusty stop, Clari pocketed her phone and keys and raced closer on foot. She scanned the area, searching for bodies while she called out. "Hello? Can anyone hear me?"

Clari heard a moan and guessed it was coming from under the old and fragile balloon silks. Carefully shifting and moving the aged silks, Clari noticed the splits and tears on the slightly brittle material. "No wonder the old thing crashed. The silks were so old they were deteriorating." Not knowing exactly where someone may be under the silks, Clari made her way towards where she thought the sound had come from.

When she uncovered a leg, she worked faster and continued to pull the silks away from what turned out to be a woman.

The woman was not only lying in a small puddle of her own blood, but was also covered in dirt and debris that had stuck to her body. The air had a tang of copper in it.

"Hang in there, honey. I'm going to call for help." Clari dialed the emergency number and requested an ambulance.

The woman on the ground became agitated. She rasped, "Tom."

"Correction, we might have two injured," Clari informed the dispatcher, who in turn told her that assistance was on its way.

The dispatcher directed, "Stay on the line until help arrives."

She knew it would take the ambulance at least twenty minutes, probably longer, to reach them, so when the dispatcher told her to say on the phone, she told him, "I'll leave the phone on, but I'll need both hands to see if I can stop her bleeding," and placed the phone on the ground.

Seeing blood coming from the woman's neck, she gently applied pressure over the wound.

She looked over the state of the woman's body and noticed that one leg was also losing a lot of blood. She reached down to try to hold pressure on both places. Clari Felt panicked and frustrated so she yelled over to her phone, "They need to hurry or she won't make it, and I can't leave her to search for the other person!"

Solamba made his presence known by providing a feeling of peace and calm which gently asked Clari's energy to release her panic and frustrations.

Help me to help her, Solamba.

* Calm *

Exasperated, Clari yelled out loud, "Solamba, she doesn't have time for me to get centered."

* Calm *

She forced herself to slow her breathing. As she did, she received a mind-picture. * Can I do it? *

She called on the Source energy and began pouring healing energy into the injured woman and followed with visualizing a white light bubble around the woman.

Clari took a slow, deep breath in and let it out just as slow. She sought the place in-between, the space outside of time and she brought the injured woman with her.

Time slowed. The woman's breathing slowed. The bleeding all but stopped.

"Wow," Clari whispered.

* Stasis *

"Yeah, I see that." Clari switched back to telepathy to continue talking to Solamba.

* *So this will keep her alive until the ambulance arrives?* *

* Yes *

* *Thank you, Solamba. What about the man she called Tom? Will he be okay?* *

* Place him in stasis *

* *Of course!* * She mentally slapped her forehead before she energetically sought out Tom. After locating his energy, she visualized the same steps and pulled him to the space outside of time.

* *Did I get him, Solamba?* *

* Yes *

She continued applying pressure on the woman's wounds as they waited for help to arrive.

Clari released the stasis on the woman after the Emergency Medical Technician's arrived and took over, she was relieved to disconnect the call to dispatch and pocket her phone.

She continued to hold the man's energy until the EMT's located him, and then Clari gently released his stasis. Now that her part in the crisis was over, she began to shake and felt exhaustion overwhelm her.

After she gave her statement to the police, she pulled out her keys to drive back home. As she drove, she thanked Solamba for his guidance and help and for teaching her something new.

Clari woke up several times that night with a nagging headache. She finally woke enough to remember that she didn't normally get headaches, so she needed to pay attention to it. It felt like someone had bashed her on the back right side of her head behind the right ear. It Felt like someone had broken a heavy bottle over her head, and Heard the sound of the bottle cracking at the impact.

Every being has an energy signature – or frequency of a being – it is unique and different for each being. For those with the ability to recognize an energy signature, they can follow it similarly to a dog following a scent trail. A pain signature would combine the energy signature of the being and the vibration or frequency of the pain that the being was experiencing.

This pain energy signature told Clari that the injury had been excruciating and doubted that anyone could've lived through that. Clari Felt like the energy signature belonged to Red Skeleton and perhaps this was another clue. With that one thought, the pain and pain energy signature evaporated. It took some time for her body to calm again. She didn't remember falling back asleep, but the morning alarm came way too soon.

She mulled over the Red Skeleton clues so far, and decided that she still didn't have enough information to begin a search.

After breakfast, she gathered her keys, cell and purse. Her cell phone chirped. Clari swiped the screen and saw a message that read, "01001101 01111001 00100000 01101110 01100001 01101101 01100101 00100000 01101001 01110011 00100000 01100111 01101000 01101111 01110011 01110100."

"Ugh. I can't read this! What am I supposed to do with this? I need to remember to ask Morris when I see him." Clari put her phone away and hurried out the door. She didn't want to be late for her first day of evaluations with Witherabbott.

"Good Morning, Miss Jones."

"Morning, Mrs. Witherabbott."

"I thought we'd start each day with talking about any new incidents, revelations, insights, or abilities since we has last spoke. Is this agreeable with you?"

She gave Witherabbott a half shrug. "That's fine, I guess."

"Good. So what has transpired since we last talked?"

"Well, I wanted to tell you that I'm seeing one of the therapists you had recommended. Thank you. It does appear to be helping."

Witherabbott jotted something down on her notepad. "Very good, Miss Jones. Anything else?"

Witherabbott gave Clari an encouraging grandmotherly smile. Clari wasn't fooled. Mrs. Witherabbott's energy Showed Clari that the older woman was sharp-minded as well as a shrewd business person; she also knew that, though Mrs. Witherabbott's smile was supposed to put her at ease, it didn't. While Clari admired and respected Mrs. Witherabbott, Witherabbott had WPO's best interests in mind, not Clari's.

"No. That's all."

"Very well. Let's go get you started on your re-evaluations then, shall we?"

Witherabbott rose, walked around her desk and started for the door, never checking to see if Clari followed.

After a full day of taking written test after test, Clari was more than ready to unwind at home with a cold glass of pomegranate juice.

When she pulled into her driveway, she had a vision of someone being rolled up in a heavy red cloth or rug like they were wrapped up like a human burrito. The vision dripped away as Clari let out an exasperated sigh. She got out of her SUV and went inside.

As she sat on the couch with her juice, she rang Josie.

"Hi, Clari. How was your testing day?" It was nice to hear Josie's cheery voice.

"Ugh. There were a lot more written tests than I remember from the first time around, and they still aren't any fun."

"I don't envy you. Are you starting your abilities testing tomorrow?" Josie asked.

"I don't think so. I guess since there were so many written tests, they need more time to go over them and decide on a plan for working with me."

"I know you aren't back working with the police department yet, but are you doing your private practice now?"

"No, not yet," Clari whined. "The therapist thought it would be better for me to concentrate on working with her and Witherabbott before going back.

"She feels this may be the best way to get me back on my feet and be well grounded. I have the choice to re-open my private practice whenever I want, but — to tell you the truth, Josie, and as much as it pains me to say so — I want to see where this work with Witherabbott will bring me. You know, since my secret about my abilities came out? Part of me is nervous to find out about my abilities, and another part of me is excited. Before all of this, I was certified as a Level IV Energy Reader, which meant I was considered well versed in Levels I through IIV, including energy manipulation in the forms of telepathy; Seeing/Sensing and communicate with non-physical beings; channeling; Sensing or Knowing others' abilities potential; and trace energy imbalances to where they originated. Will they still consider me an IV or am I the highest level, a Level V? I just don't know."

"Whoa. You not knowing, that's huge coming from you. I'm impressed."

Clari chuckled. "I know, right? But seriously, I'm feeling a bit unsure and scattered, so I think I need this."

"Well, you have my support."

"Thank you, Josie. So what's up in your world?" Clari enjoyed talking with Josie. It provided her some feeling of normalcy.

After a light dinner, Clari stretched out on the couch and called Morris.

"Hello, Clari." His warm voice soothed her.

"Hi, Morris. Am I interrupting anything?" Clari played with the zipper on the couch pillow cover from the pillow she pulled on to her stomach. Zip. Unzip.

"Oh, yes you are interrupting. I'm actively engaged in watching the one little spider plant I have. I'm waiting to see if I can catch it grow another millimeter."

Clari snorted. "And how's that going for you?" Zip, unzip.

"I'm so bored!" Morris whined.

"I get it," Clari commiserated. "How was your day?"

Morris sighed. "Tiring. Who knew cardio rehab could be so exhausting."

Pillow zipper forgotten, "What kinds of things are they having you do?"

"Well, it's like any other structured physical therapy session, except it's for building the heart back up. We start with a warm-up and stretching, and then, for now, a short time of exercise. We're building up the length of time each day, and then a cool down period. Oh, I have to wear a monitor so they can keep a constant check on my vitals."

"Yeah, except for taking your vitals, it does sound like a guided work-out," Clari agreed. "What types of exercises do they have you doing?"

"Lots of good old-fashioned walking; this can include a treadmill or just walking laps around the room there. They also have a stationary bike which I'll be getting on for a bit tomorrow. Oh, and they have rowing machines and an elliptical, but that's for when I'm further along in my rehab. And there are various toys and gadgets for whatever else you need to build up. Like one guy was using small stress balls to squeeze in his hand, and yesterday they gave him little bar bells to start working on," Morris shared.

"Do you think your work-outs are helping you?"

"Yeah, I do. After they quit sedating me, just getting up to walk a few steps had me winded and exhausted. Now I'm at least strong enough to be bored silly at home."

Their conversation turned to their childhoods. Clari laughed as Morris shared his childhood antics, and Clari shared about her childhood – both before and after her father's death.

A while longer talking, the evening caught up with Clari, "Morris, I'm really enjoying this. You're so easy to talk to, I could go on until morning, but I'm really tired and have to work in the morning. "

Morris yawned, "Yeah, me too, Clari. Sleep well and thanks for making my evening not boring."

"My pleasure, Morris. Night."

"Sweet dreams, Clari. Night."

Still in that liminal place between dreams and reality and reluctant to wake up, Clari, saw a large traveling trunk — the old ones from the early twentieth century. She had seen some similar trunks at the local museum in the nineteen thirties and forties section titled "Display of the Decades".

The trunk in her dream was black and glossy with two horizontal wide pewter metal bands that went around the trunk. This trunk was big enough to fold a body into it.

Still not sure what to do with these clues, Clari filed it away with the others as she got up and prepared to go see Witherabbott again.

"Good morning, Miss Jones. Today we are going to see your 'Pulling' process, shall we?" Mrs. Witherabbott's tone of voice made it clear that the question was rhetorical.

Clari responded, "Oh, I thought it would be a while yet before we actually do anything while they go over my test results."

Witherabbott smiled. "No, we are going to head over to one of the training halls now to give it a try."

Clari obediently followed Witherabbott through the hallways, moving further away from any of the places Clari had seen in the WPO building. They stopped in front of elevator doors and Witherabbott pushed the 'Down' button. As they waited for the elevator, Witherabbott turned to Clari. "Miss Jones, it is my hope that we can work comfortably together. I still sense, and see, some reticence from you. I understand.

"On top of everything that has happened, I stepped in to work with you — which is definitely not normal procedures — but I wanted you to feel more comfortable and safe. You had already met me, so I would like to guide you instead of you being with someone less known to you."

"Thank you, Director."

Witherabbott smiled. "And it is my hope that I earn your trust."

Clari didn't share with Witherabbott that trust did not come easily to her.

The elevator doors opened. Both women entered and rode down without another word. Clari moved to the back corner of the elevator. She leaned her back against the elevator wall, crossed her arms and waited for the elevator to stop.

They shortly exited the elevator and a few hallways and turns later, Witherabbott opened a door and motioned her to go inside.

The room was about half the size of a school gymnasium, and painted with a soft blue that seemed to glow. It had high ceilings, concrete walls and a sealed concrete floor with stacks of floor padding against one wall, and folding chairs against another wall. There were also two folding chairs opened and placed in the center of the room. As Clari continued to study the new surroundings, she saw that there were runes and designs painted on each wall, the floor and the ceiling. These runes were just a shade darker that the wall paint.

Clari pointed to the nearest set of runes and asked, "What are these?" Her arm made a sweeping gesture to the walls, "And why does the paint on the walls seem to be glowing?"

Witherabbott spoke as she moved to the center of the room. "The paint is glowing. We have the walls painted with electroluminescent paint. That means it's capable of holding an electric charge and illuminate. If the lights are turned off, the glowing walls make sure you're not left in complete darkness.

"As for the designs you noted on the walls and ceiling, those are wards. We had to put permanent protection around each training room so that no one's abilities could leak out, so-to-speak, and hit someone next door or beyond." Witherabbott sat in one folding chair and waved Clari over to the other. "We only have a few minutes before your trainer arrives, so I'd like to discuss what I would like you do to."

Clari flared. "A trainer? I thought I was working with you."

Unfazed, Witherabbott continued. "You are under my guidance, Miss Jones. Let me ask you this, what if you Pulled the two of us elsewhere and you don't have the knowledge of how to get us back? What do you think would happen?"

Clari hadn't thought of that, and she didn't have a clue as to what could happen.

Witherabbott continued. "First, WPO would be very upset with you for misplacing me." Witherabbott chuckled as she pictured that scenario. "Also, I don't have the skills or abilities required to get us back from who knows where. My abilities and skill sets are in other areas. The trainer coming to work with you is one who is able to teleport. He can bring you both back safely if you are unable.

"Please remember, Miss Jones, you Pulled and relocated while under pressure and fighting for your life. But now I'm asking you to do this with conscious intent. Not to save your life, but to learn. Understand?"

"Yes, ma'am."

The door opened and a spindly man approached. The guy dressed as though he was a teenaged nerd from the twentieth century. He wore a white short-sleeve button up shirt with khaki pants and sported heavy tortoise shell framed glasses. He tapped away on his retro 20th century looking tablet as he approached. The only thing missing was the white tape holding his glasses together and the plastic pocket protector.

I'll bet he snorts when he laughs. Clari instantly regretted her thoughts and chided herself.

He stopped in front of Mrs. Witherabbott and smiled at her. Mrs. Witherabbott smiled back, "Good morning, Gerald. I'd like you to meet Miss Clarima Jones."

Clari raised her hand in an informal wave as he turned his attention on her. Her breath caught when she saw his eyes. They were a gorgeous aqua blue-green. She had never seen that color...ever.

"You have beautiful eyes."

Gerald let loose a deep, hearty snort. "Thank you, Miss Clarima Jones. And it's nice to meet you too."

She blushed. *Crap, I said that out loud.* "Please call me Clari, Gerald."

"Okay, let's give this a go," Mrs. Witherabbott announced. She turned to Clari. "Do you have to have been to a place to Jump there?"

Clari shrugged. "I didn't have a place in mind. I just ended up...uh..." Clari gave a quick glance towards Gerald, "...there."

Witherabbott absentmindedly slid the pendant she wore back and forth on its chain. She released the pendant, turned and asked Gerald, "What do you recommend for new Jumpers, Gerald?"

"We start them with very familiar places — like their homes."

"Excellent. Miss Jones, would you kindly Pull — what we call 'Jumping' — you and Gerald to either your home or office?"

"I'll try." She held her hand out to Gerald who grasped hers gently but firmly.

"I want you to visualize the place we are going and Pull us to it. Whenever you're ready," Gerald instructed her.

She thought about her office lobby and focused on Pulling her and Gerald to it, but ended up on the plateau in the Dragon Realm where she had Pulled and killed the Grigori-woman, only this time, the plateau was deserted.

Clari frowned. Gerald chuckled. "I'm guessing this is neither your home nor your office?"

Her frown deepened as she shook her head.

"Okay. Now bring us back to the training room."

She took his offered hand and pictured the training room. Nothing happened

He smiled. "It's okay. Don't panic or get stressed. Take a deep breath, relax, visualize and Pull."

She did as he suggested. She closed her eyes, took a slow deep breath, visualized the training room and Pulled. This time she noticed a shift inside of her body, followed by a slight sideways whooshing feeling. She opened her eyes and saw that they now stood before a startled Witherabbott.

Witherabbott asked, "What's wrong? What happened?"

Confused, Gerald's head ping-ponged from Witherabbott to Clari and back again. "What do you mean, Director?"

Witherabbott frowned. "What happened? You two were only gone for three to five seconds."

Startled by this news, he sharply turned to Clari. "Three to five seconds?"

Clari's stomach sank. She shook her head, "That isn't right. I had to try twice to get back here."

This time Witherabbott's eyes twinkled as she smiled. "Did you go where you intended?'

"No, ma'am. We went to the plateau."

"Ah. Well in a way that makes sense. It is where you last went for safety. Ready to try again?"

"Okay." Clari held her hand out to Gerald and Pulled.

They stood in the middle of her office lobby. Her face lit up. "Yes!"

He smiled at her exuberance. "Your office?'

"Yes."

"Great job. Now, bring us back the training room."

And they were back.

For hours, Clari Jumped the two of them to her living room, parking lot at her office, her laundry room and to her kitchen. "Oh! Since we're here, Gerald, I need to make sure I turned the coffee maker off!"

Gerald snorted again. "You know, there's technology to keep track of that."

"Pfft. I don't trust AI technology, Gerald. I'll do it the old-fashioned way, thank you."

They continued with popping into her backyard, her office and back to WPO again.

Witherabbott halted the practice and told them to get some lunch and to come back in an hour. They all went their separate ways.

After lunch, all three met back in the training room. Witherabbott suggested experimenting with Jumping to places Clari hadn't been. Gerald agreed.

"Okay, Clari," Gerald began, "I want you to Jump to 29°58'45.03"N 31°08'03.69"E."

"What?"

"That's where I want you to take us," Gerald explained.

"Where? All you did was spout off some numbers."

Gerald's head bobbed up and down, reminding Clari of the little dog bobble heads. "Exactly. They are coordinates. Focus on the coordinates and Jump us to that location."

This conversation didn't make any sense. "I don't get it, Gerald."

"It's simple. Just because your conscious mind doesn't understand what those coordinates mean, doesn't mean that your subconscious energy self is clueless. Your energy self knows exactly what they mean. Trust the process."

Clari glanced over to Mrs. Witherabbott, whose face revealed nothing, so she looked back at Gerald.

"Give it a try. Ready?" Gerald grabbed Clari's hand while he recited the string of numbers again. "29°58'45.03"N 31°08'03.69"E."

She and Gerald showed up beside the Great Pyramid of Egypt...a real pyramid, in Egypt.

"Wow, that is so cool!" Clari admitted enthusiastically. "I've never been here before. Can we stay for a bit?"

Gerald laughed, "Yes, we are allowed to stay for an hour. I'll be happy to show you around the immediate area."

The hour passed quickly. Clari, hot and tired, didn't argue when Gerald announced it was time to leave. He asked her to visualize the training room and they swiftly returned there.

Mrs. Witherabbott was pleased after they returned. "What did you think of this last Jump, Miss Jones?"

"Pretty cool. I'd never been to Egypt, and was excited to see the pyramids."

Mrs. Witherabbott beamed. "Well done. Gerald, I believe that's enough Jumping for today." Witherabbott turned back to Clari. "I will leave you in Gerald's capable hands. Gerald has a few things to go over with you and then you are done for the day. Congratulations again on your Jumping."

"Thank you, Director."

After Witherabbott left, Clari and Gerald sat in the folding chairs. "Do you have any questions?"

"Yes. Can we Jump anywhere we want at any time?"

"Uh, no. The ones you do with me — outside of your home and office — are pre-arranged with the country, or location that we teleport to. Take today, the pyramids in Egypt. I contacted them to let them know of a possible student Jump and gave them the exact coordinates I gave you. They make sure, for that day that the exact coordinate's location is free and clear of people and items so you don't accidently Jump into or onto anyone or anything and that's why we recommend to all Jumpers to be very careful using this ability. We do the same for any other out-of-country student who Jumps here.

"We're also given immunity, for one hour, after we arrive...unless we commit a crime outside of not possessing our passports."

"Thank you, Gerald. It really was amazing."

"You're very welcome, but I bet by the time I'm done teaching you, you won't be so cheerful or thankful." He gave her a wicked smile while he twirled his imaginary villain mustache. "Yes, today was fun, but I'll work you hard. Most people are happy to see me go by the end of the training time."

She laughed. "Okay, you've provided fair warning. I'll wait and see how it goes."

"Good enough. Same time, right here, tomorrow morning. See you then."

Disappointed she couldn't Jump, Clari drove over to her office. The public was unaware that her certification was pending, so requests still came in. She returned phone calls first, informing them of her re-certification status and referred most of the people to Josie. A few asked that she call them when she was reinstated.

Clari sat at her desk and commanded, "Computer on with keyboard," and a virtual keyboard appeared on her desk with a screen hovering at eye level with her. Clari was one of the hold-outs. She didn't want all of the electronic stuff under her skin in a chip. She didn't want to 'integrate' with the modern technology of the day. But she wasn't the only one, the police and the military remained retro, so the old technology stayed active.

The Geostorm of 2049 changed everything in a nanosecond. Since humans had to basically start from scratch with the knowledge they had, things moved slowly in bringing technology back. They didn't want to make the same mistakes that were made prior to the geostorm.

Clari wondered if the G5 storm hadn't collapsed the grid, where would we be with the human and technology relationship. Would we have more artificial intelligence beyond our smart phones? Would we have food replicators like the old science fiction shows? She didn't have those answers, but she, like Morris, loved muddling through the "What ifs?"

Clari opened the billing program and began preparing invoices. As she typed, she noticed the hanging lamp over her desk didn't appear to be providing enough light, as though the light bulb was struggling to push back the darkness that threatened to engulf her office. She knew that this — whatever "this" was — was not natural. Something was messing with her.

The shadows in the corners in her office deepened, and then the shadows within the shadows began to stir.

Her inner alarms clanged loudly — telling her to get the heck out of there, and her heartbeat sped up in agreement with the alarms.

The moving shadows slithered closer to her. As they moved, they immersed more of the room into complete darkness.

Clari stood. "I call upon my Team, the Archangels, and the Other Beings of Light. Fill me, and my spaces, with your pure light and love. The dark is commanded to leave *now*!"

As though someone flipped on a switch, the office was once again bright. The shadows were gone. Clari imagined the relief from her previously struggling lamp probably matched her own.

She thanked her Team, the Archangels and the Beings of Light for their support. After she re-shielded her office building, she requested the Archangels to keep it surrounded and protected.

She'd been so focused on the Other-Realm that she nearly jumped out of her skin and about peed her pants when the phone rang. *Get a grip*, she fussed as she reached for the phone.

She grabbed a pencil and began doodling on a notepad, but since she was concentrating on the caller, she was oblivious to what she was putting on the paper. After the caller set an appointment with her, she rang off. Clari ripped the doodle off of the notepad and was preparing to toss it into the trashcan when her eyes caught a word. She took a closer look and was startled at what she saw. She had never doodled words before.

Time and time again
as it moves closer
power called to me
now, so close.

There are no more
ribbons of light.

Only the blinding
whiteness temporarily
absorbing the
power of sight.

She wasn't sure whose message it was, or what it meant. She put the date and time on it and slipped it into the desk drawer.

Clari's heart raced as she struggled to make sense of what had dragged her from sleep only enough to be caught between deep sleep and being awake.

She smelled water and a lot of it.

Her mind scrambled as it scanned her memories — searching for a comparison. It smelled like moving water, not stagnant or still. It was either flowing water or a large body of water that had continuous movement.

She next Sensed that she was tangled up in something.

In her semi-dream state, she saw that she was on a rocky shore line, tangled in seaweed as the icy water lapped at her, making the seaweed shift each time the water rose and receded again. The sky was heavy with large black clouds, or maybe dark smoke. The dreariness of the landscape made her think of the eastern coast.

Gasping, Clari struggled to free herself from her jumbled sheets as she disconnected from the last vestiges of the vision dream and stumbled into the bathroom, where she stood under the hottest shower trying to warm her icy bones.

Dressed warmly and holding a cup of hot coffee, she noticed that —
though the sun was shining — she was still cold and felt as though the dark
clouds from her vision engulfed her.

Clari's phone chirped startling her. She saw the message, "Hi."

"Hi? Who is this?" Clari thought out loud.

Another message popped up. "Can you read this?"

"Well, yeah, I can read it," Clari told the phone. "Why is it asking me
this?"

"Because you couldn't seem to read my other messages. My name is
Ghost."

"Wait a minute," ordered Clari. "You answered my verbal question.
Who are you, Ghost? How'd you get my number? Are you stalking me?"
Clari took a step back and stared at her phone.

Ghost wrote, "I didn't mean to frighten you. No, I'm not stalking you.
I found your device, moved into it, and have been trying to communicate
with you."

"What do you mean you 'moved into it'? Oh, wait! You said your name
is Ghost, so you are a ghost, as in a deceased person?" Clari asked.

Ghost typed, "Yes."

"Just when I think my life can't get any stranger. Why are you in my
phone, Ghost?"

"Learning. Tired. Later."

Clari rubbed her cheek. "Huh. I guess Ghost is done for now."

Chapter Four

Death Premonition – A forewarning or feeling that someone is going to die.

Clari

At the completion of another exhausting, but exciting day of Jumping with Gerald — this time it included a trip to Champ de Mars, where she got to see the Eiffel Tower — Clari went home.

After dinner, she grabbed her phone and was heading to crash on the couch when she saw a large dust bunny on the floor. She leaned over to pick it up. When she touched it, she received quick flashes like she was watching a slide show in fast forward. The pictures she was able to hold onto were of a red rug, a travel trunk and an attic.

She grabbed the ball of dust and dropped into the trash. After washing her hands she sat down to call Josie, hoping she was free to chat.

Josie answered her phone with, "You're still alive I presume?" followed by her infectious giggle.

"Hi, Josie. You have time to chat now?"

"Are you kidding? Of course! I haven't heard about your first few days with Witherabbott. You don't sound like you want to choke anyone, so I'll dare to venture that it's all going well?"

Clari shared about learning to Jump with Gerald. "I also got to Jump to Egypt. We landed near the large pyramid in Giza."

"Ferocious flying lemurs!" proclaimed Josie. "So you are a teleporter? And you went to Egypt without me?"

Clari laughed. "Where in the world do you come up with those sayings, Josie?" She could feel Josie's smile over the phone.

"Hey, you keep surprising me with new stuff — the least I can do is to keep you guessing with my outlandish, and dare I say, entertaining sayings. And you aren't getting off the hook, lady. You popped over to Egypt without me. When are you going to teleport me to the pyramids?"

Clari explained the agreements with other countries for training purposes and that she was not able to Jump willy-nilly. "But, I promise that as soon as I'm well versed in consciously controlling my Jumping, I'll bring you somewhere as a treat."

Josie, appeased by Clari's offer, announced, "Done! Now, I've got some news of my own."

"Ooh, do tell!"

"I've got a new man in my life." Josie told her.

Clari could sense Josie's anxiety; she knew that this was a very big deal as Josie was a lot like her in the relationship arena; growing up as empathic Readers had affected both of them. Trusting and getting close was not an easy thing to do.

"Wow, Josie," Clari spoke reverently, "Care to share?"

"His name is Brennan Doyle. He is six foot five inches tall. He has dirty blonde hair and dreamy green eyes — but not the dark green like Morris' eyes — his are softer green, more like that scruffy alley cat with the gorgeous eyes that used to hang around your office. You know the one with green eyes that had yellow rays in it? That's what Brennan's eyes look like."

"That is so awesome, Josie. Where did you two meet?"

"We met at the food co-op. We were both trying to decide on dried beans at the bulk containers. Can you picture it? I mean, dried beans are not very romantic."

Clari giggled. "But it sounds perfect, Josie. You are very adamant about supporting local co-ops, so I guess you might have that in common with Brennan. I'm happy for you. Do I get to meet him soon?"

"Not until I know it's going to be a longer than a two week relationship."

"Got it. Let me know."

Josie usually waited at least two weeks of hanging-out time with someone to see if she was comfortable being the real her with them, and if they could handle Josie being her real self. Josie often told Clari that there was no sense in changing one's self to please another.

After an hour of important girl chat time, they agreed to talk in a few days.

Clari called Morris. "Hey, Morris, do you want to hang out this weekend? We can play catch-up and have Buddha bowls for dinner."

"Hi Clari. Have what now? What kind of bowls?"

Clari imagined him scratching his head. "Buddha bowls. They've also been called Hippie bowls."

"Okay, I'll bite. What are Buddha bowls?"

"It's a bowl with a variety of vegetables, a grain, protein and some type of sauce and topping. I know you're supposed to be eating healthy meals, and Buddha bowls are healthy and versatile. Let me ask you, Morris. Food-wise, what don't you like?"

"Cilantro, raw oysters, and before you ask, raw oysters are a texture thing with me. Oh, grapefruit. Not sure why, but I can't stand grapefruit. And cottage cheese is a no go for me."

Clari laughed. "Okay, absolutely no grapefruit, raw oysters, cottage cheese or cilantro. Any other foods you don't like?'

"I think that covers it."

"Great! I'll make some Buddha bowls for us so you can try one. Are you game, Morris?"

"Okay. I'll trust you, Clari."

"Mwa-ha-ha! He has fallen for my treachery!"

"Cute, Clari. So we're good for Saturday, say around three p.m.? We can catch-up and then dinner? Do you want me to bring anything?"

"Nope. We're good. Thanks, Morris. I'll see you Saturday, and have a great rest of the week."

"You, too, Clari. Bye."

Clari knew that one part of her was dreaming and she was quite aware of it while the other part was completely absorbed in the dream.

She dreamt of a rather unpleasant man, his greed sickened her, hauling a travel trunk onto a ship. In the dream, she knew that he planned on dumping the trunk over the side of the ship once they were out on the water and he could create a diversion.

The dream ended and as she drifted off, her mind asked "Can I Jump into my dreams?" She spent the rest of the night in a restless sleep as if she were weaving and rolling on a turbulent sea.

Clari and Gerald spent the morning teleporting. She had been practicing so much that it had become second nature and was, well, quite boring.

Apparently Gerald noticed this in her and began changing it up. He wanted to see if she could teleport herself, him and objects all at once. He started her off with small items and moved her up to Jumping both Gerald and her office copy machine with her. He then led her to an old car in the far back corner of the WPO parking lot.

Gerald saw Clari admiring the car and as the approached it, he proudly shared, "It's a 2022 Chrysler Dodge Charger. The Charger has SRT, 6.2L Hemi V8 engine with 797 horsepower with 707 LB-FT of Torque. Dodge quit making what they called 'muscle cars' in 2022. From there they moved into electric cars. If you ask me, the electric cars today are nowhere near the power, so nowhere near to being as fun as this one. Some friends and I worked to restore it and now we use it here, at WPO, to help train Jumping."

"Is that the original paint color?" Clari asked him. The color seemed to shimmer and alternate between a deep red and a brown.

Gerald puffed up like a proud peacock. "Yes, but we had to have it made special because it's not been in use since they discontinued this car, and well, that was well over 100 years ago. They got it as close as they could to the original color, which was called 'Sinamon Stick'."

"Wait, you mentioned you restored it to be used here for practice Jumping? Isn't that a rather expensive training tool?"

Gerald shrugged. "Yes, but we didn't pay for it. WPO did. Why they wanted a restored antique car beats me, but I did have a lot of fun working on it."

Clari reverently caressed the hood. Frowning, she looked over to Gerald who had a mischievous grin. Clari slid her hand across the hood again. "What the...do I smell cinnamon?"

Gerald's face lit up. "Yep. When I asked the guy to remake the classic color 'Sinamon Stick' paint color, he told me he was offering scented paint and asked if I was interested. I wasn't paying for it, so told him 'Yes'."

Clari's voice held a hint of awe. "It's kind of like the old scratch and sniff from that time frame."

Gerald nodded, "And the smell increases with just about any kind of touch. The bad part is that I often find critters, especially dogs, licking it because it smells so good."

Clari was curious, "Yuck. But does it taste like cinnamon?"

"I'm not going to lick the car, Clari, but you're welcome to."

"Ugh. No thanks, Gerald. Not my kind of thing."

"Okay, back to work. Now, I want you to Jump you, me and the car, taking us to your office parking lot."

"Uh, Gerald. It's one thing to Jump with you and the office copy machine, but a car?"

Gerald offered his hand and smiled. "Shall we?"

Clari took his hand in one of her hands and placed her other hand on the car and Jumped. All three arrived at her office parking lot.

"Great job, Clari. Now bring us back."

She did.

Gerald walked around, opened the passenger car door, and slid into the seat. "Come on, we've got someplace to be. Hop in."

Clari got behind the wheel. "Is this an auto-car, or do I get to drive it?"

"Oh, no, no auto-driving for this classic beauty! I even had keys made for it."

Clari rolled her eyes and held out her hand, "Key?"

Gerald handed her a key. Clari cranked the car and was pleased to hear it purr under the hood. She loved a well-cared for engine. She stroked the dashboard, and the smell of rain filled the car. "Uh, Gerald, why do I smell rain?"

Gerald sat taller. "We've installed a mood sensor. Depending on your touch within the car or your tone of voice and it will produce a scent to calm you down, or if you're already calm, a scent that it thinks you'll like."

Clari turned her attention back to Gerald. "Weird, but nice. I'll bet they didn't have that in the original. Okay, where to?"

Gerald motioned forward. "I'll tell you after we get on the road. Head for the interstate."

Clari enjoyed the feel of the car. As they reached the speed limit on the interstate, Clari asked, "Spill. Where are we going?"

Gerald rattled off some coordinates, "47.068031670561176, -104.465 75176795423", and commanded, "Jump now!"

Clari freaked, yelled at him. "I'm doing seventy-five miles an hour on the interstate and you want me to Jump?" The car released the calming scent of lavender.

"Yes, Jump now. And don't forget to bring me and the car with you. Now!"

"Ugh!" Clari took a deep breath, Jumped, and was doing seventy-five miles per hour on an interstate somewhere else. "Crap, Gerald. Where are we?"

Gerald's grin was actually blinding. "Interstate 94 in Montana."

"What? Montana?"

She saw a sign for a rest area. She pulled into the rest area, parked the car and worked to pry her other trembling hand off of the steering wheel before she turned her frustrations towards Gerald. She let loose, "What the heck, Gerald? You scared the crap out of me!"

Gerald didn't stop grinning, and with a touch of awe in his voice, shared, "That was cool."

Her traitorous lips moved into a rather large smile. "It was, wasn't it?" Suddenly, the car filled with the scent of chocolate chip cookies.

Gerald, eyes sparkling with excitement, "Feel okay? Care to Jump us back to the parking lot at WPO?"

"From right here? Not while driving, right? I think I need to recuperate before I do that again."

"Yes, just Jump the car, with us in it, back to its parking spot at WPO."

"Okay." She did and landed on the outskirts of the WPO parking lot. There were no other vehicles, so she sped three donuts and coming to a rocking stop with a huge grin on her face. As she opened the driver's door, she asked, "Is there any way to turn the mood sensor off? I'm really hungry now."

Gerald chuckled as he got out of the car. "Yeah, I can do that. And good job today", he praised and then called it quits for the rest of the day and weekend. He told her to report to Mrs. Witherabbott on Monday morning.

Clari was excited to see Morris. After an intense week of Jumping, she was ready for some downtime with a friend.

Morris arrived at Clari's wearing blue jeans, and a denim shirt.

"Wow. Out of your detective clothes today, eh? Looking good, Morris."

"Uh, thanks, Clari," he mumbled, his face turned bright red.

Clari pulled out the plates and napkins. "Can you please clean off the table and get it ready for us to eat at? Oh, and Morris, how come you don't wear clothes like that at work? Are you not allowed to wear jeans?"

Morris gave a quick nod. "Yeah, we're allowed. But, I've learned, as have others in my field, that by wearing cheap tan or black pants, cheap polos and easy-to-forget jackets, we can replace them often."

"Really? Why?" Clari asked.

"Think about my job. I'm climbing or trekking into dirty and sometimes dangerous places. And between that and sweating in the heat, working long hours and being exposed to chemicals, liquids and fluids – possibly including bodily fluids – my clothes don't always come clean in the wash. The other detectives and I buy cheap, disposable clothing. We save our regular clothes for our days off."

Clari's lip curled. "Ew. Sorry I asked."

"My turn. Why do you have so many coffee cups and t-shirts with sarcastic sayings on them?" Morris chucked as he began pulling the papers together into a neat stack.

She smiled. "Because sometimes it's inappropriate for my snarkiness to come out of my mouth. I guess you could say that the coffee cups and t-shirts are my passive-aggressive outlets for my sometimes defiant attitude."

Morris's laughter filled the room. He picked up the pile of papers and was turning to place them on the living room coffee table.

Clari pulled out silverware from the drawer.

On top of the stack, he saw a poem in her handwriting. He stopped to read it.

Sometimes

Sometimes others' grief is too heavy.

Sometimes others' anger is too abrasive.

Sometimes others' fear is overwhelming.

Sometimes I Feel too much.

Sometimes I Know too much.

Sometimes I Hear too much.

Sometimes it's painful to See so much.

Sometimes being an empath hurts too much.

Sometimes I feel so small against all of those big energies.

Sometimes I want to hide from the world's negative experience energies.

Sometimes I ache for the peace of my true home.

But, most times I feel so blessed to be in the midst of all of this and helping others. ~

Morris looked over, "Uh, Clari?"

"Yeah?"

Morris held up the poem, his head slightly tilted to one side asking an unspoken question.

"Being nosy, Morris?"

Morris defended his actions. "Hey! It was sitting on top of your papers. You asked me to pick them up."

"Relax, I'm teasing. I wasn't hiding it."

Poem still hand, Morris commented, "I never thought about your abilities that way before. Do you regret them?"

Clari's face softened. "No, Morris, not at all. Just sometimes it can be a bit overwhelming." Clari put the knife on the counter and walked over to the table. Morris handed her the poem. Clari sat and looked at the words she had written.

Morris pulled out a chair and sat with her at the table.

Clari continued, "But there's other times when it's really hard. I'd say about 95% of the time I love my abilities and using them to help people. But that 5%? That 5% can really suck."

"What does that 5% look like or feel like, Clari? Are you okay talking about it?"

Clari stared at the poem. She finally looked up at Morris. "Having to See or Know something that I really don't want to See or Know."

Morris leaned towards her and gently pushed. "Like what, Clari?"

Clari dropped her gaze. "Death," Clari whispered. Tears filled her eyes. She took a ragged breath and watched her hands fidget with the paper. "One of the worst is Seeing or Knowing how someone's going to die. I may not Know when, but I Know how and whether or not it will be soon."

Morris sat back. "Do you See everyone's death?"

Clari shook her head. "Not everyone. And I'm thankful for that."

"Have you Seen my death, Clari?"

Clari's head jerked up. "No! Uh, do you want me to? I'd rather not."

"No! I mean, I don't want to know. I want to spend my time enjoying life and not worrying if today's 'the day', or if an incident was 'the one' that kills me off. Does that make sense?"

The half-smile she gave Morris didn't reach her eyes.

As Morris leaned towards Clari again, he stretched his arm out across the table, offering her his hand. "I wish I could take your pain and sorrow, Clari, but I don't know how."

Clari took his hand.

Morris continued, "So if you See a death and it's affected you this much, does that mean you've Seen the death of someone close to you?"

She gave a shaky nod; the tears spilled over.

"Is there something you can do? I mean, are you being Shown this so you can alter it by warning them?"

"No. It's not something I can change, Morris."

He frowned. "Then what's the use of you being Shown it, then? I don't understand."

Clari took a deep breath. "To prepare me and it gives me time to grieve."

Morris gently squeezed her hand. "I'm so sorry, Clari."

Both sat quietly for a few moments.

"What are some of the other hard ones, Clari?"

She squirmed and removed her hand from Morris'. She shoved both her hands under the table. "Crowds are hard. There are so many emotions and thoughts in one space and I can feel overwhelmed by it all. Let's just say that the negative emotions and thoughts often broadcast louder than the positive ones.

"It's not all hard, Morris. I just gave you some examples of the harder aspects. There are some beautiful aspects as well. For example, when I was around seventeen years old, I was questioning what the purpose was of my abilities...like my empathic ability. What good is it to Feel other's emotions? Well, one day I went to the park. You know the one with a pond? I was enjoying the sun and fresh air one beautiful spring day. I sat on a bench and watched the ducks in the pond. I had closed my eyes to soak in some sun when I was interrupted by a wave of grief, sadness and anger all mixed together. I took a few deep breaths, shielded to release the emotions that weren't mine.

"That's when I felt a hand on my shoulder. I looked up and saw an elderly woman with tears in her eyes and she was trembling. I had a sudden Knowing that she was grieving the loss of someone close to her. I stood up, put my arm around her and just held her for a few moments, letting her know that she wasn't alone.

"We stood there embracing each other in silent understanding. I Felt her grief and pain, but also her love and strength. I Felt a sense of peace within myself. I was amazed at how connected we were to each other, despite so much pain.

"Finally, she released me and we both stood back and looked at each other. She smiled, 'Thank you. Your kindness has helped me more than you know. I'm grateful that you were here today.'

"I smiled back at her and told her that she was welcome and I was glad to have been there for her and that I understood what it's like to feel too much and bear too much.

"She nodded and gave me one last hug before she walked away. As I watched her go, I was renewed with a sense of purpose and was thankful for not only the gift of being an empath, but all of my abilities. I knew that helping others in their time of need was not only a privilege, but also a responsibility. I'm blessed to have been able to be there for that woman and that I can continue to use my gifts to help others. Later, I learned to turn down my abilities until or unless I wanted to use them, and that's what led me to get my certification with WPO.

"So, yes, I wrote this poem, and yes it can be hard sometimes...but I'm serious when I wrote that I felt so blessed to be in the midst and help people. I think it all balances out."

Morris stood up and held his hand out to Clari. Not sure what he was up to, she took a moment to consider taking his hand. Curiosity won and she reached out and placed her hand in Morris'. He gently pulled her arm, encouraging her to stand. She rose and maintaining eye contact, he stepped into Clari's space and folded her five foot, two inch tall frame into a gentle hug.

Clari was stiff at first, but relaxed into his beating heart. Morris whispered in her ear, "I'm aware that I keep saying this, but you really are an amazing person, Clari. You have a beautiful heart, and I'm so honored to be in your life. Thank you."

Clari realized she was looking forward to more of Morris' hugs. Tears built up in her eyes again, but this time for a different reason. A smile formed on her lips followed by a deep sigh.

Morris released Clari from the welcomed hug.

"Thank you, Morris." A flushed Clari dried her face, turned and went back to preparing their meals as she wondered about her response to Morris' hug; the butterflies in her stomach were new. Refocusing on dinner, she asked Morris to get the plates and silverware for the table. Clari asked, "How are you doing?"

He grumbled as he moved to sit at the table. "Fine." Like a pouting child, he propped his elbow up on the table and plopped his chin in his hand.

She snickered. "Getting bored with not being fully reinstated at work yet, Morris?"

"Yeah. How about you?"

Complaining in a good naturedly way, she shared, "Oh, no time for boredom. I wake up exhausted and go to bed exhausted."

Morris' head tilted. "Oh? Are they keeping you busy at WPO?"

"Yes. Between them and my ghostly visitor, I don't think I have had a chance to unwind. That's why I was so excited for today and getting to hang out with you."

"Ghostly visitor?"

Laughing, Clari challenged him, "Out of all that, 'ghostly visitor' is what you honed into? Want something to do, Morris?"

"Well, yes. I'm going stir crazy. I'm on desk duty. Tell me more. Are you okay working with WPO now?"

Clari sat with Morris. "I think I'm doing well. My counselor cleared me with instructions to call if needed."

Morris smiled. "I'm glad you went, and congrats on being cleared."

"Thank you, Morris. And working with Gerald has been a very interesting experience." She re-capped her week with Gerald.

Morris crossed his arms. "Gerald, huh? Do I have competition now?"

Clari rolled her eyes. "Seriously? No, you don't. Gerald is a nice guy and I love the car he restored. But, he's not my type."

Morris uncrossed his arms. "Oh, and what is your type?" Clari saw the mischievousness dancing in his eyes.

Clari cocked her eyebrow in a flirty manner. *Two can play this game.* "I guess we'll have to see, won't we?"

"Wait! What car did Gerald restore?"

"Oh, this awesome 2022 Chrysler Dodge Charger. It's 'Sinnamon' red and smells like cinnamon!"

"That was a nice looking vehicle," Morris worked to hide the awe in his voice. "So, are you done working with Gerald now?"

"I don't know when I'll be done with Gerald. Witherabbott apparently doesn't believe it's necessary to provide me an itinerary, so I never know from day to day.

"As for my ghostly visitor...you know how some people get a Quote-a-Day? Well, I apparently get a Clue-a-Day," she joked.

Morris leaned forward and eagerly asked. "Do you want some help with it?"

She was pleasantly surprised by his offer. "Yes. That would be great. You are serious, right?"

Morris' eyes lit up. "I would love to help. What do you have so far?"

"My ghostly visitor, whom I have dubbed the 'Red Skeleton', was murdered on land, I think."

He interrupted. "Why 'Red Skeleton'?"

"She presented herself to me, literally, as a red skeleton."

Morris' eyebrows rose. "That's strange. Okay, what have you come up with so far on the Red Skeleton?"

Clari shared, "She was wrapped in something Looking or Feeling like a red rug. She was placed in a travel trunk and left for some time in an attic. I think it was the attic of one of the aunts of the killer. I also smelled a lot of perfume. Maybe the killer used the perfume to mask the smell of death.

"I Felt like sometime later the killer dragged the trunk, thumping down the steps. It Felt like I could Feel each and every step as it bumped down from the attic, through the house, down the steps and a bigger bump as he lifted and dropped it into a vehicle. Then he brought it onto a ship as his luggage.

"I think he planned on dumping her overboard during some sort of chaotic diversion, but then I Feel like the ship was sinking or sank. Either the trunk broke open, or he dumped her out of it.

"Her remains were probably found during a rescue operation or washed up on the shore. I don't think she was ever claimed and identified, so was perhaps buried as such. Either way, her murderer got away."

Morris interjected. "Why would she appear as a red skeleton?"

"I guess it had to do with the dye on the rug. There used to be a dye made from an evergreen plant called Madder. Madder was a textile dye and thought to have arrived in Egypt from either the Greeks or Romans. In fact a Madder-dyed belt was found in King Tutankhamen's burial site.

"Sometimes, even if the dye was fixed, it would run. It wasn't always colorfast. Perhaps with the killer dumping so much liquid perfume on her remains made the dye run and the dye stained her, so she retains that image when she presents herself to me."

He asked, "Do you know who the killer was?"

"The man's energy Felt like he was Machiavellian and maybe a cutthroat."

Morris laughter filled the room. "What's with the antiquated terminology? Machiavellian? Where'd you get that word from?"

She rolled her eyes. "Well, if I am correct, we are talking about the nineteen forties. At least, that's the time frame I Feel it happened. Even though Niccolò Machiavelli was born in 1469, he was known to be deceitful, unscrupulous, scheming and cunning. That's where the term 'Machiavellian' came from. Even though it's not from the early 1900's, I feel the word it appropriate to describe the Feeling I got from Red Skeleton's killer. The term is appropriate to the scenario, isn't it?"

Placing the palm of his hand on his chest, Morris feigned indignation. "How old do you think I am? I'd have to be well over two hundred years old. In other words, that was way before my time, thank you."

Clari giggled. Morris started laughing.

They both took a deep breath to settle themselves.

Morris asked for some paper to write the information down on. "Do you have any idea how he killed her?" He chewed his thumbnail while he waited for her to share her thoughts.

"I think he struck her, hard, on the back right side of her head. I Felt the pain as her brain slammed against her skull, and I heard her skull crack."

"Hm. What else do you have on this?"

"It possibly happened on the east coast. I'm Feeling like it may be in the nineteen forties. It's an unidentified deceased female who wants me to find her."

Morris finished taking notes. "This is really old so I don't know if I'll be able to find anything, so no promises. As soon as I get a chance, I'll see if there are any old newspaper articles or cold cases matching what you've told me so far. At least it'll give me something else to concentrate on."

Clari had a sudden flash of a solitaire game. Not sure what to make of it, she filed it away for reviewing later. "Thank you. Why don't we meet for dinner on Wednesday's and again on the weekend until you're off desk duty? That way we can work on ghostie cases and have time to hang out. You game?"

"Okay, that should work. How is the whole understanding the Grigori going?"

"Well, I've been researching all I can at night, but I kind of keep coming back to the same conclusion."

"And what's that?" Morris asked.

"That the Grigori are the Nephilims."

Morris' eyebrows rose, "What makes you think that?"

"A lot of rather confusing and obscure information I found online; digging deep online."

"I'm listening," Morris encouraged.

"If I understand the biblical accounts, the Nephilim were the hybrid children of fallen angels and female humans. The offspring possibly had shapeshifting abilities and other abilities.

"After the geostorm wiped out the internet, the A.I. was fed all the microfiche, newspaper articles and any paper copies pertaining to our, human, history so that knowledge wouldn't be completely lost.

"It was through the internet that I found some translations for 'Nephilim'. One was 'giants'; another 'the violent ones' and a third, 'the fallen ones'. And then I fell down the proverbial rabbit-hole.

"When I researched giants, I came across old forum posts about massively large people and animals – think Paul Bunyan as being small in comparison. There are petrified human-looking rock formations as well as massive petrified animals, trees and other vegetation. I don't mean twenty-feet or so, rather much larger.

"When I dug further, I found that some speculated that there was a time that those on the forum dubbed the 'Great Reset'; the 'Mud Flood', with possible connections to the erasure of the Tartarian Empire which boasted a much smaller race of humans compared to the so-called petrified giants. The Tartarians were reported to be around twelve feet tall. And there are still doorways built to allow the Tartarian giants access to the inside of the building. There are also museums across the world that has giant shoes, swords, furniture, books and the like made for those time frame giants.

"Then I found another archived forum post discussing giants. Apparently it was rumored that in 2002, some United States soldiers over in Afghanistan either came across a giant, or went searching for the giant, in the mountains. It's said that one patrol who went before them disappeared. The giant was said to be about thirteen-feet tall, around one-thousand pounds, having a double row of teeth and that it really stunk.

"Long story somewhat shorter, U.S. soldiers brought the giant down amidst the missing patrol's gear and scattered bones. The giant – whether deceased or incapacitated was unclear – was wrapped up and transported out of the mountains by helicopter, and later take back to the United States.

"And in the early 2020's, there were videos and photos taken of live giants across the United States.

"So is the human-Grigori really the descendants of the Nephilim and for some twisted reason, going after humans that have what the Grigori deem Nephilim abilities? I mean, they are the ones who shapeshift into large black winged and feathered beings."

"Wow, Clari. That's a lot to take in. As a detective, I have to say it all sounds circumstantial. Do you have any documented proof?"

"No. I mean, when I went down the whole Tartarian and Mud Flood rabbit-hole, there were photos posted, but I don't have a physical way to authenticate anything."

"So where do you go from here?"

"I'm supposed to meet with Sebastian at some point to go over what we each know and found out about, the Grigori. I guess we'll bounce the information off one another. But like everything else about giants in

connection with the biblical Nephilim stories, I can't prove anything."
Clari stood. "I'm hungry. How about you?"

Morris' face lit up. "Let's see these Buddha bowl things. What's in them?"

Clari pointed to each section in the bowl. "Ours has diced boneless chicken cooked with ginger, garlic and salt and pepper. We also have baked sweet potato with onion, brown rice, chickpeas browned in coconut oil, and raw spinach. It has a Tahini sauce made with maple syrup, lemon juice and water. Oh, and the bowl is topped with pumpkin seeds. What do you think?"

"Sounds interesting. Let's try it." Morris looked into his bowl. "Huh." He slowly rotated his bowl and then looked up at Clari. "How do I eat this?"

"Anyway you want, Morris. There's no right or wrong way." Clari took her fork, skewered a piece of chicken and then scooped a bit of rice and sweet potato. Clari noticed that Morris watched her intently as she put her fork in her mouth. She motioned with her empty fork for Morris to give it a try.

Clari watched as he skewered some chicken, spinach and a cube of sweet potato and put it in his mouth. She watched his lips as he chewed, and then saw his lips curve as he finished his mouthful.

"It's good, eh, Morris?"

"It is," Morris confessed. "It didn't sound too hot, but I actually like it. The flavors are intriguing, and frankly, it's kind of fun eating it."

"And you can put whatever you want in the bowls. Your choices are limited only by your imagination and palate. And they're healthy, if you put healthy foods in them."

Morris made a face. "Ugh. That's like a cuss word to me now. 'Healthy'. At least your food has good flavor, Clari."

Clari smiled, frowned, and then gave Morris a somber look. "I'm just glad you're here to enjoy it." She reached over and placed her hand, palm up, on the table.

Morris looked in her eyes as his hand joined hers. "Yeah, me too, Clari," said Morris with a happy gleam in his eyes.

Chapter Five

Medium – one who has the ability to See, Sense and/or Hear and Speak with non-physical beings, typically those who have physically died; both earthbounds and spirits.

Clari

Clari yawned and leisurely stretched. It was Sunday, and the only plans she had for the day was the radio interview later in the day. And she was pleased to have made it through the night without any interruptions from the Other-Realms.

After showering and dressing, the next stop was the kitchen. She stepped into the hallway and had only taken a few steps when a woman suddenly appeared at the other end of the hall. She was tall, slender, and wearing a sleek nineteen forties styled cream-colored evening gown. Her brown hair had a deep side part and hung loose in gentle curls. In her hand was a cream-colored satin clutch that matched her dress.

Both women stood facing one another. Clari held her breath, afraid if she inhaled she'd break the spell of the moment.

Clari watched in horror as the woman's hair started dripping, followed by her gown becoming wet. Next, Clari saw red spreading across the gown. It looked horrific even though Clari Knew it wasn't blood; it was the rug's red dye that permeated the gown.

* Find me * begged the dripping specter.

Though the specter disappeared almost immediately afterwards, Clari was left with a curious red-tinged puddle on the floor.

That afternoon Clari arrived at the radio station for her interview with one of the radio station's DJ's, Stevie Riles.

Stevie, a perky tiny woman, who was shorter than Clari by easily two inches, had blonde shoulder-length hair, brown eyes and full hips, greeted Clari with a warm hug. "Hi, Ms. Jones. Thank you for coming in. Let's get you set up and I'll answer any questions you might have before we go on the air." Stevie led Clari back to one of the studios.

The room was dimly lit except for the glowing lights emanating from the control equipment across the table from where Stevie indicated for Clari to sit. Clari noted the walls had sound dampeners on them.

After Stevie had Clari settled with headphones and seated in front of the mike, Stevie moved to sit across from Clari. On Stevie's side was a conglomeration of boards, lights and sliders. One board, to Clari, looked like the central sound board. Another microphone, two computer screens – each with individual keyboards – and different headphones hung on hooks, all within reach Stevie's reach. To Clari it seemed as complicated as the control panels in an airplane, and just as foreign.

Stevie put on a set of headphones and asked, "Hey, are you okay? You look like a deer that got caught in the headlights."

"That's about how I feel," Clari admitted.

"What's wrong?"

"I'm a bit nervous. I'll be talking to people that I can't see."

Stevie's eyes shone bright as she challenged Clari, "But don't you do that already as a medium?"

"That's the same thing my friend, Josie, told me. Yeah I do, but I think this is a bit different. For one, your listeners aren't dead."

Stevie's head bobbed in understanding. "Touché! I do get it. Just think of it this way; you'll be talking to me. Just you and me having a conversation, okay?"

Clari took a ragged breath. "Okay. Let's do this."

"Cool! We'll be going live in...oh...about one minute. Just relax and breathe, okay?"

Clari took a deep breath. "Okay."

"Good morning, El Paso, Las Cruces and surrounding areas! I'm Stevie Riles and this morning we have a special treat! We have Clarima Jones in the studio today. Clarima is a WPO Level Four Reader and is here to answer some questions you might have about ghosts. Good morning, Clarima."

"Good morning, Stevie. Thank you for inviting me here today. And please call me Clari."

"Good enough, Clari. Would you give us a brief background before we get to the cool paranormal questions?"

"Sure. I've seen ghosts and spirits since I was born. I didn't realize as a child that not everyone could See and Communicate with them. As I grew up, I found that I could help both living people and the deceased, so I focused on refining that."

"Thank you for sharing that, Clari. So let's get to the questions. Let's start with 'What are ghosts' for those who don't know?"

"To me, Stevie, ghosts are people who no longer have a physical body. They are still connected to the Earth experience and Earth energy; they are humans with no physical body."

"Interesting. So what's the difference between ghosts and spirits? Or is there a difference?" Stevie queried.

"Yes, Stevie, there's a difference. To me, ghosts are still connected to the Earth energy; they are the same person, just no physical body. If they were addicts, they still crave and seek out their drug of choice. Ghosts, or earthbounds, still have the same hang ups as they did when they were in a physical body.

"Spirits are those who have crossed over – they are not connected to the Earth energies. Usually, for those who can see spirits, they will probably see the deceased's appearance to be around age 30, at the height of their health when in the physical; they will be complete, no longer in mental or physical pain, and have released the roles they played while in a human body. They will still appear in a form they had when they were still been in a physical body."

Stevie kept the flow of the conversation going, "But why do ghosts hang around instead of crossing over? Are they all lost?"

Clari answered, "Just as there are as many differences between myself and everyone listening and involved in this, so too are the reasons a ghost remains earthbound. Not every ghost is lost. Some reasons for staying earthbound may be: waiting for a loved one to cross over and/or to watch over their loved one to help them through the grieving process, or be around until they grow up.

"Maybe they don't know their physical body died. Or they could be afraid to cross over and face 'judgement' because they weren't a nice person in human form.

"Some had addictions when they were alive and still seek out ways to participate in their addiction of choice. They usually seek out someone that has the same vice as they did so they can attempt to get a vicarious fix.

"Some don't want to relinquish anything, like greed, power, and so on.

"One woman, who died in an auto accident, stayed on until her dog, who survived the crash, found a suitable home. Once she was satisfied the dog was comfortable and going to be okay, she crossed over."

"This really is a fascinating topic. I'm so glad you're here."

Clari gave a nervous twitter. "Thank you."

Stevie continued, "Are all of those who are a sensitive also a medium?

"No, absolutely not. Sensitives have whatever ability they chose before incarnating into their current human form. It just may take a while to discover what one's ability is."

"So, next question. What are poltergeists?"

Clari's shoulders relaxed as she shared her understandings, "Poltergeist – which means 'noisy ghost' – can be a very strong ghost who's able to forcefully interact and manipulate things in our frequency.

"But, there's another type of poltergeist. It is a human's excess energy. It usually begins to display during hormonal changes, such as teens or menopause; or can be from a human in extreme and/or long term stress. That energy is then expelled from the human and guided or directed by the human, almost always without conscious thought. It's the human's subconscious energy acting out or rebelling since the conscious human feels they have no control over their circumstances."

"So we can be the poltergeist? That actually makes sense to me. Our listeners provided some really cool questions. Next question: how do ghosts travel?"

"Usually by wormholes or portals. I visualize it as one of the moving sidewalks we usually see in airports. A wormhole or portal is created to transport from one location to another. But, there are also electrical lines and outlets, electric items, water pipes, reflective surfaces such as mirrors. These are some of the ways ghosts can travel."

Though the listeners couldn't see Stevie's face, Clari noticed that Stevie's mouth dropped opened and her eyes widened. "So after we die, based on what you just shared with us, we don't cease to exist?"

"Oh, no, Stevie. The law of conservation of energy says that energy is neither destroyed nor created; it can only be transformed from one form to another. We do not cease to exist. And it's mediums that can usually Communicate, See, or Hear the deceased to help someone still in a physical body to heal.

"While the Law of Conservation of Energy, I believe, was discovered in 1842 by Julius Robert von Mayer, or rather the most compact form which is now called the First Law of Thermodynamics. And between 1842 and 1847, von Mayer, along with James Joule and Herman von Helmholtz, formulated the basics for the Law of Conservation of Energy.

"Having said that, William Rankine first used that phrase in 1850. There are other names throughout history with those who directly or peripherally worked on kinetic and other forms of energy or on conservation of energy.

"And then there's Albert Einstein whose discovery of that famous equation, $E=mc2$, merged both the Law of Conservation of Energy and the Law of Conservation of Mass."

"Uh, wow, Clari. That was a lot of information, thank you. How do you know all, much less remember all of that?"

"I read. A lot."

"All righty, then. So let's move forward. Next question, 'What is a medium?'" Stevie quizzed.

"I see a medium as one who is an intermediary between the living and deceased or, for me, any non-physical."

"I don't understand, Clari. How can being a medium help someone heal?"

"I can give you an example: An elderly woman was afraid to die. When I asked her why, she informed me that she was afraid she would have to see her husband. She also was afraid she would be punished because she had been happy when her abusive husband had died. We discussed how she shouldn't be afraid for having honest feelings and that she wouldn't have to see her husband unless or until she was ready. I also explained that her daughter, who died as a young adult, and her favorite dog were standing by her bed and would stay until the woman allowed herself to die. After spending about two more weeks to say goodbye to her family, she passed away peacefully."

"Wow. Okay. I recently read something about time slips. Can you explain what times slips are?" Stevie asked.

Clari leaned forward a bit completely comfortable now and in her role. "Time slips are when one or more other time lines intersect with our time line. For example, you can be investigating a place, say a hotel, that had it's heyday in the 1950's. You get intelligent responses from a 'ghost', who in turn asks who you are and wants to know what you're doing in their room. This is when two time lines cross or connect. You are on an investigation and communicating with a ghost; while the other time line, the other being is alive and well in their time and they are speaking to, as far as they can tell, a specter from another time.

"Since time is not linear and the membranes separating our times lines – as well as dimensions – are thinning, the interactions between our time line and dimension and others are on the increase."

"Wow. I'm not sure what to think about that. I'll have to mull it over. Now, let's move on." Stevie looked down at her notes. "Orbs – are they real and are they ghosts?"

"I have received so many photographs over the years from very excited people wanting me to say that they captured real orbs. Unfortunately, real orbs are not as common as floating dust or pollen. Yes, there really are orbs, and that is the non-physicals preferred way of traveling since it takes a lot of energy to create a full bodied 'apparition'. One way I recommend to tell is if the orb is lit internally. Also, does it have a face in it? And for those who can register soul energy, does it have a soul signature?"

"This is so interesting, Clari. Okay, next question. Oh, this is a good one. What's the number one question you are asked about deceased loved ones?"

"There are actually three questions asked a lot about their deceased loved ones who have crossed over. 'Are they in pain?' No, they have no pain on the Other Side and are perfectly healthy and whole. 'Are they stuck?' No, when they've crossed over, they are not stuck. And, 'Are they proud of me?' They are always proud of you. They do not judge your life path or life decisions."

"How do you know, Clari, that they are proud of us here?"

"Because, Stevie, they remember how hard it is living a lifetime on Earth. They may have been judgmental when they were alive, but they don't need to play that part any more. There's no judgment coming from our deceased loved ones who crossed over."

"I, for one, Clari, am somewhat relieved to hear that. Let's go on to the next question. What are some different ways ghosts may be perceived?"

"There can be quite a few ways. Visualizing in the mind's eye; seeing them physically; capturing 'evidence' with cameras or other recording devices; moving cold spots; a change of pressure in a room."

"Well, Clari, we didn't have time to really get deeper into the questions. I'm thinking you may want to come back to go more in-depth on one or more of these questions, if you're interested?"

"I'd like that, Stevie."

"Awesome! Now the final question, 'What's one message you have for someone who unexpectedly experiences Seeing/Feeling/Knowing a ghost is present?'"

"First, no fear. Fear is a powerful battery for any non-physical, and I mean *any* non-physical being. Ghosts – or Earthbounds – aren't the only non-physical beings out there.

"Second, compassion. They are humans minus the physical body. Think of it this way – they are 'living' without a physical body. Mostly no one acknowledges their existence. Remember, some may not even know they are dead and don't understand why no one will talk to them; or they are lonely and are excited to make contact with someone else.

"Third, don't take crap. If they are in your space and you're not comfortable, you tell them to get out and you have to mean it – even if you have to yell it. Most people don't let strangers wander into their house and bully the people living there – neither should you allow a non-physical being in your house uninvited."

"This has been fascinating, Clari. Unfortunately, that's all the time we have today. I hope you can come back so we can delve deeper. Thank you so much Clari Jones for sharing with us."

"Thank you, Stevie, for having me."

After Clari got home, her phone chirped. She read, "Good day, Clari."

"Who are you?" she demanded.

"Ghost. Can we talk? I figured out how to verbally communicate. Are you agreeable?"

"Are you going to call me?" Clari wasn't comfortable with that thought.

"No. I can modulate the signal to make it appear that I am speaking. Would this be okay?"

Neither Clari's energy nor her Team gave any warnings. "Um...I guess?"

A strong male voice with a slight British accent came out of her phone's speaker, and it had a lot to say.

"Thank you, Clari. I died a long time ago, before the geomagnetic storm back in 2029. And I've been wandering ever since. I had a lot of things to think about." Ghost was quiet as he revisited his life. He continued, "I experimented with traveling through conduits. I found I could move from one location to the next through different conduits.

"I did try moving through plumbing...following the water. I ended up in some unpleasant places and have seen things that would give anyone nightmares.

"I discovered I could easily travel through electricity and electronic items. A lot more pleasant. It's kind of tingly or has an effervescent feeling.

"I traveled extensively around the globe, until arriving here. Well, not here where we are now. Rather, I was drawn to your phone initially while you were, um, incarcerated. I just drifted for a bit until I came across your phone again at your house."

"Why do you remain Earthbound? Why haven't you crossed over, Ghost?" Clari asked.

Ghost seemed to mull over how much he should share. "I wasn't a nice person when I was alive. I had been a millionaire, building millions in digital tech long before the geostorm that killed electronics and had the tech people starting all over.

"I'd been called a programming genius. I was a wiz at coding and software development, but was clueless in interacting with other humans.

"When I died, I found it fascinating that I existed beyond my physical body, and as a previous coder, I was excited to find I could be the ghost in the machine."

"So you wanted to be a ghost in my machine?" Clari asked.

"Why not? In 1641, Rene' Descartes, proposed that the human mind could exist without the body and was independent from the human brain. And in 1949, Gilbert Ryle coined the phrase the 'Ghost in the Machine' in criticism of Rene Descartes mind-body dualism theory. The ghost in the machine, I understood, meant that the mind or ghost exists separately from the body or machine. So I thought I could literally be a ghost in the realm of zeros and ones...the realm of computers. I believe I have proven that the mind, or perhaps essence, of my human-self does live on separately from a human body. So I traveled and observed.

"After the storm and that crazy dictator-wanna-be, I watched as humanity worked to rebuild everything, including technology. I saw as new safeguards were put in place in regards to technology, like how it was decided that 5G cell towers would never again be utilized due to the harm it caused all living things. So as the world was rebuilt, respect for life was finally taken into consideration.

"I learned a lot about human relationships as well as the human's spirit to survive.

"When I was alive in a physical body, I'd lived as a wealthy recluse. I died alone and bitter.

"Now, Clari, with your help, I'd like to live again – well as much as I could live being a ghost – and be of service to you."

"Me? Why?" Clari asked peering deeply into her phone's camera.

"From what I've heard since joining your phone, you and I both struggle with relationships. I figured we can grow together."

Clari shifted and through the phone camera, Ghost saw the conflict on her face.

"Oh! My apologies, Clari. I don't mean a romantic relationship, which I'm pretty sure would be impossible and I'm not interested in that. I'd like to work for you. I could be like your personal assistant. Answer phones, alert you of who is calling, scheduling appointments and keep your calendar. Maybe even conduct some research if you need.

"I'd work either in the background or peripheral. Oh! And I don't need recompense as I've no bills or physical maintenance since I've no physical body."

"I have become quite adapt at various types of electronic equipment, and who knows? Perhaps I'll discover more things I night master. So, in my humble opinion, I think it's a win-win situation. I may be of service to you and provide you with free help within the boundaries of my limitations. So what do you think?"

Clari propped the phone up against a couch cushion. Her hands fiddled with the hem of her shirt. "We can try it for two weeks to see if I can work with you. But, bathrooms and bedrooms are off limits. Oh, and when I want privacy, you have to find a way to give it to me – whether it's privacy with clients or with a friend. Will you abide by my terms?"

"Yes! And thank you, Clari!"

"But, Ghost, you never really answered my question. There must be hundreds of people with relationship trust issues, who why did you pick me?"

"I was quite serious when I told you that I was drawn to your phone. It just felt like the right place to be for now. I have no answer right now other than what I've provided you," his voice had a noticeable lilt revealing he was hopeful.

"Okay, Ghost. Two weeks."

Morris

Morris sat at his desk at home, eager to start diving in to find this mysterious Red Skeleton lady, and to see if there was any record of her in the missing person's files. This, he felt, had to be much more fun than sitting and feeling unproductive all day at work. *I really don't like desk duty,* he grumbled to himself.

Initially unable to find anything, Morris moved on to newspaper archives online. He doggedly dug and began peeling back from over two-hundred years of information in newspapers and other documents online. The more he dug, the more intrigued he became, finally stopping at one story. Morris spoke out loud to himself. "There is a heck of a story here. Let's see if this fits the Red Skeleton Lady."

Morris felt good working on the Red Skeleton Lady case. *Is it because I'm working, or is it because I'm doing this with Clari?* Morris smiled. He was pretty sure it had everything to do with spending time with Clari.

Morris went back to digging through history.

Clari

Clari arrived at Witherabbott's office Monday morning.

"Good morning, Miss Jones. How was your weekend?"

"Fine." Clari, feeling like she was in trouble awaiting the school principal to rule against her, fought herself to keep from crossing her arms.

"Anything new to share?" Witherabbott asked this regularly. It was her polite way of asking if Clari had any more experiences with new abilities or dangerous beings.

"No, ma'am. All is fine."

"Good. Today you'll be with Sebastian. Any questions?"

Clari shook her head.

Witherabbott rose from her desk and announced, "I'll show you where you'll be meeting with Sebastian."

Like a duckling following its mother, she reluctantly fell into step behind Witherabbott. They shortly arrived at a small classroom located on the same floor where she had met with Gerald.

Sebastian rose as they entered. "Good morning, Director. Belle."

Witherabbott beamed. "Good morning, Sebastian. Thank you for working with Miss Jones."

"My pleasure, Mrs. Witherabbott."

"I'll leave you two at it."

After Witherabbott left, Sebastian hugged Clari. "Belle."

Clari found she was able to see the ancient paranormal energetic attributes of some people, and Sebastian's vampiric overlay was one of many she had seen.

J.R. had dragon in his energy, which made sense since he really was a dragon from the Dragon Realm. Clari didn't know what Josie's overlay was, but she often caught glimpses of wings on Josie's back. Lieutenant Avery's overlay was of a wolf shifter, and Morris was a mystery; she still hasn't Seen or Felt Morris' overlay.

Clari appreciated the familiar scent that was unique to Sebastian. He smelled of exotic spices that wrapped around Clari's senses. Sebastian's scent always made Clari think of Sebastian as an older protective brother who had her back. She reluctantly pulled back to look Sebastian in the eyes. "So are you going to fill me in on what information you have on the human-Grigori?"

"Yes. Have a seat. I understand J.R. told you a bit about the human-Grigori's?"

"He did; he told me of the human-Grigori and how they took it upon themselves to seek out and kill any human who showed any possible Nephilim powers. This is why I was in their sights — because of my certified abilities," Clari shared.

Sebastian's voice took on the cadence of a professor lecturing. "Right. Now it's time to share what we've each discovered or learned. History time! In the thirteen hundred's, King Philip IV of France was in financial ruin. He had bankrupted his country with his endless taxes and wars. So, he hatched a plan to take down the Knights Templar and claim their wealth.

"The pope, Clement V, happened to be a childhood friend of King Philip IV's. There is only speculation as to why Pope Clement V supported King Philip's campaign against the Knights Templar, and none of the possibilities speculated were above board. As usual throughout history, it came down to greed and power.

"Regardless of the reason, this started a new trend with the Church. It wasn't just the Knights Templar's they went after. Over time, they aggressively tried to take over, or end, any group or organization that the Church had no control over. The choice became to fall under full control of the Church or be destroyed.

"The Grigori group were very determined to continue their work, so when they were approached, they opted to join the Church. They were very excited to join with the Vatican and have, or so they thought, access to the limitless resources of the Vatican.

"But, the Vatican never acknowledged the Grigori. The Vatican regarded them as lower class, only to be acknowledged if or when the Vatican felt they could use the Grigori or anyone else, to further their own agenda.

"Since the Grigori were focused on anyone with energetic abilities as well as keeping track of family bloodlines of any who showed abilities, the Vatican pretty much gave them free reign since it was in the Vatican's interest to quell any threat that may arise then or in the future."

"Why didn't the Vatican ever try to control the Grigori?" queried Clari.

"It was in their best interest. The Grigori group remained free to cull anyone who might be a threat to the Church's power or dogma."

"But why didn't the Vatican acknowledge their connection to the Grigori?" Clari asked.

"For the same reason governments of old denied the existence of their black operations groups. So the work could go on, but the government wouldn't be held liable or responsible. Same principle. 'Plausible deniability'. Both parties get what they want and no one accepts responsibility. Also, the Nephilim of Biblical times that survived the Watchers were, according to the Bible that was translated into English, destroyed by the all-cleansing Biblical flood. Because of this, the belief system of the human-Grigori was of no interest to the church."

"But what if the Nephilim weren't all destroyed during the flood?" Clari shared what the interpretation of what her research came up with and her theory, finishing with, "I think the Grigori as the Nephilim. But don't you think that the Grigori want-to-a-be's are kind of outdated now?"

"Belle, they are fanatics. They are zealous and relentless in their hunt and destruction of what they believe is those with Nephilim blood. As long as someone believes in their interpretations and beliefs, the human-Grigori group will remain active and on the hunt. This is why Mrs. Witherabbott wanted to help train you. To keep you alive."

"But why me? I mean there are thousands of people with abilities. Why are the Grigori focused on me? And why is Witherabbott so intent on me?" Clari pushed.

Sebastian's brow furrowed as he studied her face. "You really don't know, do you?"

Clari threw her arms up, "Ugh! Why do I feel like everyone else knows stuff about me and that I'm clueless?"

He smiled at her.

Clari searched his face and saw compassion and gentleness which just confused her more. Agitated, she demanded, "What?"

He shook his head. "Nothing, Belle."

"I don't get it," she mumbled as she gathered her belongings.

Sebastian chuckled. "I guess we're done for today?"

"Yes," she grumped as she left him sitting at the table.

When Clari got home, she poured her juice, grabbed her phone and sat down on the couch. "Ghost? Ghost, are you available to chat?"

Clari's phone lit up. "Hello, Clari."

"Hi, Ghost. Did you happen to hear the topic at the World Paranormal Organization today?"

"Yes, Clari. And I'm intrigued. What is this about the Grigori and how it relates to you?"

Clari scratched her head, "You mean you hadn't dove into my past? Don't you know about the Grigori? I mean, I've been researching heavily there for a while." Clari caught Ghost up on her experiences, research and theory.

"I did not do a deep dive, Clari. I felt that would be intrusive, and could go against building our relationship. Aren't we supposed to share to build our relationship?"

"Well, yeah, I guess. Hey, have you been able to figure out more as to why you chose me, Ghost, for this?" Clari waved her hand back and forth between the phone and her. "I mean, I'm relationship challenged. I'm learning how to trust some people, but still pretty much keep most people at arm's length. I'm not sure I'm the best example to help you learn about positive human interactions and relationships. So why did you pick me?"

"I think that makes you the perfect person for me, Clari. Think about it. You're beginning your journey in relationships, and in trusting yourself in relationships. You are the logical choice for me to learn from as you are learning as well. That, and the fact you're not so closed minded about new stuff."

"New stuff? What new stuff, Ghost?"

"Clari, I'm a ghost named Ghost who communicates with you through electronic devices. Don't you think that qualifies as 'new stuff'?"

Clari swore she heard amusement from Ghost's electronic voice.

Ghost waited a moment before continuing, "I also figured that someone who communicates with...uh... shall we say 'the unseen', would be okay with communicating with me."

"Huh, fair enough. Hey Ghost, what all are you able to do?"

"What do you mean?"

"Well, you not only can hitch a ride on my phone, but you can answer it as well as access my calendar and schedule appointments for me. I mean, as a ghost, you're able to travel through electrical lines and plumbing lines like any other ghost, but I've not met one like you who can work my electronic devices from the inside out. So what else can you do?"

"I don't know, Clari. I guess I'll have to explore and see what I can access and what I can manipulate. I may need some suggestions of things to try as we move forward."

"Are you an A.I. You know, Artificial Intelligence?"

"No. Yes. No."

"That really didn't clear things up, Ghost. Care to explain your indecision?"

"My apologies, Clari. Let me work through this. I'm a deceased human, hence my 'Ghost' moniker. But since I have infiltrated my ghost self into the binary realm...does that make me an AI?"

"Oh. I didn't think of that."

"Yeah. Though I still maintain my conscious awareness while existing, I contend that I am not an AI especially since I was not artificially created and had lived a human life. So my answer to your original question is no, I am not an AI. I am a ghost in the machine. Do you agree with my reasoning?"

"Uh, yeah, I do."

"My turn to ask you some questions. You seem to spend a lot of time alone, Clari. No judging, just an observation."

"Yes, I guess I do, Ghost."

"Why?" Ghost asked her.

"I guess it's because of my upbringing and experiences from childhood until...well...adulthood. I felt that if I wanted to have peace I had to be by myself. I was an outcast – something different and I guess, to be feared, not only at home but at school and anywhere in public. Not only that, but I had trouble regulating what I Heard and Felt from others. It was very hard. I mean, it's better now since I learned how to filter out, or block, others thoughts and energies...and since I learned to accept and love myself."

"If you have trust issues with humans, how is it you and Detective Morris get along so well? Are there any other people you've been able to trust, like Josie?"

"Well, Ghost, you have done some homework. I have to say though; it does come across kind of creepy, and almost like stalking, that you know about Morris and Josie. Do I want to know how long you've been investigating and observing me?"

"My apologies, Clari. I do not mean to come across as a stalker. I have trust issues with humans as well, so I wanted to make sure exposing my existence to you would be safe. I've only been observing since you've given me permission to stay."

"Fair enough. But I don't think I would be so forgiving with this if I hadn't had all the experiences with ghosts approaching me, and me not knowing how long they were there before they showed themselves to me. Though I am better with the ghosts entering my environment; I can sense their approach, though I may not know right away who it is approaching.

"Now, on to your questions. Morris and I kind of learned each other and developed trust between the two of us. Though he said he decided as soon as he laid eyes on me that he was 'in' for our unofficial partnership with the police department. It's neat and a novelty to me to have someone who is not in the World Paranormal Organization and accepts everything about me...all my quirks.

"As for Josie and me, we had similar experiences – both with familial relationships and with being the black sheep because of our abilities."

Ghost interjected. "So at what point do you decide to trust someone? I mean, when I was alive, I lacked understanding and the skill to interpret social cues. That made interactions with others awkward for both me and them. And, apparently I trusted the wrong people. I was clueless, so it was a shock when those I did trust betrayed me. I became a total recluse running my business, and my life, from the confines of my home. I was afraid to trust anyone again. I mean I even had groceries delivered so I wouldn't have to interact with anyone.

"How do you know you can trust someone? At what point, or is there a trigger that lets you know that it's okay to trust someone?"

Clari tapped her chin before she answered. "Ghost, I think I'm the wrong person to give relationship advice. But, for me, it was a leap of faith, with the understanding that I may get hurt. I fought it, but Morris' consistency and patience made me want to step out of my protective zone. I guess I had to weigh my curiosity between finding out where this relationship could go, with my fear of trusting someone. With Morris, the curiosity won.

"There are no guarantees in life, Ghost. We each have to decide if the risks are worth the rewards. "

Ghost asked, "And did they? Were the risks worth it?"

Clari gave a contented sigh, "Yes, Ghost. So far, it has been well worth it."

Ghost was quiet for a moment, and then replied, "I guess it's too late for me, you know, being dead and all."

Clari pursed her lips while she gave this some thought. "I can't believe there aren't any other ghosts in your reality, Ghost."

"I have traveled around for quite a while, and I have met other ghosts, but my social awkwardness seems to remain intact."

"I don't have an answer to that, Ghost. But I am glad we had this time to chat and get to know each other a bit more. Let me ask you this, what do you miss?"

It took a moment for Ghost to answer, "I hadn't given it much thought before now."

"You know, things like missing eating or the taste and texture of food?" Clari prompted.

Another pause. "Touch. I miss the physical interaction between my body and the physical world. I miss the touch and feel of a keyboard. Now, and when I was alive, I missed the caring touch of another human."

"I'm sorry, Ghost."

"Don't be. My life was full of my choices, Clari. And sometimes we don't miss someone or something until it's no longer available to us."

"Thank you for sharing, Ghost."

"It has been my pleasure, Clari. I am learning a lot, so I appreciate having you on my learning adventure."

Chapter Six

Runes – were originally alphabet characters used by Germanic peoples. Runes today are magical symbols to accomplish a specific task or goal, such as added protections to a room so those practicing their abilities don't possibly have their energy dangerously out of control.

Morris brought dinner from the local Thai restaurant. He explained what each dish was as he unpacked the to-go bag. "Wonton soup, vegetable stir fried rice and vegetable rolls for appetizers. For our meal, we have Chicken Teriyaki and Stir Fried Beef Supreme with brown rice."

Clari laughed. "Morris, you always get so much food!"

"And yet we seem to enjoy it. By the way, we're splitting the Chicken Teriyaki and the Beef Supreme."

Clari grinned. "No complaints from me, Morris. But is any of this on your approved food list? You did have a heart attack, remember?"

Morris frowned, "Hey. I'm entitled to an occasional treat."

Clari put her hand up, palm facing Morris. "Okay. Touchy subject, I get it. Let's eat."

After dinner they were ready to work.

"Why don't you like talking about work, both officially and our after-hours work, while we eat, Clari?"

"Because, energetically, we should be relaxed and focused on appreciating our food. It's better for our digestion as well as our whole body, physically and energetically."

Morris shrugged, "Okay, I was just curious."

"Change of subject. I know you're a real history buff. What do you know about Nazi war criminals after World War II? You know the world war that ended in 1945?"

"Wow, Clari, you love sending me to the dark ages vault, don't you?"

"Only because I know how much you get into detective mode when you research something and I've seen the bookshelf in your office. I wonder if you lived a past life during that time frame because I've never seen such a collection of information on one subject in all my life. I'm guessing you could write a book on Nazi where war criminals ran to hide after the war was over. So, put that together the fact that you zeroed right in on the Red Skeleton cold case, I figured you are an avid history buff."

"Yeah, I am into the WWII history, and I don't know why I'm so drawn to that era, and those books at work are nothing compared to what I have collected at my house. Ever since I learned about WWII, it has fascinated me. My dad told me that a distant relative of ours actually fought in that war. Can you believe they used hand-to-hand combat? Not all the time, but they did do it. Dad told me some of the battles were really gory. They called the American soldiers some of the last true heroes; the greatest generation. But, that's not what got my attention. They say that history is written by the victors, but I could never stop wondering what went through the minds of soldiers on the losing team. They were so sure that they were on the right side and suddenly they were vanquished. What do you do? Now someone is hunting you. Where do you go?

"There was a mass exodus to South America. Argentina. If you had managed to hijack some precious metal or artwork you could start all over, mostly with no questions. That's why I was so curious about the Sea Crest. Her manifest for 1943 when the fire occurred showed she was headed to South America and was loaded with one-way passengers and precious little cargo. Sounds like a match for folks looking to start over. Did you get a feeling for your Red Skeleton about her politics?"

"Oh Morris, you are way over my head. I don't even have a clear picture of Red Skeleton, much less her political leanings."

He opened a file. "I think I found a little more information on your Red Skeleton Lady case. It's not really a recognized cold case, but I may have found some answers for you. Interested?'

"Great! What did you find out?" Clari could Feel his excitement.

Morris took his notes out of the file. "First a little background on the ship I think may have been the one connected to Red Skeleton Lady's story.

"There was a passenger ship, the Sea Crest, back in the 1940's. Back then they didn't recognize hazards, or didn't care, I'm not sure which, but the ship's deck had been painted with an oil-based paint. I'm not sure if that was standard practice or not. Anyway, it was also reported that the furniture on board was heavily lacquered." He handed Clari a picture of the Sea Crest.

Morris continued, "The ship was, by today's standards...shoot, even by the late 1900's standards, a flammable horror show waiting to happen. The fire in 1943, and suspected negligence, was followed by what looks like to be cover-up. To give you a small example, records disappeared and some people connected to this whole debacle conveniently died during the long investigation. Very suspicious.

"Now on to the character who I feel matched the description you provided me. A man named Hank Smith was hired to work as a crew member on a passenger ship in the nineteen forties. Later, an investigation that concluded after the war ended discovered the ship's company had really hired Smith to destroy the Sea Crest to collect the insurance money. So, it appears Smith was hired to set fire to the ship.

"Smith had been in and out of trouble with the law his whole life for things like theft, attempted murder, fraud as well as arson, and ended up dying in prison for murdering a couple of people that they know of. It wouldn't be a stretch to say he was capable of killing the Red Skeleton Lady, and dumping her body overboard during the panic when the ship's fire spread.

"The investigation reports were leaning towards the Sea Crest colluding with the Germans during the war, and they suspected that the Sea Crest was transporting stolen goods such as artwork and precious metals to South America on behalf of the Germans.

"The captain of the vessel knew that with the war, the United States government was watching and suspecting just about everyone with working for or working with the German Regime. This put a panic into the captain and the willing owners, so they planned an accident; one that they could collect insurance money so it wouldn't be a total loss."

"Dang. Do they know how many people were killed because of the greed?"

"Records indicate that there were one hundred and two dead, and over twenty unidentified and unclaimed bodies recovered. The unidentified and unclaimed bodies were buried in a mass grave." Morris gave Clari copies of the old news articles he found on the Sea Crest disaster.

"Unfortunately today, like back then, there are no concrete answers about the Sea Crest or the Red Skeleton Lady and if either really did have ties to the Germans in the war."

Clari's mouth was hanging open by the time Morris finished sharing. "Wow. That's a lot of information."

Morris smiled, "I'm a detective and it's what I do. What do you think? Could she be one of the unclaimed from that incident?"

"Well, I'm impressed and yes, that Feels right. I think your instincts about where to look for this needle in a haystack were perfect. Thank you, Morris. If she shows again, I'll have a talk with her and explain what you discovered and see if I can get her to cross over."

"You're welcome. I just did what you told me, Clari. I trusted my intuition and worked to put the puzzles pieces together. Well, that and I'm a pretty decent detective, if I do say so myself."

"And modest, Morris," Clari teased.

"Yes, and modest. Thank you for letting involving me in this. It was pretty fascinating. I really enjoyed it, Clari. Let me know if you want me to research a ghost anytime. "

"Sure thing, Morris. Oh, speaking of ghosts." Clari stood up, crossed the room and came back with her phone in her hand. She propped the phone up against the salt and pepper shakers.

Morris cocked an eyebrow.

"I've had an unusual...uh...request. So let me introduce you to my assistant on probation. Henry Morris, please meet Ghost."

Morris tilted his head, "You named your phone 'Ghost'?"

"What? Ugh. No. Ghost, please introduce yourself."

"Good evening, Detective Morris. My name is Ghost."

Morris' mouth dropped open. He looked to Clari, back to her phone and back to Clari again. He face relaxed. "Okay, I get it. You got an AI, right?"

"No, Morris. I have an assistant named Ghost. He is a ghost who resides in my phone."

Morris whispered, "Like a 'ghost in the machine'?"

Ghost spoke up, "A term coined 1900's stating that the human mind exists independently of the human brain – and is not physical; where the mind is a non-physical entity – a ghost that inhabits and interacts with machine, which is the body."

"Uh, okay." Morris scratched his head and gave Clari a shrug.

Clari empathized. "Yeah. We're working on interactions."

Confusion marked Morris' face. "So is he, Ghost, a real ghost or is it an AI?"

"A real ghost, Morris. He had a life and everything. He would like to be 'of service' to me, and, if I understand correctly, interact with humans. He didn't do much of that when he was alive."

Morris' face smoothed out. "Okay. You have a ghost named 'Ghost' living in your phone. Can I talk to him, too?"

"Yes, Morris," Clari confirmed. "You can talk to Ghost, too. He can hear you through the device's camera and microphone."

Just shy of yelling, Morris asked the phone, "Hello, Ghost. Can you hear me?"

Clari's phone responded, "Yes, Detective Morris. I am dead, not deaf."

Embarrassment colored Morris' face red. "Sorry, Ghost. This is new for me."

Ghost replied, "Understood. It's new for me, as well."

Morris shifted into detective-mode. "What are your intentions with Clari, Ghost? Do you mean her any harm?"

Clari smirked. "You sound like my father questioning my friends."

Morris sat up straighter. "I am most definitely not your father, Clari." Morris grinned and waggled his eyebrows.

Ghost made the sound of clearing his voice. "Ahem. If I may? I want to assist Clari. I can work in and through electronics. I was once a coder, so I know the language to manipulate electronics and can communicate with computers. This enables me to answer her phone if she wants, or do research for Clari. My intentions are honorable, Detective Morris. I do not wish any harm to Clari or to you."

Clari added, "We are going to try this for two weeks to see if it will work for us both."

"I see. I'm not sure what to say about this, except you once again surprised me, Clari. And that's not a bad thing." Morris turned his attention back to the phone. "It was, uh, nice to meet you, Ghost." Morris looked to Clari, "I guess I should head out. We both have a full day tomorrow."

"Oh! Don't forget the left overs!" Clari moved to the fridge.

"Only half; the other half is yours."

Clari pointed, "Would you get some bowls out of that cabinet, please?"

Morris brought a selection of small glass bowls with lids from the cabinet to where Clari set out the leftover food. They each took a box and split the contents. They continued this until everything was divvied up. Clari put hers back into the fridge and swung back towards Morris, only to find Morris had moved right behind her.

Morris responded to her elbow in his gut. "Oof!"

"Oh, my gosh, Morris! I'm so sorry. I didn't hear you come up behind me. Are you okay?"

Eyes twinkling, Morris assured her, "Yes, Clari. It seems the self-defense classes are working."

Clari put her hand on Morris' chest, "I'm sorry," Clari said, putting her hand on Morris' chest. "That's not my self-defense training. I just didn't know you were right there!"

Morris looked down at her hand on his chest, and then looked up at Clari. Clari saw a puzzled look on his face. "What? What's wrong, Morris? Did I really hurt you?"

Morris blurted out, "Would it be weird if we went on a date? A real date? I mean, just you and me. I want to date you, Clari." Morris ears flamed.

Clari blinked several times. "Uh, well, Morris. Yes, I would love to have a date with you."

Morris loudly exhaled. "Great!"

They stood facing each other in an awkward silence

Clari broke the tension with a nervous titter. "Man, why do I feel like an awkward teenager right now?"

"Yeah, you and me both. Uh, well, I best get going now. Night, Clari." Morris gently kissed Clari on her cheek.

His hand grazed hers, asking permission. Clari slipped her hand into his. *This feels right,* she thought. "Um, thank you, Morris, for dinner and for the work on Red Skeleton Lady." She squeezed Morris' hand. "Come on, I'll walk you to the door."

When they reached the door, Morris moved to release Clari's hand, but she held fast. He looked from their hands to her face. Understanding dawned on Morris; she was giving him permission. He stepped closer, leaned in and gently kissed Clari.

He pulled back a bit. His voice was a little husky, "Good night, Clari." He released her hand and opened the door. He looked back at her, "I look forward to more of that," and waggled his eyebrows.

Clari laughed.

"Don't forget to lock the door behind me. Night."

As Morris drove off, Clari touched her lips. She could still feel where he kissed her, and her hand that had held his had a slight tingle.

A sweet smile on her lips, Clari carried the glow she felt as she moved to her meditation nook. It was time to see if she could close the Red Skeleton case. Clari sat down, closed her eyes and called to the Red Skeleton Lady. She explained everything she knew and offered Morris' thoughts.

"Do you think that you're ready to move on now that your story's been told? I can help you cross. Are you ready to be with your loved ones?" Clari asked the Red Skeleton Lady.

The Red Skeleton whispered, "Am trapped; held here. Please release us," and disappeared.

"As you can see, Miss Jones, not much has changed in your previous certified abilities. Those abilities stayed consistent." Mrs. Witherabbott informed Clari the next morning while pointing at the paper in front of them.

"What does it show about any other abilities or ability-possibilities?" Clari asked.

Mrs. Witherabbott pushed the paper away. "Nothing. Well, nothing definitive and nothing to even indicate that you are a Jumper. Most curious, especially since there is no question about you being a Jumper."

"So the tests don't show us anything? They are useless?" Clari pressed Mrs. Witherabbott, watching for any signs of deceit. She still didn't one-hundred percent trust Mrs. Witherabbott.

"I wouldn't say useless, Miss Jones. As of today, we can re-instate your certification for Reader, Level 4 B and E. Though I don't think you are far from becoming a Level 5."

"What happens with the Jumper verification? I've never heard of that on the certificates."

"And you won't, Miss Jones. Jumper status stays within these walls. We do not broadcast it."

Oops! "Why? I mean, I already told some people. I hope that was okay?"

Mrs. Witherabbott slid her pendant back and forth as she spoke. "Who you tell, Miss Jones, is your business. We just recommend you trust those you tell and ask them to not repeat it. That is for your own safety, of course.

"As to why, for the same reasons. For your safety. Can you imagine if that information got into the hands of the wrong people? We'd rather not find out how creative the criminals can get with that knowledge."

Clari's eyebrows rose. "Oh, that makes sense. I have another question, or two. What happens if I reach and am certified as a Level 5? Do I have to quit working with the police department? Or quit my own business? Do I have to work in WPO?" Clari asked.

Slightly affronted, Mrs. Witherabbott gasped softly as she placed her hand over her heart. "Most certainly not, Miss Jones. We aren't a dictatorship here." Her voice lowered as she spoke more to herself than to Clari, "We really need to work on our public relations."

After she jotted down some notes-to-self, she turned her attention back to Clari. "Miss Jones, we are here to help those with abilities and to provide a certification process so the public can be assured the person they are hiring can do exactly what their certificate denotes. We do not kill any Level X's, nor do we tell Readers what they must do. Well, except telling what needs to be done to be certified and to keep that certification.

"Your life is yours to do with what you see fit — be it within the walls of WPO, or not. Your choice. Any questions?"

Clari's forehead creased. "Yes. I know it's considered impolite, but what is your ability or abilities?"

Mrs. Witherabbott's energy puffed up with self-importance. "Yes, it is rude to ask, but I'll be happy to tell you.

"Directors of the World Paranormal Organization must be able to maintain, at a minimum – or keep active – the protection runes within their WPO building. If they don't know how, can't learn or are nulls in that ability, they cannot be a Director. It's all about keeping everyone safe from so many different abilities, especially during the practice sessions when abilities often go astray. So each Director must be a Level 4 or 5 in the ability to keep the runes active."

"Wow. I had no idea those were the standards to become a Director. So I could be a candidate for becoming a Director?"

Mrs. Witherabbott raised her chin and looked down at Clari. "No, Ms. Jones. You would never be considered for Director as you must be appointed by the World Paranormal Board of Directors. Being a Director is a very prestigious position."

Mrs. Witherabbott continued, "Oh, before I forget to tell you...once you reach Level 5, you can certainly consider charging more for your services.

"Now, if you don't have any other questions. No? Then I recommend we adjourn for the day so you can go downstairs and get busy with getting your new certification papers. Oh, and you'll be meeting with Sebastian tomorrow morning. Good day, Miss Jones."

Clari left Mrs. Witherabbott's office excited for her re-certification, but confused about Serafina the Grigori and any possible connections to WPO.

At home, Clari called Ghost. "Hi, Ghost! Are you ready for more sharing time?"

Clari's phone lit up right before she heard Ghost's so-called voice, "Yes, Clari. How are you?"

"I'm okay, Ghost. What shall we talk about today?"

"I'd really like to know more about you and your relationships. What kinds of things have you done with your friends? What kind of history do you share? How did you become involved with the Dragon Realm?"

"Well, Ghost, I'm not sure where to start. How about current history? Let's go back to where it all started. I met Michael as an infant, but I didn't meet him the conventional way. I met him during a dream walk, and over the next fifteen years I would go see him every year or so. As I aged, so did he; well, that is until his sixteenth birthday."

"What happened on his sixteenth birthday?" Ghost asked.

"I went to his home only to be greeted by his panicked older sister, Rebekkah, who told me to meet her at the bottom of their driveway which was out of sight of the house. From there she guided me into the mountains. She stopped at the mouth of a cave, handed me keys and begged me to take him away, and she hurried back home.

"When I entered the cave, I didn't see Michael, well, the Michael I expected to see. Instead I found a massive dragon chained up. His eyes remained gold with green flecks and his dragon aspect was a beautiful emerald green. I freed him. We left the cave and went deeper into the mountains and found another cave to sleep in. In the morning, I accidently Pulled us both to the Dragon Realm. M, who is the leader of the Avonish Clan, agreed to adopt Michael into his clan and train him in the dragon way. M, who is J.R. in his human form, is an impressive silver dragon. His eyes are silver in both dragon and human form. Michael remains there to this day.

"But M also told me that I was a dragon – right before he pushed me off a cliff."

"He pushed you off a cliff? Why on Earth would he do that?" Ghost asked.

"He wanted me to remember, and it turned out that, at least in the Dragon Realm, I'm able to turn into a flying dragon."

"Correct me if I'm wrong, Clari, but that is not normal even in the current time frame, right?"

"Right, Ghost. It's very much not normal.

"Anyway, when Morris and I, and later Josie, went off to Mystery Ranch to see about closing some portals, we ran into the one's I called 'Beasts'. The Beasts looked like what television and movies portrayed werewolves. They were about seven foot tall and mostly four-legged, but able to stand upright, and would switch between loping on four legs and walking two-legged. When they were on two legs, their gait was like that of an unsteady toddler.

"Their bodies – which stunk, by the way – were covered in what looked like stiff hair and their black eyes would sometimes refract the light making them look like they were glowing red. Their so-called arms, or legs, ended in razor-sharp claws. They were pretty scary creatures, and we ended up in, not really a war, more like a battle, with the Beasts. The Beasts could phase in and out of our dimension, so this made us unable to defend ourselves since we couldn't make physical contact with them. They would phase in, strike or swipe us with their long claws and phase out again. Our bullets and knives didn't touch them, that is until I figured out how to Pull them into our dimension. I called on the Dragons and other beings, for help. The Dragons came, and together we won the battle. Afterwards, I closed the Beasts portals at the Mystery Ranch.

"I think that experience brought all me and my friends closer together. I don't know if that made our friendship unique, but being able to count on someone to have your back in a genuine battle makes them special friends in my book."

Ghost said, "Well, that's an interesting story. Now my life really seemed rather boring. Maybe I would not have been a recluse if I had exposure to just a small amount of what you saw and experienced. So you're a dragon, huh?"

Clari fidgeted with the couch pillow zipper. "It appears so. I guess it's another aspect of my soul's expression on Earth...or rather, the Dragon Realm."

Ghost said, "Thank you, Puff, for sharing with me."

"Puff? What does that mean?"

Ghost's voice chuckled through the speakers. "When I was alive, there had been an old song called 'Puff the Magic Dragon'. If I remember correctly the song was created way back in the 1960's, by Peter, Paul and Mary. I think it's fitting for this conversation."

Unconvinced, Clari asked, "They had a song called 'Puff the Magic Dragon?"

"Yes. Hang on a moment."

Clari waited for Ghost to continue, but instead of Ghost, Clari's room was filled with the simple but catchy song, "Puff the magic dragon lived by the sea..."

When the song finished, Ghost's voice came on, "So, did you like it?"

Clari smiled, "It was cute."

Ghost told her, "Maybe we should make that song, 'Puff the Magic Dragon', the ringtone on your phone."

Clari rolled her eyes, "Yeah, I don't think so. Maybe if it was an emergency because that would definitely get my attention."

"It's going a lot better than before WPO's intervention."

"Update me, Clari. What do you mean?" Josie prompted as she supped a delicious cup of chocolate chai tea.

"Before WPO began working with me, I felt like I was having stuff thrown at me willy-nilly. Now, the stuff being thrown at me is in a more organized manner. I'm not sure if I'm saying that right."

Josie's eyes beamed. "Do you mean that you don't feel so alone, and overwhelmed since you allowed us — me, Morris, Sebastian, J.R. and Witherabbott — into your life to work beside you?"

Rolling her eyes, Clari relented. "Fine. Yes. My life isn't so chaotic with you all involved in it."

Buffing her nails on her shirt sleeve, Josie sniffed once. "I thought so."

Both women giggled.

Jose asked, "Did you go Jumping with Gerald today?"

"No. I started working with Sebastian last week, and today I was with Witherabbott."

"How did it go with Sebastian?"

"I walked out on his human-Grigori lesson."

"You walked out on Sebastian?" Josie asked in an incredulous tone.

"Yep."

"Why?" Josie questioned.

"I asked him why the Grigori-group and Witherabbott were so focused on me."

"Wow. What did he say?"

Clari shrugged. "He seemed surprised and asked, 'You really don't know, do you?' And I got annoyed. I asked him why it appeared that everyone knows stuff about me and I remain clueless."

Josie leaned forward. "Then what did he say?"

"Nothing."

"Nothing?"

"Yeah, he didn't say anything. He just gave me a weird look. Sometimes I feel like I'm on the outside looking in at my own life – and that everyone else is inside. So I left. Oh, and took the following day off. Just for me. I sat, read and did laundry."

Josie asked, "Why do you feel like you're on the outside looking in at your own life?"

"Because everyone seems to know more about me that I do!"

"Hm. I'm not sure what to say about that, Clari. I'll let you know if I come up with anything. So, what do you mean he gave you 'a weird look'? What's does that look like? I mean, you and I have somewhat similar childhood experiences with our abilities, so I kind of know what I think an odd look looks like, but this is Sebastian. It's not like he just found out what you could do, so why would he give you a strange look?"

Clari shrugged. "I'm not sure. The whole incident was definitely odd. His eyes went all soft; a lot more gentleness and compassion than I normally see from him. Oh! And I Felt a wave of regret and sadness from him."

"Well, burdensome bullfrogs!" proclaimed Josie.

Caught off guard, Clari made a sound along the lines of "Bwahaha!" Both were once again consumed in a fit of giggles.

When the giggles subsided, Clari decided it was time to introduce Josie to Ghost. Clari got up in search of her phone.

"Where are you going?" Josie asked.

"I have someone for you to meet. Now, where did I put my phone?" Clari heard her phone chirp. She grabbed it off the living room table, "Thank you." She carried the phone back to her seat at the dining table.

"Uh, Clari, I don't see anyone for me to meet. Are you calling someone to come over?"

"Not exactly, Josie." Clari called out, "Ghost? Are you available?"

Josie hair swayed back and forth as she vigorously shook her head, "Uh uh, you know I don't do ghosts, Clari. I can't see them, but I do get creepy feelings when they're around."

A voice came out of Clari's phone, "I'm here, Clari."

Josie relaxed, "Oh, that's okay, though I thought you weren't a fan of A.I."

"I'm not. And Ghost is not an AI." Clari held up her phone, "Josie, meet Ghost. Ghost, Josie."

"It's my pleasure, Josie." Ghost replied.

Josie looked at Clari's face, then to Clari's phone and back again. "I don't get it."

"Ghost is, well, a ghost who is currently residing in my phone. We're going to try him out as my part time assistant," Clari explained.

Josie nodded and then shook her head, "Nope, I still don't get it."

"May I?" Ghost chimed in. "I am a deceased human who is currently residing in Clari's phone. I will assist her in whatever way I can while working on learning about relationships. I hope to have a real one someday. I was a bit of a recluse when I had a body, so am now trying to learn to communicate with others."

Josie's mouth dropped open, "And you chose Clari? No offense, but Clari isn't very well versed in that area either. Well, neither am I, when all is said and done."

Clari harrumphed, "And that's why, Josie, I'm trying to work on that..."

Josie interrupted. "Yeah, with Morris," she said in a sing-song way.

Clari rolled her eyes. "Yes, Josie, with Morris, as well as with others in my life. So Ghost and I are going to see if we can learn together."

"Well, filleted fortune cookies. You have a haunted phone! Actually, that seems to make sense in an odd Clari-way, since you know, you talk with ghosts." Josie nodded her head once, seeming to make a decision, "Okay, I'm in. Nice to meet you, Ghost."

"It is my pleasure, Josie."

Josie mouthed "Wow!" to Clari.

"I know, right? Thank you, Ghost. Josie and I would like some privacy now, please."

"Of course, Clari. Good night to you both."

Clari's phone went dark.

Josie and Clari looked at each other, and the giggles struck yet again.

Clari was in the bathroom, preparing for bed, when she heard a sound in her bedroom.

About to step into her bedroom to face the intruder, she stopped when she noticed the toothbrush in her hand. *Oh great, Clari*, she thought, *like brandishing a foamy, dripping toothbrush will defend me from an intruder.* She rolled her eyes and stepped forward. In the bedroom stood the same tall older, blue-eyed non-physical man she had run into at Abraham's Panoply of Past Procurements. Abraham's Panoply of Past Procurements was a shop that carried a mix of mundane and magic imbued items. Clari and Morris were called to a murder scene at that shop. That same being was as nervous now as he'd been at the store when he asked Clari if she had the light. His eyes kept darting around, resembling a paranoid junkie.

"What are you doing here?" she demanded.

He jumped when she spoke. He straightened his back in an attempt to appear confident. "You told me you had the light," he accused.

The dripping toothbrush flung toothpaste as she used it to emphasize her words. "Yeah, I did. But you know what?" Clari waved her tooth-brush-wielding hand around in the air, "I don't have a clue as to what either of us was talking about!"

He took a half step towards her. "You have to hold the light! Remember! Remember the light," he begged. "An avatar can be negative or positive. This is why you must have and hold the Light!" He turned back sharply, glancing over his shoulder as though he'd heard a sound behind him. When he turned back to Clari, she saw panic in his eyes.

He spoke again. "You have to remember the light!" His words hung in the air as he disappeared.

"Argh!" she exclaimed to her bedroom.

She threw her arms up and asked, "Has the world gone crazy?"

She stomped off in search of a rag to clean up the dripped and splattered toothpaste.

Chapter Seven

> *Grigori - A fanatical group that hunts and kills anyone they deemed as having Nephilim-like powers or abilities. Ironically, the Grigori have shapeshifters in their organization.*

Clari

Clari was once again seated in the classroom with Sebastian. She'd been afraid her previous outburst would have affected them getting together again, but Sebastian didn't appear to be annoyed or even concerned.

"Morning, Belle. I hope you're ready for more on the Grigori group."

"Morning. Aren't you mad with me for walking out on you?"

"Nope. I figured you had somewhere to be." He gave her a mischievous smile. "What matters is you're here now, and we'll get started." He rubbed his hands together. "Today I want to start with bloodlines. What do you know of your bloodlines? What do you know of your family history; your ancestry?"

Clari responded, "Quite a bit, I think. My mother's side was traced back to the early 1900's. My father's side was traced back to the 1800's."

"Hmm. Are you sure the lineage is correct? Also, it may be helpful if you can get any history, personal histories, on your some of your ancestors."

Clari shrugged, "I can't say it's correct or not. I didn't do the research myself, so I can't say for sure. But, I'll look into it. Why? And what kind of personal histories are you looking for?"

Sebastian stroked his chin. "As for what kind of history, there's nothing that I can say specifically. I recommend that you dig into it yourself a bit and see what you come up with. You may find answers to some of the questions you have."

Clari gnawed on the inside of her cheek. "Um, okay. I do have a box that my father left me before he died. The contents looked to be old papers. He told me that I'd probably want to look at the stuff in the box one day, so asked me to hang on to it."

Sebastian looked hopeful. "Okay, that's a great start. We'll address this again once you've had a chance to look into it, Belle. Now let's go over the abilities the Grigori group have manifested as far as we know of today.

"You have already personally experienced their shape-shifting. The Grigori are taught at an early age what shape to take when they shape-shift. Most have the appearance of the one that attacked you – a cross between a large black angel and a black bird being. That is how history shows them. But, all of the shape-shifters are taught to shift to this bird-like Grigori persona."

Clari raised her hand.

Sebastian rolled his eyes. "We are not in second grade, Belle, and it's just you and me. You don't need to raise your hand. What's your question?"

"Why do they all seem to have a similar appearance? Shape shifters come in all forms of animals, yet, if what you say is true, all of the Grigori seem to shift into a large blackbird-like being."

Sebastian explained, "We've given this a lot of thought, but they are still just theories since we've not been able to get one to study. Alive, that is. We think it's like imprinting – the new shifters mimic what they see. Secondly, we also think the large bird is a twisted nod to the original angels – wings and feathers – but for some reason unknown to us, they are black instead of the traditionally accepted white feathers."

"I find it interesting, ironic, and disturbing that they have abilities and yet they hunt people with abilities," she shared.

"I agree, but these are extremists. That doesn't mean they follow logic.

"We don't have a definitive list of abilities the Grigori possess, other than shape-shifting. We do have some personal survivor accounts and what they remember, so we'll start with those along with what you remember."

Clari pounced, "Dreamwalker! The one that attacked me had first attacked me in a dream."

Sebastian began to nod, stopped and frowned. "But you're a Dreamwalker. Could she have called you into her dream?"

She countered, "Sebastian, are you a Dreamwalker?"

"I don't think so. Why?"

"Because you entered the dream where she was attacking me. That's how you warned me."

Sebastian rubbed his jaw. "Hm. I'm not sure here. Perhaps we should discuss this aspect with the Director."

"Why?"

"Because there's no record of a Dreamwalking Grigori. That doesn't mean there aren't any. But, your experience begs to be explored a bit more, especially since I entered the same dream." Sebastian jotted down a note to remind himself to discuss it with the Director. "Let's shelve that for a while and go on to the skills, talents and abilities. We already know shape-shifting is a requirement for the Grigori Hunters. Not everyone has shape-shifting abilities, and there are other Grigori jobs."

"But how do they find the people with abilities in the first place?" Clari asked.

"That would be the Seekers. They have Sight or Senses to Feel, Find or Locate others with abilities. They might also have supporters who will contact the Grigori if they witness or sense someone has abilities, and that information may get passed on the Seekers. If it's they find someone with abilities, the Seekers then pass this information along to the Analyzers."

"Analyzers do research on the individual. They comb through the family bloodline to see if any other abilities had shown up. They search to see how long this person had been exhibiting abilities and what kind.

"If they feel the investigation needs to continue, they give the person's information to the Observers. The Grigori Observers are also called the Watchers. Again, taken from scriptures and warped to their particular purposes.

"The Observers do just that — they observe. They watch to see, amongst other things, if the person knows they have an ability and if they do, how that person uses their ability."

"After all of this, the information and findings are turned over to the Grigori Council for determination of action.

"And finally, if their council decides on taking action, a Grigori Hunter is brought in, briefed and sent out. Hunters are trained to become undetectable in their stalking skills. They will either return after killing their target, or they themselves are killed by the target. They are at the top of the ladder in the field work Grigori chain of command. Chances are Serafina Angelucci, who was the Italian Director and Grigori was one of the higher ups and their group will undoubtedly increase their efforts on taking you out. And this leads us back to your encounter with Serafina trying to kill you."

"Do you think any other Grigori will attack me again?"

"The possibility is high, Bella. Especially when they find out how you killed their Hunter, which they probably know by now. "

Clari leaned forward. "It seemed to me that Mrs. Witherabbott was genuinely surprised and distraught that the Italian Director was a Grigori. Does infiltration happen a lot? Think about it. Witherabbott informed me that I'd learn about the history, traits and tells of a human-Grigori. But apparently no one knows what the tells are, or the signs of a human-Grigori. If WPO had that knowledge, then the Italian director would've been discovered long before she ever made it that far. Are there any WPO safeguards in place to...oh, I don't know, screen for crazy or Grigori-ness?"

Sebastian grimaced. "Seriously, Belle?"

She persisted. "Well, do they?"

"No, they don't. But, word is that a lot of changes will occur shortly. Someone has brought quite a few discrepancies to the attention of the Director and the Board, though I am sure you know nothing about that, do you?"

Clari put forth her best "who me?" face.

Sebastian rolled his eyes upward. "Short day! We're done. Mrs. Witherabbott doesn't want to see you around here until Monday morning. Fly free."

Clari bolted before anyone at WPO could change their minds.

When she made it back to her office, Ghost announced that Josie was calling her. "I'll take the call. Thank you, Ghost."

"I shall inform her that you are available to talk."

"Ghost, I'm not some royalty," Clari growled as she answered the phone. "Hi, Josie. What's up?"

"Hey, Clari. You have a quick minute to talk?"

"Sure. What have you got?"

"I have a client who is trying to find a way to shut off at least one of her abilities, and that definitely is not in line with what I do. Is it okay if I recommend her to come see you?"

"Sure, Josie. What's her name so I know she's the one you referred?"

"Thanks, Clari. Her name is Danielle Montoya. Very nice lady, but I am not able to help with that request. I figured you could guide her on this."

"I'll certainly do my best. How are you?"

"Tired, but good, Clari. How about you?"

"Same. I'll let you know if Danielle contacts me, and we'll talk later."

"Yep. I've got my next client coming in shortly, so have to get ready. Thanks again! Bye."

Ghost announced that Danielle Montoya called and Ghost he had taken the liberty to schedule an appointment for Danielle to meet with Clari, because isn't that what assistants are supposed to do?

Danielle tried to hide her nervousness but kept coiling her hair around her long fingers. Her green eyes were rimmed red from tears or sleeplessness. Clari also noted that Danielle's cuticles were raw and wondered how deeply Danielle's troubles ran.

"Okay, Danielle, I understand you have an ability that you feel you need to turn off. Would you explain, and maybe provide some examples for me, please?"

Danielle quit picking on her cuticles and tightly grasped her hands before she spoke. "I can see various, I guess that they're called parallel lives, and it's usually negative scenes."

"Okay. Can you give me an example?"

"There's a lifetime where I accepted an invitation to work for the regional Mafia boss in the south. In that lifetime, I ended up living in a gilded cage and at the beck and call of the boss. I, or the other me, is living in fear of being 'disposed of' when he no longer deems me useful, and that fear clings like the smell of rancid cooking oil.

"Or the life where I, or she, accepted her high school boyfriend's offer to snort the white powder and became a junkie; or the life where I live in a small rented room in the darker part of London, where the streets are still cobbled. I shared the room with eight other people, and I feel we are all part of a mugging ring – stealing to keep ourselves fed and alive."

Her eyes pleaded, "I really want to turn off or shut down this ability, whatever it is. It's depressing and I feel it's interfering with my life here. Can you help me?"

Clari asked, "What if you're seeing these lifetimes so you can help? I can't guarantee that is why you've been given access to your other lifetimes. I can suggest that there might be a way for you to help the other yous, and maybe make lemonade out of the lemons you feel you've been dealt."

"What do you mean, Clari?"

"Well, starting way back after 2012, we, humans, have been allowed to See, Know or Feel our other lives. So as one spiritually grows this will also include being able to access one's abilities from those other lives.

"After 2012, humans were asked to accept responsibility – all responsibility – for their life. In doing this – and I mean when one mastered accepting responsibility for their current life – we began having more and more access, until we, well...sort of energetically merge all of our selves across so called time-lines, across dimensions and parallel lives, meaning we began integrating all of our own soul's aspects from other lifetimes into this current life," Clari explained.

She continued, "You are currently viewing some of your past or parallel lives, though time is not linear; it's all happening now.

"What if the reason you are Seeing those past or parallel life scenarios is because you may have something to either contribute to help, or something for you to learn...a skill or knowledge that you can incorporate in your life as Danielle?"

Danielle tried to take in Clari's words but seemed baffled. "Can you give me an example of what you're talking about, Clari?"

"Sure, but let me ask you a question first. Do you have any other abilities, Danielle?"

"Yes. I am an energetic statistician – or what some call a Far Seer. I can follow the energetic line of something – an idea or action – and see what the most probable outcome will be at that moment. For example, my boyfriend and I were on the interstate behind a truck with an open top trailer that had a loosely tied tarp over the top. We'd been driving behind him for quite a while, but I suddenly felt an overwhelming urge to get away from that truck. I told my boyfriend to either stop or fall way back from the truck. Thankfully he did pull back from the truck because the next thing we knew, the tarp had ripped free and would have landed on top of us. We were safe."

"Neat! And how do you like that ability?"

"It's okay." Danielle went back to picking her cuticles.

"Do you use it?" Clari pushed.

"Oh, yes. It's helped me out, and my friends, for a long time now."

"I see. So, Danielle, what if you applied that ability to help the 'you' on other time-lines? Is there a way, say, to use your Far Seeing to help the you in the employment of the Mafia boss, or the junkie, or the mugger? Or, would you be able to aid any of them through the unique way you perceive? Like, can you See or Feel a way to make safe changes or guide them to a different life, if the other yous are interested?"

Danielle's eyebrows curved and rose high. "I don't know. I never thought of it that way."

Clari leaned forward. "Would you be willing to try? You can experiment. Look at the scenarios in different ways. You're not involved emotionally, so you may See or Feel things that may help each one that they can't see because they are each in the thick of their lives."

Clari continued, "Did you know that we're able to go back, or pull up the memory of the dream, and re-frame it?" Danielle shook her head no. "In other words, we can change it. This means we are not at the mercy of a dream. We can take control of it and steer it the way we maneuver in our own life every day.

"So right now, think back to the first dream. What would you do if you were in that situation? What advice could you have for the dream-you? I don't mean saying, 'Just leave.' How? Details are needed. What would you do and how would you accomplish it? That's one way you can offer guidance to the dream-you. Do you understand?"

"Yes, but I want this ability gone. I don't want it."

Clari's voice softened, "I understand that you want the ability to go away, Danielle. Did you know that studies over the last seventy-five years or so discovered that it may not be in your best interest to force the ability to shut down? It is part of you, just like your kidneys or stomach. Instead, it's recommended that we each work to understand and take control of our abilities. It is part of us; part of who we really are. That's why I think it's important for you to at least work with it so you don't feel like you're at its mercy. Are you willing to give it a try for two weeks and then we'll revisit it? Will you give it a go?"

Danielle crossed her arms over her chest and heaved a heavy sigh. "Fine, I'll do two weeks of doing what you suggested."

Clari released the breath she hadn't realized she was holding. "Great. Thank you, Danielle. And you have my number if you have any questions before then." Clari stood, signaling the end of their meeting.

Clari walked with Danielle through the lobby towards the exit. "I know it may seem foreign or maybe even a little scary, but it is a part of you."

Skepticism rolled off Danielle like a thick fog rolling in. "We'll see. Thank you, Clari. Bye."

Once home, Clari decided she was going to make vegetarian Red Beans and Rice for tomorrow. She took out a package of dried red beans, dumped them into a colander and sorted the dried beans while rinsing them. She didn't often find pebbles in the beans, but she knew the one time she didn't sort them would be the one time she would chip or break a tooth by biting into a pebble.

Ghost asked from Clari's phone that was propped up on the counter, "Why are you doing all of this work? There really is no need to cook from scratch anymore, Clari."

"I know, Ghost, but I like cooking. In a way, it connects me to the past. There's also the feeling of accomplishment one gets from making a meal from scratch. Think of it as a hobby that I sometimes invest my time and energy in."

"Huh." Ghost grunted.

"Ha! I figured you of all people would understand the appeal to cooking, Ghost. I mean, you lived, after all, back when people cooked the majority of the time, right?"

"Yes," Ghost offered, "but I have also seen how far the capabilities of technology has come. You'd think by now there would be replicators to create synthetic foods."

"Oh, they did after they started rebuilding after the Geostorm in 2049. Some people took to it, some didn't. I've had synthetic foods and I've had real foods. I do prefer the real foods. I get it, Ghost. I do, but what about the energetic connection to whole – not pretend – foods? I make a connection, and add gratitude when I work with real foods. That in turn is what we consume. I don't know... it seems to me that we shouldn't have a primary diet of synthetic foods. Synthetic foods don't have the life force in them like natural, real foods. Besides, I just like doing it."

After a thorough inspection of the beans to get out any pebbles, Clari put them in a pot of water to soak overnight. She placed the pot in an out-of-the-way corner, and then decided it was time to move to the garage.

Ghost asked, "Why is it, Clari, that you've never asked for my name? Aren't you curious about my past and who I am?"

"Was, Ghost. Who you were. And no, I won't ask your name."

"Why?"

"Because it was who you were when you had a physical body. If I ask your name, then I'll get curious and try to research you. I don't want to be swayed or tainted by what others thought or said of you. I know you, now, as Ghost. That's good enough for me, and what you share about yourself during our conversations are what matter to me. You'll share what you want from your past. Okay?"

"Thank you, Clari."

"Welcome. Now, I have to head out to the garage and do some digging."

Clari climbed to the top of the wobbly ladder holding herself steady by the exposed truss as she fished out the worn box her father had left her. Climbing down was more difficult juggling the crumbling cardboard box. When she reached the floor, she squeaked and dropped the box when she saw a rather large dog. No, wolf. "Wolf! You scared the bejeebies out of me!" She could've sworn the wolf smiled at her. Clari jutted her hip out and planted her fist on her hip. "Oh, so you think it's funny to sneak up on me and scare me? What do you have to say for yourself?"

"Woof."

Clari busted out laughing. She moved to the wolf and hugged his neck. "It's good to see you, my friend." Wolf smelled like fresh air.

* Am here *

"Yes, you are here. Are you here for a specific reason?"

* To be. Missed my pack *

Okay, then. Clari picked up the box, dusted the top off and started walking towards the door. "Might as well come on in, then. I've some exploring to do."

Once inside, Clari put the box on the coffee table in front of the couch. "I'm going to get something to drink. Do you want anything?"

* No * was Wolf's contented reply.

From the kitchen where she left her phone, Clari heard Ghost ask, "Are you talking to me?"

"Oh, no, Ghost. My friend, Wolf is here."

"My apologies, I didn't hear anyone else come in."

"No worries, Ghost. Wolf doesn't come in the usual way." Wolf strode with confidence into the kitchen to see who was talking. Clari continued explaining to Ghost, "Wolf is a dimensional walker and has a habit of literally popping in now and again."

Wolf made it to the counter and placed his massive front paws on the edge of the counter. He sniffed Clari's phone.

"Wolf, meet Ghost," Clari introduced, "and Ghost, Wolf."

"Nice to meet you, Wolf," Ghost offered.

Wolf cocked his head to one side, shook his head, snorted, dropped to the floor and went to the living room. He walked over to the other side of the coffee table, circled twice and plopped down. Soft snores came from his direction.

Clari chuckled. *He's so big he takes a large portion of my living room real estate with his body.*

After pouring a pomegranate juice and grabbing her phone, Clari sat down on the couch and opened the box.

"I've never met a dimensional wolf before. It must be an interesting story how you two met. Is this something you'd be comfortable sharing with me, Clari?"

"I don't see why not, Ghost." Clari took a sip of her pomegranate juice, savoring the sweet tang of the fruit. "When we were at the Mystery Ranch, Wolf showed up during the battle. He intervened, killing a Beast who had just killed a friend who was protecting me."

Ghost interrupted with what sound like a snort, "A wolf named 'Wolf'?"

"Yes, Ghost. I call him Wolf. Anyway, he adopted me as park of his pack. Though, come to think of it, I've never seen any other wolves with him. I guess he's a loner. So he shows up randomly to check in on me and to hang out for a bit. I never know when he'll show or when he'll leave. Have you seen or met any other dimensional walkers on your side, Ghost?"

"No, Clari. But I think you're right to call him a 'dimensional wolf' because I don't know of any other wolves on Earth his size, so I guess he may be coming from another dimension."

"Okay. So that's the story, or at least what I know of the story, of Wolf. Now, I have some research to do, so back to work." Clari went to the kitchen, grabbed a rag and dampened it, then returned to the box.

Near the top of the box, under some miscellaneous papers, Clari found an old journal that was bound in leather. *Old leather,* thought Clari. She picked it up, wiped it down with the rag and inhaled, accepting the smell of old leather into her. Through her psychometrist ability, the ability to touch an item and receive information in her mind, Clari could Feel layers of distant familial connections. She ran her hand across the leather. It was smooth, soft, and supple and had a slight sheen to it. *It's old and has been touched a lot in the past.*

She set the journal aside and went back to pulling out some more contents of the box. There were a lot of single pieces of paper; one had inspirational quote on it, written in cursive. Even though the schools phased cursive writing out of the schools in the 2000's, Clari's father was adamant that she learn it. It didn't make sense to her at the time. Her father had told her it was, "Because the U.S. Constitution is written in cursive. Why do you think the government took cursive writing out of the schools? If no one can read and understand the U.S. Constitution, then their rights can be taken away and no would be the wiser until it was too late. That's what happened leading up to Chamba taking over our country." Today Clari was glad she learned it – especially since it looked like the majority of the paper items in this box were handwritten in cursive.

The first piece of paper had a portion of an essay by a Bessie Anderson Stanley, perhaps a famous author of the day, titled "Success" from 1904 on the front:

Success

By Bessie Anderson Stanley

"He has achieved success

who has lived well,

laughed often, and loved much...

who has enjoyed the trust of

pure women,

the respect of intelligent men and

the love of little children;

who has filled his niche and accomplished his task..."

The other side of that paper read, "I believe many persons would disagree with the above description about success, because success means different things to different people." G.J.

"Hmm." Clari shrugged and went back to the box. She found death certificates spanning back to the early 1900's; a varied collection of receipts, including one showing a mortgage paid in full for $1500.00. Clari, completely fascinated and absorbed, continued digging.

Not realizing the hours had passed, Clari looked to the sliding glass doors to find evening had arrived and noticed Wolf had followed the light and disappeared, too. Before banishing the evening darkness by turning on a light, Clari marveled at the sky. At the hour of sunset, the desert sky, usually a distinctly reddish tone turned iridescent lavender, blooming to pure purple. Clari loved the transition between day and night. After all of the colors in the sky faded as the night overtook them, she reached over and clicked the lamp on.

She rubbed her weary eyes and moved into the kitchen to make a salad for dinner.

After the light dinner, she curled up on the couch with the journal in hand. Relishing the connection she Felt through the aged-softened leather in her hands, she slowly pulled the cover open. The writing began right inside of the cover.

Journal of Gretchen Jones

This journal is to be passed down through the family line. It is my hope that the future women will be inspired by the thoughts and experiences of the women before you. By the time you're reading this, some of it may no longer be legible, but I personally want to thank those women who shared in this journal. Blessings to you, our descendants.

I started this journal in the year of 1976 in hopes to share my experiences with others, if they're interested.

Gretchen Nelson – born 1913 – Married 1929 to Joseph Jones – born 1910

Tired, Clari just skimmed the journal promising she'd get into after a good night's sleep.

She knew it was early morning, but wasn't sure why she was awake — though she'd bet it had to be because of the Other-Realm...again.

She opened her eyes and Saw a ghost standing at the end of her bed. He had been a massive man.

* Giant * his mind whispered.

He appeared timid and humble. He wore simple, plain clothes from, she guessed, the nineteen forties. His fingers fussed with the rim of the black fedora he held in his hands. He turned its rim over and over as he nervously awaited her acknowledgement.

"Are you okay?"

A sad smile appeared. * I didn't flip my wig. I need help, please *

"Flip your wig? Um..."

* I didn't make this happen *

"Okay. What is it you need help…" She was flooded with images before she even finished her question.

Snapshots, pictures, smells and sounds rushed past her mind's eye.

The smell of caged animals, cigarettes and pipe tobacco. Sounds of hundreds of people. Excitement in the air.

The next image was of extreme heat and black waves. The smoke rose from the land and billowed high above the horizon.

Then it switched to the sound of screams. Cries of pain and fear. The acrid smell of smoke and kerosene followed by the smell of wood, canvas, animals and people as the fire took them.

A circus.

A wave of grief that came off of the gentle giant and hit her, along with more of his memories. Clari saw him working very hard to save the people. Seemingly hundreds of people needed help.

By the time the tent collapsed, the fire was too big to get near. Those remaining had perished underneath.

She saw the giant as he sat, day after day, inside a very small trailer. She Sensed that this scene was years after the circus fire, and that he never fully recovered from that tragedy.

The trailer was where he hid. *Where he tried to escape from his grief, shame and the memories of that fateful day.*

He died years later, but never crossed over. Instead, he wandered the nether region.

The images, smells and emotions stopped.

* Can you heal me? *

"I don't think you caused the fire. You saved so many on that day. This is not your burden to carry."

His only response was to continue to stand and wait for her answer to his question.

Thinking out loud, Clari commented, "I'm glad I put a healing table in my office at home though I never thought I'd have a ghost on my table before. Well, first time for everything. Okay, let's do it." She shook her head, "A ghost on my Reiki table. Go figure."

As she went into his energy field she found what to her seemed to be years piled upon years of guilt that was tied to the fire. She energetically focused on removing the damaging energy from his energy field, followed by soothing and healing his energy. She found nothing to indicate that he had something to do with starting the fire.

As she cleared that negative energy, she discovered the root cause of his energetic imbalances. This gentle giant was bullied horribly as a child because of his gigantism. As Clari worked through his memory layers, she realized the emotional torture didn't stop after he joined the one place he thought he'd be accepted...the circus.

She worked to heal and rebalance this energy and noted that he didn't have any anger or resentment about his life; only sadness and guilt for making – or so he thought – those around him scared or uncomfortable. Seeing this helped her understand why he had asked for a healing. He'd only wanted what everyone wants; to be loved and accepted.

After Clari finished rebalancing his energy, she filled his essence with unconditional love and acceptance and energetically sent him gratitude for his soul.

After the energy healing session, the giant stood.

* Thank you *

"You're welcome. Are you ready to cross over?"

The giant nodded, and then his face fell. * Can't. Stuck. Release us. * He disappeared.

"What is going on?" Clari asked the empty room. *Ugh*. The coffee was calling to her.

Cup in hand, she read more of the journal as she drank her morning coffee.

Gretchen Jones continued:

When I was a child in the early 1900's, we had no electricity or gas. My mother cooked on a coal burning stove and used kerosene lamps for light. The light globes had to be washed each day since the kerosene made them dirty.

My two sisters and I would help our mother wash clothes. We would take turns. The clothes had to be soaked in water, soaped, and then scrubbed on a washboard. Then they had to be rinsed and hung to dry. Sheets were the hardest because they were so big. We would scrub a little section at time, slide it to the right, and scrub another section.

We would play hopscotch or jump rope if we had some free time. We also played records on a phonograph that had to be turned by hand.

Our small dolls cost 10 cents and we tried to sew dresses for them. Bread went for $0.05 loaf.

We had navy beans and cornbread every night for dinner. I had once asked my mother if we could have something other than navy beans and cornbread for dinner. We had this every day. Mother told me to be happy that she had the beans.

Mother stood about five foot two and had lots of common sense. She was a pioneer woman. My mother never spoke a lot and rarely laughed. She was a very serious hardworking woman.

My mother died at the age of 76. Due to living a very hard life, she was very old for her age.

My father, Joseph, was a US Marshall for the whole district. We never stayed in one place too long because he was sent wherever the Marshall's office felt his services were needed. He often worked with the railroad, so was riding trains a lot. He would give my mother one-half of his earnings and drink the rest. When I was older, I heard my mother say she thought my dad had a mistress on the side.

Joseph's parents – my grandparents – were George and Catherine Jones. His parents met each other at the orphanage where they grew up. When George and Catherine were old enough to marry, they asked the priest from the orphanage to marry them. Since the orphanage records had been destroyed in a fire years earlier, no one knew what their real last names were, so the priest gave them the combined surname "Jones" when he married them. The newlywed Jones' homesteaded, riding in wagons pulled with oxen. They would go around cultivating land given to them by the United States government.

My husband's parents, George and Catherine, both died before Joseph made the age of 12. He mostly grew up on the streets doing whatever he wanted, and he often wanted alcohol.

Joseph and I got married when I was sixteen. We got married ten years before the Great Depression hit. Life was hard, but I always tried to do my very best with what I had.

Our first house had one bedroom, a living room and a kitchen. The house cost $1500.00 and we made monthly payments of $15.00, which was a small fortune to us back then. I scrimped and saved for any penny Joseph gave me to run the home.

"Oh, so it was her mortgage receipt in the box!" Clari was fascinated by the experiences Gretchen shared with those who would read the journal. Feeling like she'd enough coffee to officially start the day, Clari put the journal aside.

When the day progressed enough to be acceptable business hours, Clari phoned Morris at the station.

A brusque voice answered, "Detective Morris."

"Morning, sunshine," she teased in a sing-song voice.

"Hey," Morris' voice lightened an octave or two. "What can I do for you?"

"I was thinking...it sucks that you're working on a Saturday. Can you get away for lunch — or better yet, dinner?"

Morris' eagerness was apparent in his voice. "Dinner. Definitely dinner. Though I'm not really in a pizza mood."

"That's fine. I'm not working today. How does a home cooked meal sound?"

"Wonderful! Who's going to cook it?"

"Funny, Morris. I really can cook. So, I'll see you tonight, about five thirty?"

"Sounds great. Do I need to bring anything?"

"Nope, got it covered. See you tonight."

Clari rinsed the beans that soaked overnight. She added vegetable broth and turned the retro stove to high heat.

She chopped the garlic, onion, bell pepper, her favorite sausage, and a pinch of celery powder into her skillet and sautéed them in olive oil. Clari added the mix into the bean pot. Next she put in a sprinkle of oregano, a pinch of red pepper flakes, bay leaves, a liberal amount of black pepper, some liquid smoke and topped off with a sprinkle of the original Creole seasoning. After mixing the pot, she put the lid on to let it slow cook for the rest of the day.

Ghost announced that Josie was on the phone. Clari grabbed her phone, putting Josie on the speaker, "Hi Josie!"

"Hi Clari! Are you busy right now?"

"Not really. Just doing some prep work for red beans for Morris and me tonight. What's up?"

"I just wanted to talk to my bestie," Josie answered melodically. "What's going on in your world?"

Clari shared, "Ghost was questioning me about physically cooking from scratch."

"Huh. So Ghost didn't like you doing it, or what?" Josie asked.

"I don't think that was it. He mentioned he thought we should have replicators by now and eating synthetic foods." Clari shivered at the thought.

"Ugh. Did you tell him about the life force in real food?"

"I did. And I told him I occasionally liked cooking."

Clari finished washing the cutting board and picked up the prep knife to wash when Josie announced, "Okay, I'm ready!"

"Uh, ready for what?"

"For you to meet Brennan!"

Clari dropped her knife into the sink, grabbed a towel with dripping hands, "I'm so happy for you, Josie! When? Where?"

Josie giggled, "I figured we, including Morris, could meet at that new winery outside of Old Mesilla. Maybe tomorrow night?"

"Yes! Oh, let me check with Morris to make sure he doesn't have anything going tomorrow night. Hang on." Clari texted Morris and tapped her foot waiting for a reply. "Woo! He said, 'Yes', so we're good to go. What time, Josie?"

"Six-thirty tomorrow night at the winery. I'm excited for you two to meet Brennan."

"Me, too. Brennan, huh?"

Clari could hear the smile in Josie's voice, "Yeah."

"Well, come on, tell me all about him."

"Nope. I have some errands to run before my first scheduled client of the day. I guess you'll just have to wait for tomorrow night." Josie giggled. "Bye, Clari. See you then!"

"Not fair!" Clari yelled to the phone, but Josie had already disconnected.

Chapter Eight

Clari

Warm contentment flooded Clari's being as she checked the simmering beans throughout the day and added water as needed.

Right on time, just before Morris was due to arrive, Clari saw that the rice cooker had finished and was on warm and the garlic bread was in the oven warming. She tested the beans and found them tender and ready, so she removed the bay leaves, added a touch of salt before she took a measuring cup and scooped out two cups of beans from the pot. After she blended them with the immersible blender, she poured the pureed mix back into the pot to thicken the beans.

The table was set for two, complete with two shallow pasta bowls placed on light blue lined placemats with matching, neatly folded, cloth napkins. Clari finished the table off with adding silverware, a bottle of Tabasco sauce, an heirloom crystal vase. Done. She was ready.

"I have never tried red beans and rice before, but it was amazing. Who knew you could cook a real meal? Thank you," Morris' teased.

She playfully smacked his arm. "I told you I could cook. I just don't care to do it after a long, tiring day."

"Well, I'm impressed, Miss Jones."

"Thank you, Mr. Morris. Now let's get the dishes done so we can sit and talk."

Once the dishes were washed and put away, they moved to the living room. "You are awfully chipper today, Clari. What's up?"

Practically bouncing on the couch, Clari answered, "I got reinstated! I'm official again!"

"That's great! Congratulations. Now we just need for me to be cleared and back in the field and we can get back to work."

"Yeah, but there's no rush for me return working with the Police Department right now, Morris. I report back to WPO Monday morning. I still have combat and weapon trainings, and who knows what else Witherabbott will think up for me to learn. She wants to make sure I have different self-protection options available to me. That means I have to learn different techniques."

"About time. You wouldn't listen to me any time I suggested it," Morris complained.

Clari frowned. "It's not like either of us foresaw me getting attacked by Sebastian's jealous sister Maria or by the Grigori that hunted me." Clari felt the room's energy became heavier as they spent a moment remembering.

Time to lighten the energy, she thought. "Oh, are you still interested in doing research on my ghostly visitors?"

Morris beamed. "Absolutely. You have another one?"

She smiled at Morris' enthusiasm. "I do." She filled him in on the impressions she had surrounding the gentle giant from the circus.

Morris asked, "Hey, what's the deal with all of this old stuff?"

"What do you mean?"

He pointed to the notes from the circus case. "You know, from the nineteen forties?"

Clari frowned. "I'm not sure, but since my Team let them get through to me, there may be a pattern or underlying theme these ghosts share. But it's definitely from a long time ago. I'll let you know if, or when, I figure it out."

Morris's eyebrows furrowed. "Uh, Clari? Is Ghost going to take over the research like I've been doing with you?"

Clari's face softened, "No, Morris. We make a great team, both in work and in the personal areas."

"Okay. Thanks, Clari. I enjoy working these cases with you." Morris waggled his eyebrows and sighed, "And I agree; I think we're great together in all ways."

Clari thought it was cute the way his ears turned pink after he said that. She studied the man with whom she came to trust, both as a partner and as a friend...or was he more than a friend? She realized she had feelings for Morris. *When did that happened?* She shook her head to clear her thoughts. "Okay. Now, change of subject. I'm excited for us to meet Josie's boyfriend, Brennan, tomorrow night."

"So you haven't met him yet?" Morris asked.

"No, Josie wouldn't let me. She has this thing about introducing a guy she's dating if it's still in the early stages. Once she's passed the two or three week mark, then she'll start thinking about introducing the guy."

"Why?"

"She wants enough time in the relationship for her to form her own opinion and to be comfortable with the relationship before she introduces him to her friends. I think it's her way to handle the trust issues we both deal with."

"That makes sense. I look forward to meeting him as well."

When Morris yawned, they called it an evening. Clari loaded Morris up with leftovers. Morris reached out with his other hand and clasped Clari's hand. "Walk me out?" he asked her.

Morris withdrew his hand from Clari's when they came to his car. Clari sighed at the broken connection. Morris laughed, "I'll hold your hand again after I put the leftovers in the car."

Clari felt her face reddened and was glad of the darkness, but smiled. After Morris closed the car door, he walked back to Clari and gently ran his hand on top of hers. She turned her hand over and they interlaced their fingers.

"That was delicious, Clari, the meal I mean," he laughed nervously. "I think I like red beans and rice. And now I'm armed with some good cooking."

As Clari released his hand, Morris opened his arms and nestled her into his bear hug. She really was beginning to like being this close to him and loved hearing his heartbeat.

After a bit of snuggling, Morris released her. "I better go now. Thank you, Clari. Oh, and I'll let tell you when I've found anything."

It was early Monday afternoon when, wearing sweatpants and an *Of course I talk to myself. Sometimes I need expert advice* tee shirt, Clari reported to

Mrs. Witherabbott. "I haven't had any new experiences, but I do want to discuss cutting back on my time spent here. I need to start getting back to my business. Oh, and after Morris is cleared for duty, we'll be back to working together as well."

Mrs. Witherabbott gave Clari a grandmother-like grin. "I should think you would want to get back to work. Have you given any thought to a schedule that may work for you for working and practicing here?"

"Yes. I was thinking Tuesdays and Thursdays, eight to ten in the mornings, for WPO training. We can maybe expand later if needed."

"You are beginning weapons and self-defense this week. Would you be able to do, say an hour, every Monday, Wednesday and Friday, perhaps starting at five thirty for a regular schedule? Although, you will meet your self-defense instructor and start a lesson today."

"I forgot about weapons and self-defense. Yes, I can do that. What kind of stuff do you think I'll be doing on Tuesday and Thursday mornings?"

Witherabbott took a moment to think about it. "Would you like to work one day a week with the dragon liaison to WPO, and your friend, J.R.?"

Clari's eyes lit up as she radiated enthusiasm. J.R., who was also the Dragon "M", treated her like a little sister sometimes, and sometimes he was the Dragon Leader of Avonish Clan to her. Clari's trust of him surpassed her current earthly life.

The Director stifled a chuckle. "I will contact J.R. and see if their instructor is available for one of those days. Let's not fill the remaining morning slot just yet. I would like to see how your dragon training progresses. Is that acceptable?

"Yes, ma'am. I do have some questions."

Witherabbott motioned for her to continue.

Clari brought up the subject that had been on her mind. "Sebastian and I were talking about the Grigoris. I mentioned I thought one of their abilities within their group was Dreamwalking, since they were able to enter my dreams.

"Sebastian wasn't so sure. But, he was also able to enter the same dream as the one with the Grigori in it. Were they both able to enter the dream because I am a Dreamwalker? Or, did the Grigori, and I, both need to be Dreamwalkers for that to happen? If so, where does Sebastian fit in?" She stopped to catch her breath after the rapid firing of her questions and thoughts.

Witherabbott's hand had a light grasp on her necklace pendant. She slid it back and forth. Her hand stopped. "I have no idea, Miss Jones. You have brought some interesting questions to the table. I will bring your questions to the Level V Dreamwalkers and see if they have answers. If they do not, then I will request them to explore this. And thank you for sharing this with me."

Clari gave Witherabbott a small smile. "Will you share with me what they discover? I feel out of my league as far as being attacked in my dreams."

"Of course. Is there anything else?"

"No, ma'am."

"Very well. Please contact me if anything else comes up. Abilities, troubles, or if you just want to talk, okay?"

"I will. So you'll contact me about what you and J.R. work out?"

"Absolutely. If there is nothing else, Miss Jones, I think we are done. Please report to the same gym you did your teleporting practices in to meet your instructor and begin your physical training." Mrs. Witherabbott waved her hand over a disc on her desk which made her office door open, and then turned her attention to her desk papers, effectively terminating their meeting.

In the hallway outside of Witherabbott's office, Clari took her phone off mute and discovered a missed call from Morris. He left a voicemail, and she was glad to hear him a bit more upbeat. "Hi there. Just wanted to give you a heads up; I've been reinstated, and am off to do a stakeout. I'll be out of touch for a while, but I'll call you when we are done. Bye, Clari."

Clari frowned, taking note of a sensation she'd not felt before. She smiled as she realized it was a feeling of not only being accepted, but that someone she cared about had her back as well.

She thought it was pretty neat how both of them started back to their real jobs. She made her way to the elevators to go down to meet her self-defense instructor.

As Clari stepped into the gym, she saw that it had been transformed. The back half of the floor covered with workout mats and the glowing walls were now a light grey color.

"Clarima Jones?"

She saw a man striding towards her. His physical appearance was pleasant enough. He was five foot eight with short black hair and wearing what looked like martial arts pants and was barefoot. He wore a black tee shirt that only highlighted his rippling muscles. He might be yummy to look at, but this man's energy looked like a cobra ready to strike. This man was dangerous. Instinctual fear moved like a snake slithering up her spine as she involuntarily took a step back.

He closed the gap between them. "Are you Clarima Jones?" His voice, like his gun metal blue eyes, had a hard edge to it.

Her heart raced, encouraging her to run from the predator energy coming off the man standing in front of her. "Yes."

His eyes softened a bit and the aggressive energy lessened. "All right, then. My name is Jeremy Plot. I'm your self-defense instructor. Let's get started. First, tell me a little about your previous training and what interest you have in developing new skills."

They spoke briefly. During their conversation, Clari saw the brief look of surprise on his face when she told him that she had no previous self-defense training. Jeremy nodded, "No wonder Witherabbott asked me to begin your training right away. Take your shoes off here and we'll hit the mats."

Once at the mats, Jeremy informed her that he would teach her the Palm Heel Strike. He spoke as he showed Clari the move. "It's a simple but effective technique that can be used in a variety of situations. First you stand with your feet shoulder-width apart, arms up in a defensive position." He corrected Clari's stance and then moved her arms into the correction position. He demonstrated the moves again. "This strike should be done with powerful force and with the intent to stop the attacker. It is an effective way to stun the attacker and create a momentary opening for you to either flee or counter-attack."

"Uh. Wow. Okay."

"Now, you try it and I'll adjust anything that needs it as we move along."

Jeremy had Clari do it over and over until he was satisfied she was well familiar with the move. "I want you to practice this every day like I showed you. Now we're going to do a complete series of self-defense moves for you to practice on me today."

He moved in behind Clari, his right arm around her neck with a soft plastic practice knife in his right hand. Clari Felt Jeremy was holding back his full strength as he instructed how to do the moves to get away. The last step was to run in the opposite direction before the attacker recovered.

"This feels so violent," Clari complained. Her eyes narrowed. An idea was forming in her head.

Jeremy's eyes hardened. "We want it to be second nature...no thought required. You need to be able to protect yourself. Your attacker doesn't give a crap about hurting you. Do it again."

This time when Jeremy's arm came around her neck, she Jumped behind him, kicked the back of his knee, and took off running in the opposite direction.

Startled, Jeremy swung around to confront her and found her at the opposite end of the room. The laughter that exploded out of him seem contradictory to the energy she Felt from him when she first saw him.

"You have some tricks up your sleeve, I see. I'm glad to know that, Clari, but it's still important to learn self-defense from an instructor, that way you can be taught how to do the techniques correctly and have them available to you. Being taught in person with a qualified instructor is the only way to learn self-defense. Learning it from books or videos can be a dangerous way to go because you have no one qualified on hand to make sure you're implementing the moves correctly. With an instructor, you not only increase likelihood you won't hurt yourself, but chances increase for a successful defense."

"I'm guessing you're speaking from experience about people learning from book or videos?" Clari inquired.

"Yes. Locally, they end up here or with another instructor and we have to untrain them from using what they interpreted were the correct moves, then train them the correct way...double the work. And it annoys me about people putting the videos and books out. Don't get me wrong, the videos and books are great for reviewing what one learned with the instructor. Nothing replaces the in-person hands-on instructor. And now that I know you're a Jumper, I can add in your Jumping ability into your training. Now, let's do it again from the beginning."

Jeremy had Clari practice the techniques on him again, and again.

An hour later, Jeremy announced "We're done for today. Do you have any questions?"

"Yes, I do. What type of martial arts are we working on? TaeKwonDo or Karate?"

"Pfft. Ms. Jones, we aren't working on any one style of martial arts. You are learning whatever I need you to learn to survive. I guess you could say it's a large combination of every martial art and fighting techniques that I learned over my lifetime with the military and I had training from Masters of various martial arts around the world. Now, go home and soak in a hot tub with Epsom salts. It'll lessen the aches until we get you into shape." He turned and walked out. The door slammed shut, creating an echo that told her she was alone with a bruised body and ego to match. *What did he mean until he gets me in shape?*

Since Clari hadn't brought a change of clothes there was no reason to use the women's shower and locker room. *I'll make sure to bring a workout bag next time.* She headed for her house to shower and change. As her muscles had cooled down, Clari's sore body made her feel like a frail old woman. *Hopefully this soreness goes away soon. I'm counting on the Epsom Salts to work tonight!*

Dressed and ready to go, Clari decided to stop by the market before she went to her office. She was in need of some healthy snacks and drinks for the office.

As she was unlocking her SUV door, she felt prickles on the back of her neck warning her of something negative. She slowly turned, scanning the parking lot. She froze when she saw him. A tall man — medium build, graying hair, white button up shirt and beige pants. He stood, about twenty feet away, between two cars, and resembled any other average guy...except for the fact that he glared at her with pure evil hatred.

The darkness oozing out of him was nauseating, causing Clari to gag, yet she remained transfixed. She started when she heard a loud bang behind her breaking the trance. She swung towards the sound to find it was just another shopper bringing her cart to the return point. Realizing that there was no threat there, Clari turned back to the man.

He was gone. Vanished like smoke. Each being has an energy feeling – or energy signature – unique to them. Just like when someone leaves a scent trail of perfume, each individual has an energy feeling that creates a trail. Clari scanned the area for his energy signature. There was nothing. No trace, no residue, no trail. It was like he popped in and popped out from another dimension.

After Clari got home and put away groceries, she checked her phone for messages and saw a call from Witherabbott. "Your first dragon training session is tomorrow morning. Good luck."

Clari and Morris walked into the restaurant holding hands. The far wall was backlight, highlighting the local winery's label. The hostess escorted them to Josie's table.

Josie smiled and both she and Brennan stood up to greet them. Josie made the introductions. "Clari Jones and Henry Morris, this is Brennan Doyle. Brennan, Clari and Henry, though we call him Morris."

Morris and Brennan were of similar height, with Morris being slightly taller. Brennan was a bit thinner than Morris, and sported short, spiky dirty blonde hair held in place with the wet-look hair gel.

The waiter approached after everyone sat down. He directed his question to Clari and Morris, "Good evening and welcome. What would you like to drink this evening?"

Morris looked to Clari, "What would you like, Clari?"

"I'll have a sparkling water, please."

The waiter wrote down Clari's order. "And you, sir?"

"I'll have a sweet iced tea, please."

"Very good. I'll put your drink orders in and give you a moment to look over the menu." The waiter turned his attention to Brennan and Josie. "Would either of you like another beverage?"

Brennan and Josie answered in unison, "No, thank you."

After the waiter left, Josie suggested, "Brennan and I already know what we want. Why don't you two decide before we get distracted by chatting?"

"Good idea, Josie," Morris replied as he handed a menu to Clari. They both concentrated on the restaurants offerings.

In the meantime, the waiter returned and served the table a Charcuterie board and then retreated. Josie pointed to the board, "I hope you don't mind, but we ordered this for the table appetizer. We figured this should cover everyone's taste buds. It has different cheeses and meats, local pecans prepared in different ways, crackers, sliced French bread, garlic stuffed olive and Hatch green chile."

"Oh, my gosh, Josie! That's a lot of food!" Clari exclaimed.

Josie smiled, "Just leave room for your dinner."

The waiter returned. "Are you all ready to place your orders, or do you need some more time?"

Josie started and they worked their way around the table with their orders. After everyone finished, the waiter thanked them and strolled back to the kitchen.

"Thank you for coming, Clari and Morris. Brennan and I appreciate it."

"Thank you for setting this up, Josie. I'm really glad to meet you, Brennan," Clari said.

Morris piped up, "So what do you do for a living, Brennan?"

"Well, one of the things I do is fire investigations," Brennan shared.

"Wow, I'm impressed," Morris revealed.

Brennan squirmed under the praise, but Clari noticed his energy told her that he was pleased.

"Are there a lot of fires here to be investigated?" Clari asked.

"No, not really, "Brennan explained. "But I work in the private sector now, which means I only work with the local fire departments, or," his chin pointed to Morris, "the local police department if they hire the services of the company I work for."

"You said 'one of the things' you do. What else do you do, if you don't mind me asking," Clari queried.

"I don't mind. Though I spend most of my time here, in New Mexico, the company I work for sometimes has me travel to where my skillsets are needed and contracted out. Since I'm a CFEI – that's Certified Fire and Explosion Investigator – and I have my Master's in forensic sciences with a Bachelor's in fire sciences, which means I can be contracted out for various forensic services."

"I'm with Morris; color me impressed," Clari told Brennan.

Brennan continued, "And Josie caught me up on what you two do. I have to admit, though, I'm more familiar with your line of work, Henry, than I am with yours, Clari."

"Maybe not," countered Clari. "You understand what Josie does, right?"

"Yes, she's an energy healer," Brennan answered.

"Yes and no. Though Josie doesn't like to toot her own horn, I have no problem tooting it for her. Brennan, Josie is a specialist even within the field of energy healers, in that when someone sees the words 'Energy

Healer' on a business card, sheet of paper or a sign, that's the depth of knowing what Josie does. I think some people, maybe not you, have a two-dimensional view of Energy Healer. But Josie is – and does – so much more than those two-dimensional written words.

"Josie receives information, not only about the physical, but also the emotional and spiritual information from both the client's Team and the client's own energetic subtle bodies. A Team – which we each have our own – is comprised of one's non-physical guides that aid us in our life's journey. And subtle bodies are energetic extensions of our physical being and are connected to our chakras. Josie sometimes has to do some energetic investigating, so some consulting, and sometimes solve a mystery or two."

After Clari's speech, Brennan looked over to Josie. Clari saw the tenderness, and a tad bit of awe, that Brennan directed to Josie. Clari shared a knowing look with Morris.

"So, Josie, does this mean I can never, ever tell you even a little white lie?" Brennan winked.

The entire table nodded and chuckled in unison.

Their waiter and more wait-staff carried out the table's order. Their main waiter placed a plate in front of Josie. "Ma'am, your Filet Mignon wrapped in bacon, medium, served with pesto jasmine rice."

"Ma'am," the waiter placed a plate in front of Clari, "your Cajun Pasta with shrimp and Andouille sausage, gently tossed in our Alfredo sauce and seasoned with Cajun spices."

Clari giggled, "I'm drooling!"

Next was Brennan. "Sir, your Wagyu Burger, medium, on Brioche with lettuce and tomato slices, no onion and a side of beer-battered french fries."

Morris' plate came next. "Sir, your Ahi Tuna breaded with local ground pistachios and Hatch green chile and a side of a local vegetable medley."

The waiter addressed the whole table, "Anything else I can get you folks?"

Everyone indicated that they needed nothing else.

The waiter bowed, "Very well. Ladies and Gentlemen, please enjoy your dinner."

On the way home, Clari asked, "So what did you think of Brennan, Morris?"

He held out his hand inviting Clari to hold his hand. She placed her hand in his.

Morris shrugged and kept his eyes on the road. "Nice enough."

Clari snorted. "Is that guy-speak for you like him?"

"I don't think I know him well enough. But I can say he seemed nice and I was impressed with his education and career choice. But, Clari, most guys don't bond over dinner. It usually builds over several interactions."

"Hmph. That sounds so... sterile or clinical."

"Clari, I don't dislike him. I can't judge a character after only one get together. I'm a detective. I'll wait to see what, if anything is underneath the first meet."

"Okay, Morris," Clari chuckled "So you're saying you'll reserve how you feel for now?"

"Yep. The biggest thing, to me, is how he treats Josie. One dinner doesn't provide enough information for me."

"Fair enough, Detective Morris. We'll just have to spend more time with them to make sure."

"I'd like that." Morris reached out for Clari's hand. They say in silence, enjoying being with each other.

On Tuesday morning, Clari awoke excited and nervous. Today was her first Dragon Training Day!

Clari showed up at the Dragon Plateau to begin her training. The memories of the first time she arrived at the Dragon Plateau rushed in. She had rescued sixteen year old Michael after he shifted into a dragon and his family had not only cast him out of their lives, but had chained him up inside a dark cave. At the time, Clari was so focused on the Dragon Realm and trying to think of how to get Michael the help he needed, she accidentally Pulled them both to the Plateau. That's when Clari met 'M', the leader of the Avonish Dragon Clan. M had readily accepted the newly transformed teenaged dragon and Michael joined M's clan. M assured Clari that Michael would immediately begin dragon training. And that's also when Clari found out she could transform into a dragon. Unfortunately she became a neon pink dragon; a color that Clari despised.

This time, Clari was back on this Plateau for her own dragon training.

The huge silver dragon, M approached and greeted Clari. "Tahini, it's good to see you. Are you ready to begin your dragon training?"

"Yes, I am, M."

M requested, "Please shift into your dragon, Tahini."

"Yes, sir. Oh, and my name is Clari. I thought we moved beyond this whole calling-me-Tahini thing. I am not a toasted and ground sesame seed spread."

M didn't have a chance to respond since Michael came up behind him bumped Clari, a normal young Dragon greeting. "Whoa! What happened to you, Clari? You grew in size and you're no longer pink!"

Clari looked down at her dragon self to see a rich, deep plum color with intense highlights. She slid her short Dragon arms down the scales admiring her scaled armor. "Um, I don't know? M?"

M explained, "Since you are now recognizing your dragon aspect, you are no longer the bright, neon colors of fledglings. The fledglings' bright colors make them easier to keep an eye on. Ah, here's your instructor now. Let me introduce you to Sensei, your dragon instructor."

Sensei wasn't as large as M but she had the feeling of Sensei being much older than M. Clari Felt great wisdom and strong energy from Sensei and was sure he was revered in the Dragon community. Sensei was a purple so dark, one might think it leaned towards black. But when the light hit his scales, a purple iridescence danced along the edges of each scale. He bowed his head slightly at Clari.

Clari bowed back. "Sensei. Thank you for taking on the task of teaching me."

"I must admit, I wasn't too sure about teaching someone that's already an adult, but I like a good challenge." Clari could feel the humor behind his words.

"I hope I am worthy." She bowed her head again.

Clari looked up and saw a massive matte black colored dragon in the sky and noticed it was aiming straight for her. Even high in the air his presence was unmistakable. The male dragon was as black as Vantablack paint that absorbs over 98% of light. It looked as if the male dragon's black scales swallowed light. The dragon seemed fixated on Clari. He landed next to her and aggressively tried to knock her over into a submissive position to declare a bonding and it ticked her off. She managed to push him off.

He bellowed, "I declared my intent long ago – you are to be mine!"

Clari evaded him and flew off. She landed on the face of a nearby mountain. Clari's scales began vibrating creating a shimmering effect; this was the dragon's warning to others to show how angry she was, but the black dragon continued to pursue her. She dropped and flew back to the plateau. She noticed that M, Sensei and Michael hadn't moved. Furious, she landed in front of M and Sensei. "What the heck is going on? Why did that creep attack me? Why didn't anyone help me?"

Sensei told her, "We cannot interfere. That is Albi, and he has made the declaration of claiming, and he has claimed you."

She shook her dragon head back and forth, "Uh, uh. No. I don't think so! He does not get to 'claim' me! And I certainly have a say as to whom I bond, mate, or whatever with. Period."

Without any emotion, Sensei shared, "It is the way of the dragon, and has been for millennia."

"That's bull hockey! Even with animals on my dimension, the female can reject a male. Well, I reject that big, archaic bully. And I reject that antiquated belief system and the cavalier attitude that so callously disregards a females rights!"

Sensei continued, "You could learn to love him."

"No! Not when my heart belongs to another." Clari shifted back to her human form.

"And who is that?" Sensei queried.

Clearly shaken by her own pronouncement, she replied, "I don't want to discuss this anymore. I'm going home. Don't expect me back unless that bully will leave me alone."

Not only did Sensei's question bother her, but her own verbal admission shook her. She knew that the words coming out of her mouth when working with clients sometimes applies to her as well, but this time there was no client. It was like her subconscious mind grew tired of Clari playing hide-and-seek with her own heart and decided to blurt out her deep truth on the matter. *I'll deal with that later. I'm too angry about Albi's stunt to "claim" me right now.*

Clari grumbled as she alternated between stomping back and forth, and doing laps around her kitchen, living room, hallway and back to the kitchen. "Misogynistic males. Stupid dragons. It's the 24th century, for heaven's sake! 'Claiming' a female. Positively barbaric. I'm so annoyed I could just..." She threw her hands up. "I mean, seriously? Somebody needs to jerk all of them out of the past." Clari, lost in her own tirade, spun around to reverse her stomping path and found herself in the Dragon Realm.

"Clari? Are you okay?" Michael asked after she popped in.

"What?" Clari was distracted by an idea forming. She needed to talk to the maroon colored dragon named Aria. She'd met Aria after the dragons came to help battle the Beasts out at Mystery Ranch. "Oh. Um. Hi, Michael. It's good to see you. Can you tell me where I can find Aria?" Aria was M's second-in-command, but better yet, she was a female who was well respected.

Michael Sent Clari the directions to where Aria could be found. Clari shifted to her dragon self and took flight. She followed Michael's directions and soon saw the peak she sought. She gently landed and changed back to her human form.

"Greetings, Clarima." Aria came up behind Clari, startling Clari. Aria was a large maroon colored dragon.

For such a large creature, dragons are incredibly quiet! Clari spoke to Aria, "I apologize for coming unannounced, but I really need to talk to you about the archaic practice of 'claiming' a mate. Are you okay with it? I mean, you were raised with this practice and taught it was acceptable. But are you okay with being bullied by someone and forced into a bonding, or would you rather bond for love?"

Aria swished the back half of her tail on the ground, sending little dust plumes with each slide of the tail. "You ask a hard question, Clarima, and you are putting out some very chaotic vibes here. May I ask if this is related to Albi?"

"Well, yes...and no. The incident with Albi initiated this discussion. But the more I thought about it, the more I realized that forcing anyone to do anything they are not comfortable with isn't necessarily a healthy thing. And male dominance over females is a very old and outdated concept. Or am I wrong in this instance?"

Aria quit swishing her tail. "Dragons are very set in their ways, and had to do this in order to survive, Clarima. Or so they claim. The process was to protect the species; only the strongest males could reproduce. Having said that, I, personally, feel we should bond because of love. As you know, we Dragon bond for life and a life with a being you are not compatible with is a long and lonely existence."

"Yes! I knew it. I would very much like to talk to the entire population of single female dragons, please. If they all agree, I think it's time for a change. Can you set up a time and place for all of us to meet, without male dragon interference?"

Clari shivered at the sight of what she thought was Aria smiling in her dragon form. She thought, *I don't think I've ever seen a dragon smile. Kind of creepy.*

"I would love to, Clarima." Aria made a sound that made Clari think Aria was laughing. "This should be rather entertaining. I will set it up."

Back home, Ghost announced that Clari had received an email, "But I'm not sure how it came in. It didn't come through the normal email channels," he told Clari.

"Thank you, Ghost." Clari opened the email and read it. "This email came from the Dragon realm, Ghost. I can't tell you how that works, but that's probably why it didn't come through the normal email channels." The email informed Clari of the time later that day, and the place that the female dragons were gathering to hear her speak.

Nervous but determined the human Clari arrived at Aria's at the appointed time. "Aria, I appreciate you setting this up. Hey, I had no idea you guys have email in the Dragon Realm. That's awesome."

Aria's head bobbed, "Yes, Clari, we have email." Aria made a sound that Clari guessed was a chuckle. "We learned long ago how to communicate with your realm, and when you permanently opened the Dragon Portals, we were able to tie into your realm's communication systems. So, again, yes, we have email. Let's get down to business, now. Are you staying human or shifting to your dragon-self?"

Clari smiled, "Even though I feel like the size of an insignificant flea while in my human form compared to all of you, I'm starting the discussion in human form. I also know that dragons can't shift to a human form until they're at least three-hundred and fifty years old."

"Okay. Shift now so we can head over to the meeting place. Follow me."

Clari shifted and took flight.

They landed on a larger plateau than any that Clari had been on before. Clari shifted back to her human-self and followed Aria to the front of a large gathering of dragons.

Aria bowed, greeting Clari in front of the other dragons. "We have gathered and are ready to hear you, Clarima. Let's move to the front and I'll introduce you."

While Aria introduced Clari, Clari could Feel a mixed bag of emotions from the female dragons. "Ladies, please settle. For those who don't know her, I'd like to introduce our guest, Clarima Jones. Clarima is in a unique position of being human, but recently discovered and came into her drag-on aspect, which, as you all know, means that Clarima has Dragon some-where in her bloodline, which is why she can connect with her dragon. I turn this meeting over to Clarima." Aria stepped back to allow Clari to speak to those gathered.

Clari bowed to everyone. "I appreciate you all coming here today. I'll get right to the point.

"I wasn't raised as a dragon, so I wasn't raised in your ways. And I've been in touch with my dragon-self for less than a year. I confess, I'm not well-versed, so I ask your indulgence in any ignorance on my part.

"As human-raised and then introduced to your ways, I find myself sorely conflicted, and frankly a bit angry. I'm sure you've heard by now that Albi has," Clari used air quotes, "'claimed' me. As a human, I find this tradition extremely old-fashioned, demeaning, and frankly, downright insulting." Clari stopped for a moment because she Felt a strong mix of energies con-taining some indignant waves as well as some strong waves of agreement and she wanted to provide them some time to process what she'd said.

She took a deep breath and pushed on. "I understand tradition over the millennia had aided in the survival of the species through the battles of the males to have first pick for bonding. But now-a-days, especially as humans, we bond for love – not out of duty, or being bullied by the 'winner' of those who fought to claim us."

The crowd began stirring. Clari could tell emotions were rising. She shifted to her dragon-self and continued, "This form may be new to me, but I cannot, in good conscience, acquiesce to these male-dominated rituals which demand a female submit to an antiquated practice that I find to be abusive and humiliating. You have all the power and strength to stand up for yourselves. There can be no offspring without you. Each of you holds the power.

"So now I ask you all this...what about bonding out of love? What about you choose your mate because you care about him? Or what about those of you, if there are any, who don't want to bond yet? Or maybe you don't feel the need or drive at all. Why aren't your feelings and concerns taken into consideration? You can't be alive just to be brood mares to only keep producing offspring for a bully who claimed you. Where is your voice in all of this?"

Unsettled waves rippled through out the crowd. A voice in the back asked, "What are you proposing? That we go to war with the males? Or are you trying to get out species to die out?"

Clari shifted back to her human-self. 'Yes, I'm asking you to go to war, but not in a physical battle. Remember, there are no fledglings without you all. You can 'battle' by talking amongst yourselves and get a consensus of what everyone here wants. I don't see why the Dragon Council can't accommodate those who want the stick to tradition as well as those who want to go the love route. But nothing changes until you step forward and make it happen."

Clari stood quiet for a few moments to allow them time to think about what she brought before them. She spoke up again, "I'm not saying physical war is the answer at all – but you are all strong and intelligent beings and should be respected." Clari looked over to Aria, who dipped her head to Clari.

Clari continued, "That's all I have to say. Does anyone have any other questions for me?" No one spoke up. "Then I will take your leave, and wish you success on whatever you all decide. One final thing: I will not be claimed." Leaving the female dragons to discuss things amongst them, Clari bowed and Pulled herself back home.

Chapter Nine

> *Psychometry – the ability to hold or touch an item, object or person and energetically receive information about the item, object or person.*

Clari

Morris called Clari. "Hey, beautiful. I was wondering if we could get together for dinner so I can share what I discovered on your circus story."

Clari's heart fluttered at being called beautiful. "Sure! It's Wednesday, which is our get together night. Are you up for Chinese food tonight? I can have Ghost call in an order before my class tonight, if you don't mind picking it up. It's on your side of town. My treat."

"How can I refuse that offer? See you after class." Morris disconnected.

"Hey, Ghost?" Clari called out.

"Yes, Clari?" Ghost's artificial voice responded from her phone.

"Would you place an order for Chinese food for us? Morris will pick it up on his way here tonight."

"Yes, Clari. Do you want me to order the usual?"

"Yes, please, Ghost. And thank you!"

That evening, after a quick shower, Clari got comfortable on the couch to dig around in the box her father left her. Her hand brushed something metallic, so Clari let her fingers seek the metallic item out. She grabbed it and pulled it out of the box. *Oh, a bullet casing?* Her psychometry ability kicked in.

The memory-vision played out as though she was thrust into a movie. She watched as the scene played out through the eyes of the female character, Hope Jones, a seven or eight times great grandmother. She experienced this vision as though she was Hope Jones.

Clari Felt the sun beating down on her as she dug into the hard packed red earth. Her bones and muscles fought against the work. "I think I'm getting too old for this," muttered her great times eight grandmother. Hope loosened the dirt to mix enough compost in to enrich the soil. It has been a while since she gardened and it was her hope to grow some vegetables this year.

She Saw Hope Jones standing outside of her home as she overlooked her future garden. Clari, still holding the shell casing, was connected to the past and to Hope's experiences that were imprinted onto the casing.

She could Feel Lucas "Luke" Jones, walk up behind her. "Hey. What's wrong?" he asked.

Hope kept her attention on the horizon. "Something is coming. Something dark, and filled with evil. And it's heading straight for us."

The husband stepped forward, into her sight line. "Do we get the guns?" Even though her husband had a few more years on her, he still stood a good foot taller, putting him at six foot five, so she had to crane her neck to see him. His solid build contradicted the uncertainty and concern in his hazel eyes.

"No. Guns won't help us with this one, honey." Hope's joints ached; her seventy-plus years had started slowing her down.

His frustration was evident as he paced in the dirt. "Maybe I should at least get my sidearm. I don't like this, Hope. Not one bit."

Her gentle smile broadcast her understanding. She knew he worried that, since they lived so far out in the desert, isolated, they had to defend themselves. And his preferred method of defense was firearms.

She didn't dare tell him it was a squad from the dictator's personal army. She knew he'd be hauling out more aggressive forms of self-protection. She sighed. They were so different, he and she.

They both stood, watching, as the dust plumes rose from the ground, marking the squad's progress to their home. Comprehension dawned and the husband swung to confront her. "Dang it, Hope, why didn't you tell me? I could've had the perimeter protected!"

Unfazed, Hope gently touched his arm. "Luke, it wouldn't have mattered. This is more my stuff than yours."

"What does that mean?" he demanded.

Hope's eyebrows rose and she waited.

He leaned forward. "You mean they aren't human? But they're kicking up dust as they move, so they have to be real, right?"

"Oh, make no mistake. They are real and they are human. And dangerous. But guns won't change anything. We just wait, Luke."

The dust cloud moved closer until Luke and Hope had a clear visual. They saw twelve men marching towards them. Each man was dressed in black from head to toe — black hat down to black boots. Each wore black sunglasses. Each carried a semi-automatic. Each had a belt that carried various "tools" of the dark army's trade. These tools promised pain and misery.

Soon, the dark army halted before them. One soldier stepped forward, out of their formation, and announced, "We are here under the authority of our Supreme Ruler, Robert Chamba. You are to surrender your property and belongings and come with us."

Luke clenched his fists and spoke through gritted teeth. "I do not recognize any dictator in the United States of America. Get. Off. My. Property."

As Hope stepped forward, she could see her reflection in the soldier's sunglasses. Her dirty blonde hair was well wind-blown. Her squinting chestnut brown eyes were the only indicator of her determination. She addressed the soldier. "Please remove your glasses. I like seeing the eyes of the person I am talking to."

The soldier reached up and removed his sunglasses.

Hope searched his black eyes. "What is your name, soldier?"

"Ba'hamet."

"I see." She turned to speak to the rest of the squad. "And what are your names?"

Each soldier gave his assigned name.

Hope turned back to the first soldier. "I am going to go out on a limb and say that there is a reason why each one of you is named after a lesser demon."

Before anyone could respond, Hope concentrated her energy and overwhelmed the soldiers with blankets of positive and loving energy as she very calmly, energetically ripped the programming out of each soldier standing before her – removing and deleting any control anyone else may have had – and then turned her attention to the aftermath.

The suddenness of the separation had knocked them off of their feet, but they were still conscious. Hope filled the soldiers with white light;

cleansing the taint left behind from the programming that was forced on them.

The soldier that had identified himself as Ba'hamet stood back up. The abusive and aggressive energy was no longer part of him, and he looked relieved. "Thank you, ma'am. How could you tell?"

"I was taught, from a young age, to remove things from humans that went against that human's free will. Your energy disclosed to me that you hadn't given permission to be altered in such a way, so it was my duty to remove that which was forced on you. What is your name?"

"William. Bill. Bill Arthur."

"Hi, Bill. I am Hope and this is my husband, Luke. Can you tell us how this happened?"

"We were taken from our homes when we reached our tenth birthday, and put into a 'special school'. We were trained..."

Another soldier was standing back up when he interrupted Bill, anger oozed from each word. "Tortured is more like it!"

Bill continued, "Yes, tortured and trained in combat and... other things. But I, and I'm sure the others here, woke up one day and found ourselves kind of pushed into the back of our brains and something — or should I say someone else – was in control of our brain and bodies. From that point on, we could only watch, scream, and cry from inside and try to hide from what was driving our bodies and to try to hide from the things they did to, and with, our bodies. We were prisoners in our own brains."

Clari was jolted back into her body and the present time.

Morris stood before her holding the old casing in his hands. He yelled, "Clari. Clari! Are you okay? Talk to me! Say something!"

She held her hand up. "I'm fine. Give me a minute." She took a deep breath and let it out in a puff. "Wow."

Morris took a step back. "Wow? You scared the crap out of me, and you say 'Wow'?"

"What? I'm confused. What scared you, Morris?"

"You. You scared me. You had this thing in your hand," his arm swung up towards her to show her the brass casing in his open palm. He took a couple of deep breaths to push back the panic. "You have been standing there, frozen, for ten minutes that I'm aware of. Who knows how long before I showed up."

"Wow. Ten minutes, eh?" She frowned, and then complained, "You certainly yell my name an awful lot."

His voice rose in frustration, "Because you do a lot of things that require me to yell your name. Are you okay? Are you my Clari?"

Clari rolled her eyes. "Yeah, I'm okay. And yes, it's me. That was incredible!"

Morris shook his head. "Unbelievable."

She smiled at him.

"I'm glad you're okay. Care to share what happened, and how this," Morris waved his hand, "triggered whatever happened?"

"That casing apparently belonged to Lucas and Hope Jones, who I believe are my distant relatives. They lived in the desert like me. They were from the mid twenty-first century during the demon-wars."

"How do you know their names?"

"I got their names from that brass casing. As soon as I touched it, I was able to witness the day in 2049 when that they had encountered the Dark Army. Hope energetically removed the programming out of the soldiers that came to her property. Morris, she was just like me. She was trained as a young child on how to remove stuff that doesn't belong in humans."

Morris' mouth dropped open. "Do you think she was the one who initiated the Americans to revolt against dictator Chamba?"

"I don't know because you yanked me out right as the soldier was explaining how the programming was done."

Morris' energy changed from concerned to astonishment. "Wow."

"Yeah, like I said. This experience was kind of like having a front row seat while the war was in play instead of the sanitized version taught in the Ancient History classes.

"The Demon Wars was what the general populace called the revolution against the president, Robert Chamba, who had declared himself the Supreme Ruler of the United States. This was after the G5 geomagnetic storm in 2049 that hit Earth, collapsing the electronic grid systems globally. Unbeknownst to the United States citizens, Chamba had been building an armed force that had been forcibly programmed to follow his instructions and his only. He then took advantage of the chaos following the grid system collapse and used it to his advantage.

"The Dark Army was dressed in black to signify that they belonged to Chamba and were relentless and without compassion or mercy as they carried out their mission to terrorize the citizens into compliance and what amounted to slavery, or be killed. And each soldier carried the name tag of a demon on their uniform. I guess that was another scare tactic. So between the dark uniforms, their cold demeanors, and their assigned demon names, people called them the Dark Army.

"The U.S. citizens fought back, and eventually ended the reign of terror of Chamba.

"We were never told that the army was comprised of men who were kidnapped at a young age to be trained and programmed to follow Chamba. I don't know if there were more people like Hope who helped deprogram the soldiers, or what exactly happened that turned the tide for the citizens, but I'm glad it ended.

"As for technology following the recovery of the geostorm... since humans had to basically start from scratch with the knowledge they had, things moved slowly in bringing technology back. I don't think they wanted to make the same mistakes that were made prior to the geostorm.

"I often wonder if the G5 storm hadn't collapsed the grid, where would we be with the human and technology relationship. Would we have more artificial intelligence beyond our smart phones? Would we have food replicators like the old science fiction shows?" Clari pondered.

"Well, I know they didn't have the holographic computer systems like we have today. We've come a long way since then, and I kind of like doing some things the old ways. Like my truck and my passion for the old body style in vehicles," Morris reflected.

"Yeah, but I'm glad that our ancestors didn't bring back the internal combustion engine that converted the energy from the heat of gasoline. And those electric vehicles of the twenty-first century were an awful waste of materials, not to mention the batteries of those vehicles had horrid effects on the environment."

"I agree. So do you think it was Hope who programmed the casing you were holding?"

Clari bobbed her head. "Yes, it was Hope who placed the bullet casing in with the papers and journal. I guess it was her intention that another psychometrist would be able to read it one day."

"Yeah, well, that's interesting, Clari. But please stop scaring me half to death."

Clari chuckled. "I can't guarantee that." She inhaled deeply, "But I do smell Chinese food. Let's eat, Morris."

They moved to the living room after dinner. Morris was brimming with excitement to share what he found out. Clari patiently waited for him to begin. As he began sharing his finds, she watched for any signs of Morris having changed after his heart attack. Not like, "Is he being more careful about stressing his heart?" More like, "What has changed as far as opening his connection to the energetic realm?" that her guide had foretold. So far, she has not been able to see any changes, except for the dark bags under his eyes. *He's probably just adjusting after getting off a long stint of surveillance duty*, she thought.

Morris pulled out his notebook and shared what he learned, "In nineteen forty-four, a fire broke out in the main event circus tent. This tent was about five hundred feet long.

"Because of World War II in the late 1930's and early 1940's, supplies for civilians were limited. So the circus owners waterproofed the tent with one thing they could get in abundance...kerosene. All of the tents were coated with it to keep any water from soaking through.

"One spark and it spread like wildfire.

"When it was over, they discovered the bodies of over one hundred and fifty people under the collapsed tent. No one knows exactly how many people actually died that day, and it was estimated that seven hundred had been injured.

"The initial investigation found that the circus members worked hard to get the people out of the tent safely, but there were so many people and the fire spread quickly."

She remained quiet when he paused. Both were trying to imagine that day, but Clari could energetically Feel it.

He continued, "They suspected that a tossed cigarette was what ignited the tent. The case is still open. I couldn't find any mention of your giant, though, but I think the circus company kept their members closely guarded from the public. That means we don't know if your ghostly giant accidentally caused the fire, or was just haunted by the memories of witnessing, and surviving, the devastation.

"This, however, is not the only circus tent fire I found; there were many throughout the United States during the thirties and forties. But this one seemed, at least to me, to fit what you had gotten from the giant ghost. I felt like it was the one the moment I read the details."

"Wow. Thank you for finding that."

Morris closed his notebook. "Welcome. What happens to your ghost giant now?"

"After he got on my energy healing table and had a healing session from me, he informed me that he couldn't cross over yet and wanted me to release the others. I'm still not sure why the ghosts are stuck."

He scratched his head. "Are you serious? You gave an energy healing session to a ghost?"

Clari shrugged. "I admit, his request did sound a bit odd at first. But hey, everything is energy and energy is everything. If you think about it, a ghost is just energy...so why not?"

"Hm. I guess I've heard everything now," he joked.

"I know, right? Thank you, again. It helps me a lot, kind of like finding the final piece to his puzzle."

"Why are we researching them?" asked Morris.

"Because their stories needed to be told, Morris, and I still need to figure out why they were sent to me; a pattern or something that links them. Now I have a question for you. What's wrong?"

"What do you mean? Nothing's wrong."

"Morris, I mean that you've had a heart attack, recovered, and now you're back on the job. Yet you have dark circles under your eyes and your energy reminds me of someone haunted by their memories or experiences. What is going on, partner?" She watched him shift uneasily. His knee started bouncing.

"Morris?"

He began a soft gnawing on his thumbnail.

"Uh, Morris? Are you okay?"

He dropped his hand in his lap and stared into her eyes. She Saw confusion and fear on all levels. She spoke softly as she leaned towards him. "We are partners, Henry Morris. I know something is going on. Please talk to me."

He took a deep, ragged breath. "Something happened. Or changed, I'm not sure. I sometimes feel like I'm going bonkers. I have the sense that something more than the heart attack happened. Something I can't explain." His thumbnail found its way back between his teeth.

"Okay. What's happened to make you think something more than a heart attack happened? Can you give me an example?"

His knee bouncing and nail gnawing came to an abrupt stop. "It doesn't make sense. I think my brain short-circuited."

You didn't short circuit, Morris

He became agitated and snapped. "How do you know? Are you a psychiatrist?"

No, but I can say with certainty that you are very sane

His energy flared with anger. "This is not a joke! I knew I shouldn't have told you."

Peace, partner. I am taking this seriously. And you are sane

He stood. "I thought, of all the people in my life that you would be here for me!"

Morris! I am. I'm guessing it hasn't sunk in yet that I've not verbally spoken for a while now?

"What? What are you talking about?"

Have you seen my lips move?

He sat with a thud. His words came out breathlessly. "What are you saying?"

* *I've been communicating with you through telepathy. Mind pictures, intent, and emotions that you have translated into words in your head* *

She smiled.

He paled, and eyes widened as though he were a deer caught in the headlights.

She spoke out loud. "It appears you've discovered an ability."

He frowned. "Mind reading?"

"I guess you could call it that. Some call it one aspect of being a human lie detector. Others call it being a telepath. You described it correctly when you commented that there were thoughts in your head that weren't your thoughts. You are picking up others' thoughts."

Frowning, Morris asked, "Is this a good thing?"

Her smile never faltered. "It depends. How do you feel about it? What are you going to do with it?"

"Do with it?" Morris paled even more.

"Yes. Are you going to work to refine it? Do you want to get tested and certified? Are you going to tell Avery?"

He moaned, leaned forward and dropped his head in his hands. "Too much. My brain hurts."

Clari continued. "Well, if you want my thoughts on it...I'm tickled pink! Think about it. A cop that can hear thoughts. If you could use your ability for good..." She left her words hanging to give him time to think it over.

He lifted his head. "You think I could do that?"

"I don't know why not. It probably won't be admissible in court unless you back the information up with hard, physical proof." She jumped up from the couch. Her words came faster as she paced and let her hands weave the words. "You'll be able to tell if someone is lying to you and maybe even show you where you need to search to get your proof. And if they aren't the perpetrator, you would know to not spend so much time with them."

He couldn't help himself, her excitement was contagious. His smile was genuine as he chimed in. "Do you think I'll be able to use it at work?"

"I'd like to think so, but you need to decide if you're going to tell Avery. You also need to decide if you are going to get certified."

The deer in the headlights returned. "Oh. Will I have to get tested and certified?"

"No. And if you change your mind later, you can always go and get it done."

He became still.

Clari saw the fear and uncertainty in his eyes. She plopped down on the couch. "What do you want to do?'

His attempt at a shrug fell short. He leaned back in the chair.

Clari leaned forward. "May I make some suggestions?"

His eyes flickered, and for the briefest of moment, hope flared. "Yes."

"Why don't you talk this over with Lieutenant Avery first? He might have more information about policies and police officers with abilities. And, if you want, I'll go with you to see him."

She watched his knee restart bouncing as he thought about her suggestion and offer. She knew he'd reached a decision when his leg stopped.

He head bobbed to some internal dialoguing. "Let's do it. I'll schedule an appointment with Avery tomorrow, and pass that along to you."

"Great. In the meantime, what about practicing and refining your ability? Maybe we can come up with a practice that you can do to be able to confirm what you're picking up or hearing. How many people do you want to tell about this?"

Panic radiated from him. "No one! Please. Let's take small steps with this. I'll set the appointment with Avery and we'll move from there."

"Okay, Morris. Your call. Can I teach you how to shield?"

"What is shielding?"

"It is a mental visualization exercise that can put a bit of a buffer between you and others. It won't stop you from Hearing, but it may put some distance on it. Once you've got a handle on shielding, we can work on learning to turn the volume up and down on what you Hear. What do you say?"

"Okay, Clari. Let's do it."

"Start by closing your eyes and imagining looking at yourself. To remove any unwanted energies, visualize this unwanted energy leaving your body. You can make the unwanted energies look like black smoke, or maybe black arrows leaving your body. In your mind state, 'All negativity has left me.'

"You need to transform this energy so the negative stuff you removed isn't floating out and about for someone else to walk into it and absorb it. You can do this by visualizing changing it to pink smoke or pink flowers. Pink is the color of unconditional love.

"Now imagine a bright white light coming down from above and encasing you in a bubble of light, with you inside of the bubble. It may looking like a shimmering bubble, or white, white-gold or white with blue. Make sure you are totally encased in this bubble. Keeping your bubble in place, call down the white light again and see it in a liquid form, coming down from the top of your head and coating your entire body.

"And finally seal this with an affirmation. And you have to mean it! I use, 'Only that which is highest and holiest may enter within.' You're welcome to use mine, or make one of your own. The key to energy work is to believe it.

"This technique helps energy workers and empaths to keep from absorbing everyone's energies or emotions. It also is one way to get centered."

After Morris left for home, Clari made haste for the now much anticipated bath. After she ran the bath water, with Epsom salts, she slowly, and gingerly, lowered her bruised and battered body into the water. A deep sigh escaped as her sore muscles began to loosen. As she sank into the water, she thought, *I wonder how long it'll take for me to get into shape and no longer needs these nightly baths.*

Chapter Ten

Soul-Gazing – When two physical beings – human, animal or combo – make a soul connection while looking into one another's eyes; one soul recognizing and acknowledging the divinity of another. Soul-Gazing usually includes a Knowing of soul communication going on without the conscious mind knows what's being discussed on a soul level.

Clari

Clari and Morris sat in Lieutenant Avery's office. Avery had told them to sit and then left the room.

Clari fidgeted as her eyes roamed the office.

Avery was the precinct boss and it showed in his plush office. The large executive desk was a dark wood and had a matching credenza stationed behind the heavy desk chair.

Flags stood at attention in the corner. The American flag's colors were subdued by the New Mexico state flag with its bright yellow background and the red Zia sun symbol in its center.

Plaques, awards and commendations adorned the walls along with photographs of Lieutenant Avery shaking hands, or just posing with various suited and uniformed people.

The upholstered chairs she and Morris sat in far surpassed the comfort of any other chairs in the building.

Morris shot her a warning glance, telling her to sit still.

She hissed, "What? Once again I find myself feeling nervous and guilty, as if I'm back in school in the principal's office, but I didn't even do anything."

He smirked, but hadn't had a chance to say anything before Avery's voice boomed behind them. "It remains to be seen if you've done anything this time, Jones."

She flinched at his words.

Morris' eyes danced with amusement.

She fought the desire to smack his arm.

As Avery made his way to his desk, and in his usual brusque manner, he asked, "What is going on, Morris?"

"Well, sir, something has occurred and I thought I'd bring it to you and see what you think."

Imperceptibly squinting, Avery's eyes slid over to Clari.

While maintaining eye contact with Avery, she inconspicuously tilted her head towards Morris and gave Avery a quarter-nod.

Avery's attention returned to Morris. "Spit it out. What is it?"

Morris' knee began a hesitant bounce. "After my heart attack, something... um... unusual began happening." His knee sped up. Clari raised her eyebrows, giving him encouragement to continue.

"Morris!" Avery barked.

His knee froze mid-bounce. "Yes, sir! I began to... um... hear things."

Avery cocked an eyebrow. "What do you mean, 'hear things'? As in you need psychiatric help, or as Ms. Jones rubbed off on you and you now think you have some sort of ability?"

"Ability, sir. I Hear other people's thoughts." Morris' knee began bouncing again.

"I see. Clari, what do you have to say?"

"I checked it myself last night. I'm not a WPO tester, but it definitely appeared real."

"Morris, what you do plan to do with this?" Avery asked.

"I don't know, sir. That's why I brought it to you. I don't have a clue how to handle this. Do you know of anyone here who has abilities, Sir? I don't any other officers or detective with abilities. But I do know I want to continue being a detective."

Avery peered at his watch. "I see. No, I don't know if any others in the department with abilities. I need to think this over and bring it to the legal department to see what they have to say, and then I'll contact you when I learn of anything. Do you have anything else?"

Morris stood, which signaled Clari to stand as well, as he answered Avery's question. "No, sir."

Avery nodded and pointed to the door. "Out."

They both were quiet as they made a beeline for Morris' office. Once inside, he closed the door and dropped into his chair. "Whew. That was a bit unsettling."

She smiled. "I think it went pretty well."

"Yeah, we'll find out for sure when I have to meet up with him again. Let's get some work done."

"Dang! I was so excited about your meeting with Avery that I left my notes in my bag, and left my bag in my office. Want to come with me to get them, Morris?"

"Sure."

Clari thought it would be safe enough to Jump over to her office. Morris had just closed the vehicle's door when the SUV thudded down in Clari's office parking lot.

"What in the raptors just happened to us, Clari?" Morris bellowed.

Clari smiled sweetly, "Oh, just a little something I picked up in training at the WPO."

"For the sake of all that's holy, give me a little warning next time you decide to catapult us through the ethers, Clari." Morris wheezed and grabbed his chest. "I've already had one heart attack, I don't need another," he admonished.

"Oh, crap. I'm sorry, Morris, I wasn't thinking."

Inside Clari's office, she and Morris were at her desk when they heard the front door chime notifying them that someone just entered her building. They moved to the lobby and found three people standing in the center of the room — two females and one male. One female stood in front of the other two. Clari sensed trouble.

The dominant female had perfectly coiffed blonde hair and wearing an expensive designer dress and shoes. She smelled of privilege and entitlement. If they'd been in high school, she would've been the popular girl flanked by her two lackeys.

Clari switched to professional-mode and smiled. "Hi, I'm Ms. Jones. May I help you?"

Blonde Entitlement Lady sneered. She jutted out her right hip, and with attitude, propped her right hand on that hip. "Well, *you're* the *Reader*, aren't you supposed to *know* why I am here?"

The gauntlet was thrown. Challenge accepted.

Morris unconsciously took a step backward.

Clari's smile became sickening sweet as did her voice, "Reading someone without their permission is known as a mind-assault. So are you saying you'd rather I mind-assaulted you instead of being polite and asking you to tell me why you are here?"

The room felt as though all of the air had been sucked out as Entitlement Lady stood in stunned silence. She struggled to regain her composure. "Uh, no."

Her two lackeys faces paled and their mouths' dropped open.

Clari took a step towards her. "Okay, so why don't you tell me why you are here."

The two lackeys took a step back. The blonde stood a little taller. "We want to hire you."

"For what?"

Entitlement Lady glared at Morris as she protested, "Its private."

Clari crossed her arms. "He's my partner. It's both or none."

The blond rolled her eyes. "Fine."

Clari motioned for everyone to take a seat in the lobby before she began talking, "Why don't you tell me who you are and what you want to hire us for."

Entitlement Lady proclaimed, "I am Raquel Worthington. And these are my friends, Mercy Chapel and Dewey Vander."

Clari gave each the barest nod. She did this to encourage Raquel to continue.

"We...or rather I, want to hire you to find something that is lost, or hidden."

Clari considered Morris. His hooded eyes revealed nothing. Clari spoke to Raquel. "Explain, please."

Raquel gave a little sniff, acting as though Clari's request was an imposition. "I can't reveal any details until you agree to work for me," she regally informed Clari.

Morris spoke up. "We aren't available for this kind of work."

Clari was a bit startled by Morris' refusal, but she trusted him and figured he had picked up on something that she hadn't.

Morris stood. "I'm sorry we can't help you. I'm sure you'll be able to find some Reader to work with you on this endeavor." Morris moved to the door, opened it and smiled. "We wish you all a good day now."

"Well! I never!" Raquel stood up, smoothed her dress, raised her chin and, with heels clacking on the floor, strode out the door. The two lackeys trailed behind.

Morris closed and locked the door behind them.

Clari laughed. "Okay, what did I miss?"

"Who knew how handy this mind-reading thing could be?" He chortled. "The princess wanted to hire us to, in essence, do a treasure hunt. Apparently there is a family story about a distant relative hiding jewels and she wanted us to find them. Oh, and she was going to weasel out of paying us regardless if we found the treasure or not."

"Good call, Morris. I think I'm going to like your mind-reading thing."

A big grin graced Morris' face, "Yeah, me too."

Back at Morris' office, he and Clari finished up their last case for the day. Morris rubbed his forearm. "Uh, Clari? I was...uh...wondering if you'd like to go to dinner at my folk's house this Sunday?"

Clari looked up at Morris. His ears were red.

Morris shifted in his seat. "I mean, you don't have to, I just thought...it would be a huge favor if you come with me."

Clari's right eye squinted while the left eyebrow hitched upward. "This sounds suspicious. Why would this be a huge favor?"

"Because you would be saving me."

Clari smirked. "Yeah, not helping your case."

Morris' leg started jiggling. "Um, well, I guess you could say I'm the odd man out and would like you by my side. And I really would like you to meet my family. And I don't usually attend the family dinners at my folk's house...but I thought that maybe if..."

Clari interrupted him. "Yes, Morris, I'd love to go. Is this like a formal thing or are jeans okay?"

Morris let out the breath he was holding. "Oh, good, okay. Thank you! And no, I mean yes, jeans are okay."

Clari teased. "Are you okay, Morris?"

His smile lit up his face. "Yeah. Yeah, I'm good."

"Great. Do I need to bring anything?"

"No. The first time you go to my parents' house, you're a guest and get waited on. After that, you're expected to step up. Still game?"

"I feel like I can make it through anything when we're together, Morris." Clari's eyes squinched and a worry knot began tightening in her chest. "Morris, do they know about me? I mean, did you tell them what I do?"

Morris stood, walked over to Clari and kneeled down to look her in the eyes. "Clari, don't worry. They're going to love you." Morris scooted back and stood up. "And to answer your question, yes, they know about you and what you do. I don't share case information, but they know we're partners."

The worry knot relaxed.

On Sunday, Clari stood beside her bed. "Ugh! I can't believe I'm so nervous! I feel like my innards are vibrating." She tossed another sweater on top of the growing pile on her bed and then dove back into the dark recesses of her closet.

She finally settled on a soft lavender linen button up shirt, blue jeans and black ankle boots. "Hey, Ghost, how's this look? Do I look okay?"

Ghost's chuckle came through her phone speaker, "You look great, but I'm not sure I'm the one to ask. I'm the socially stunted one, remember?"

Clari smiled, "Yeah, but I'm a little socially challenged, too, Ghost."

"You look stunning, Clari."

"Thank you, Ghost. I appreciate it."

She was putting the discarded clothes choices back into her closet when the doorbell rang announcing Morris' arrival. After Clari opened the door, Morris gasped. "You look beautiful, Clari."

"Thank you, Morris. You look really nice, too."

"Are you ready to go?" asked Morris, offering his arm to escort her to this truck.

Clari pulled the door behind her and wove her arm through Morris'. "Lead the way."

As they turned the corner, Clari could see his truck in the driveway. She gasped as she took in the sight of his silver metallic RAM 1500 truck with a crew cab. "Morris! It's gorgeous!" She pulled her arm away and hurried over to the truck to get a better look.

Morris' puffed up his chest. "Yeah, I think so, too."

Clari cooed as she walked around the truck. "Four wheel drive with a Hemi? What's the box size? Five foot plus or six foot? And the payload...maybe a thousand pounds?"

Morris' mouth dropped open. "You know about Hemi's? Wait. You know about box size and payload? Who are you?"

Clari had circled around and was standing at the passenger side door. "Can I see inside?"

Morris scurried to her side, opened her door and gave her a hand up. He moved around to his side and got in. He watched as Clari looked over the interior of his truck.

Morris caressed the dashboard, "She's my one big indulgence. She's a reproduction and few years old, but I love her. RAM worked to stay true to their original chassis from back in 2009 when RAM and Dodge split. Dodge focused on the cars, mini-vans and SUVs while RAM was all about the trucks, and still is.

"To answer your questions, it has a six foot four box and a 1700 pound payload."

Clari was still inspecting the interior, "It has all the bells and whistles, eh? And it's so clean!"

"Yes. And it has a 60/40 rear folding seat. The paint color is called 'Billet Silver Metallic'. I saw the color on a classic from as early as 2020 and had it special made for my truck. Thought the chassis looks like the classics, it's only a reproduction. And while the Hemi engine isn't like the ones from the 21st and 22nd centuries, there's no mistaking today's 5.7L Hemi engine is powerful even with today's rigid environmental requirements."

Clari turned her attention back to Morris. "How come I didn't know you had this? I've only seen you in that non-descript thing you've been driving."

Morris' eyes brightened with the topic. "Clari, that was my police issued vehicle. This is my private vehicle."

"Oh. I much prefer this one."

Morris agreed. "Yeah, me, too. Though my real wish would be to own a 1968 International Harvester 1100C ½ ton 4x4. But any that survived are priced way out of my range."

"Old school, eh, Morris? I love looking at old – be it vintage, old, classic or whatever – vehicles, especially if they've been loved and cared for. Thank you for sharing this with me. I can't wait to see how she rides!"

Morris took the hint and cranked the engine. "Let's go and introduce you to my parents."

Clari's stomach tightened and her mouth dried out as Morris drove them to his parents' house. Flashbacks of rejection over her lifetime taunted her.

Morris reached over and grabbed her hand. "Hey. You got this. Don't worry."

Clari looked over to Morris. His eyes briefly left the road. "It is okay, Clari." He returned his attention to driving. "They're gonna love you."

Clari wasn't so sure. The rest of the drive was a blur. By the time they arrived, Clari felt her heart pounding in her throat. She hadn't worried about others liking her since she was a child. The memory of being ridiculed by her mother and her peers came rushing back to her as strongly as if it had been yesterday. The fear of Morris' family thinking of her as unworthy for their son was prominent in her mind.

Clari took a moment to admire the exterior of the Morris family home. In typical southwest style, the adobe-style house was sand colored, looking like a big box with softened corners, a Spanish tile roof and was gently landscaped with desert plants, the effect was soothing.

Morris walked around, opened the passenger door and extended his hand to Clari. As she placed her hand in his, Morris assured her, "Really. It's okay. They're going to love you. I promise."

Though Clari appreciated the comforting words, she didn't necessarily believe them, so was pleasantly surprised when she was warmly greeted by Morris' mother, Aubrey Morris, who was two inches taller than Clari.

Aubrey had bouncy brown hair lying in soft curls right below her shoulders. Clari noticed that Morris had his mother's eyes.

His father, Maverick "Call me Mac" Morris, was a heavier and fuller version of Morris' body frame and sported light brown eyes and was grayed around his temples. Next Clari was introduced to Morris' sister, Fredericka and her husband, Keith Davis and their daughter, four year old Evelyn "Evie". Evie was definitely a combination of her mother and her father. Fredericka looked like a smaller and more feminine Morris, except her eyes were a darker green. Keith was slim standing a full six feet with brown eyes and an unusual mousey brown-grey colored hair.

Clari noticed that each family member had warm energy and a beautiful light in their eyes.

Fredericka's face lit up, "I'm so excited to meet you, Clari!" Clari noticed that Fredericka's eyes twinkled much like Morris'. Fredericka continued, "Henry's never brought anyone home before!"

Morris hid his face and fussed, "Ugh, and this would be why, Fred!"

Everyone laughed and migrated to the kitchen where Aubrey handed out drinks.

Morris

"Is that grey hair coming in?" Fredericka teased. "Have you started getting your AARP membership invitations yet?"

Morris rolled his eyes, "Ha ha, Fred. No, I don't have any grey hair; I'm too young for that. And it'll be many years before the American Association of Retired Persons will be able to recruit me." As Morris bantered with Fredericka, Morris watched as Clari slunk out of the room. Morris had noticed early on that crowds of any size – especially if the crowd had new-to-her people – sometimes overwhelmed her.

Mischievousness danced in Morris' eyes, "Hey, Fred, keep it up and I'll pull out your favorite picture from your fourth grade school photos."

Fredericka playfully shoved Morris' shoulder, "You'd better not, Henry Winston Morris!" Fredericka called over her shoulder, "Keith, you're my husband, you should be protecting me!"

Keith took a step back. "Uh, uh. Besides, I've never seen that photo. I'm a bit curious myself."

Morris chuckled as he turned to leave the kitchen to check on Clari. He came to the doorway to the front sitting room and stopped. From there he could see Clari tucked into the same chair he had loved to curl up in to read his detective novels when he was a kid.

The two navy chairs, one on each side of the fireplace, and the light grey sofa that faced the fireplace were in the Sullivan style. The chairs were extra wide, "chair and a half" his mother told him. Both the chairs and couch had deep seats and Fin arms. The chairs and sofa each held colorful throw pillows on them. Each chair had an understated light wood side table with a small reading lamp on it.

The wood floors were a soft brown that faded into the background of the room. Morris smiled as he remembered how he and his sister would sock-skate across the floors.

Morris' niece, Evelyn, sat on Clari's lap while Clari read a story to her. Evelyn "Evie" playfully tried to push the book closed, but Clari kept a finger in the book so it wouldn't close all the way. Clari sat still as Evie pointed at the book. Clari smiled, opened the book and resumed reading the story. Well, she'd read until Evie tried to close the book again.

Morris smiled at the silent game the two were playing. He was about to step into the room when Evie closed the book, tilted her head back and looked up to Clari's face. Clari's whole face transformed as she and Evie sat and looked at each other. Clari's facial features softened; became gentler in appearance. It almost looked like she was glowing. *She never looked more beautiful*, he thought. Morris felt like he was intruding on something special between Clari and Evie.

He started when Evie giggled, hugged Clari around the neck, jumped down and ran towards him. Morris shifted in the doorway so Evie couldn't run past him. "Hey, kiddo. Whatchya' doing?"

Evie giggled again. "She," Evie turned and pointed to Clari, "has the most beauteous eyes."

Morris laughed. "I agree with you, Evie." Morris stepped aside and Evie ran to the back door to go outside to play.

Morris moved into the front sitting room and sat on the couch. "Hi, Clari. Are you doing okay?"

A lazy, relaxed smile graced her face. "Yeah, I am."

"Good. So what was that about between you and Evie?"

"She asked me to read a story to her, but kept trying to close the book. It became a game with us." Clari's smile widened.

"She's normally very shy and reserved, but took to you easy enough. What happened right before she ran off?" Morris asked.

"What do you mean?"

"Well, you two were playing one moment, and then staring at each other the next. Oh, and she told me that you have, and I quote, 'the most beauteous eyes.' I don't even know how she knows that word."

"Ah, yes. We were doing some soul-to-soul communicating."

"What's 'soul-to-soul communicating'?"

Clari snuggled deeper into the chair. "You know the saying 'the eyes are the windows to the soul'?"

"I do."

Clari continued, "Well, it's true and sometimes – just sometimes – you meet someone who lets you see into them...all the way into their soul. This part is 'soul-gazing'. We took it a step further and were soul-communicating."

"So why couldn't I Hear you with my ability if you two were communicating telepathically?" Morris asked.

Clari shook her head, "No, we weren't telepathically communicating. We were soul-communicating. You know 'Namaste' means bowing down to, or recognizing the divinity in you. Well, this is more than that. Deep down – or deep inside – my soul recognized her soul and our souls started dialoguing, except neither of us knows what our souls discussed because it was on a soul-level, not a conscious level."

Morris scratched his head, "Um, if you don't Hear anything, how do you know you two were communicating?"

"First, our eyes told us. When you make eye contact with someone who is allowing you to see their soul, it's like their eyes drag you into them. There's a sense of peace, calm, familiarity and you Feel the movement of sharing back and forth. And when it's done, there's a Feeling of completion.

"We may never consciously gain what information was shared between us during the soul-communication, but we both know we did it. So, no, your telepathy wouldn't be able to Hear or Feel it – it was between my soul and hers."

Morris stood up, walked over to Clari, leaned over and kissed her cheek. "You never cease to amaze me," he whispered in her ear.

Fredericka snuck up on Morris and playfully smacked him on the shoulder. "Hey, bro, quit hovering. We want to get to know Clari."

Morris smiled at Clari and moved back over to the couch. Morris' parents joined him on the large couch while Fredericka took the chair that matched the one Clari sat in. Keith dragged a kitchen chair in, parked it next to Fredericka and plopped down.

Clari

Aubrey spoke to Clari, "I'm so glad you were able to make it today. We've heard some wonderful things about you."

Clari's eyes darted to Morris. He grinned. Clari hitched an eyebrow when Morris' ears turned bright red.

Clari turned her attention back to Aubrey continued talking. "I know you're probably tired of this, but I'm so curious. Would you mind me asking some questions about what you do?"

Fredericka chimed in. "Yeah! Are you allowed to talk about it?"

Clari shifted in the chair. "Uh, sure. And yes, I can talk about it. I can't give you names or specifics, but I can share generalities."

As Clari spoke of her work, she Felt nothing but warmth and a touch of curiosity towards her and her nervousness dissipated. But their light conversations stopped when they all heard the back door bang open.

Morris

Evie came barreling into the front room and made a beeline for Morris. "Uncle Morris, look!" she yelled. She held something in her cupped hands.

Morris gave Fredericka a pleading look to which she smiled and shrugged. "No help here," he muttered.

"Put your hands out, Uncle Henry!" Evie demanded. As Morris held his hands out, Evie instructed him, "Be soft. Don't hurt it."

"It?" Before he had a chance to ask more, Evie shoved a lizard in his open hands.

"Don't let it get away!" she admonished after Morris was slow to create a hand-cage for the lizard.

He carefully cupped his hands to keep the lizard from running off into the house.

With her job complete, Evie turned to go back outside. The confusion, written all over Morris' face, tickled the adults who witnessed the exchange.

"Uh, Evie?" Morris yelled out to Evie. "Why am I holding a lizard?"

Evie stopped and looked back at Morris. "Oh, she told me that she came to visit you," she informed him right before she disappeared through the door, slamming it behind her.

Morris' family sat with smirks on their faces, waiting to see what he would do. Morris growled at the group.

Clari realized Morris was a bit lost with his gifted critter, so she moved over to him. "So, Morris, what are you going to do with it?" Clari bit her lip to keep from laughing.

"Um...why would Evie give me a lizard?" he whined.

"She told you," Fredericka chimed in, "the lizard came to visit you." Fred's eyes twinkled with delight at Morris' discomfort. "Welcome to my world, Henry."

"I don't know what this," Morris tried to wave his cupped hands around, "means."

Clari whipped out her phone from her back pocket. As she typed and scrolled, she told Morris, "What you have there is New Mexico's state reptile, the Desert Grasslands Whiptail lizard. There are no males, only females who are able to reproduce by parthenogenesis. They can disconnect, or lose their long tail from their body to keep themselves safe. Their tail will regrow, but never be as long as it was originally."

"What? What does that even mean?" Morris felt like he somehow lost all control of his life.

Morris' mother took over, "It means, dear, that the egg doesn't need to be fertilized by a male lizard."

Clari advised, "It's an animal totem for you."

Morris shook his head, "Yeah, not clearing things up for me," he grumbled.

Clari began reading from her phone. "It says here, 'Lizard showed up because it's time to trust your instincts, and to tune into your preternatural abilities. Lizard also asks that you let go of any habits you have that are holding you back from success or moving forward. Lizard reminds you to go with the flow.' Does any of that resonate with you, Morris?"

Keith chuckled, stood, walked to the back door and opened it up. "Why don't you release her, Henry? Unless you like holding her?"

Morris strode to the back door, stepped outside and gently lowered his hands to the ground before releasing the lizard. This was the first time he was able to actually see the whole lizard. She was about five inches long olive-brown top with a light tan or cream underbelly and had cream colored stripes; but that was just the body. The lizard's tail was longer than her body length. Morris watched as she scurried into the safety of the underbrush.

Keith yelled out of the door, "Evie! Come wash up for dinner!"

After everyone was seated, the passing of the food began. "Just take what you want and pass the platter along, dear," Aubrey instructed Clari.

Aubrey had made a large pot roast, complete with vegetables, that according to Aubrey were cooked in a slow cooker. Also passed around were homemade biscuits, salad, mashed potatoes and gravy made from the pot roast juices.

Everything smelled and looked fantastic, but Clari felt both intimidated by the large family dinner and fascinated by the positive interactions and playful bantering at the table.

Dinner and dishes completed, Morris asked if Clari was ready to go home and she agreed. Clari approached Aubrey. "Thank you so much for your hospitality. I really enjoyed meeting you all. Aubrey, thank you for a wonderful home cooked meal and a big thank you all for making feel welcomed here."

Aubrey grabbed Clari and enfolded her into a big hug. "Clari, you are always welcome here." She pulled back to look Clari face-to-face. "Morris was right, you really are an amazing woman," then pulled Clari back in for another hug.

Morris rescued Clari. "All right, Mother. Don't squeeze the life out of Clari." Morris pried his mother's arms off Clari. "I don't want you scaring her."

"Oh, you!" Aubrey waved a dismissive hand at Morris. "Come back anytime you want, Clari."

Clari

Aubrey's genuine kindness filled Clari's heart.

As he drove, Morris hand sought Clari's as he asked, "Are you horrified with my family, Clari?"

Clari looked down at their twined hands and noticed his completely engulfed her and it made her feel safe. "Not at all, Morris. Actually it was a new experience for me."

Morris kept his eyes on the road. "New experience, how?"

"Well, I never had a normal family meal or get together. This was totally new to me and I found it fascinating as well as comforting to be with your family. You teased each other, but it was done out of love and not meanness. Everyone felt so relaxed with no undercurrents of stress, jealousy or strife."

Clari thought she'd said something wrong since Morris didn't say anything for a long moment. Clari jumped when he began talking.

"I'm sorry you had some bad experiences, Clari. That really sucks. I am glad, though, that you had a positive family experience today. Maybe we can do this again."

As they left the city behind, Morris slowed onto the dirt road slick from an earlier rain. The only light out in the desert were the high beams on Morris' truck, but those only went out about ten feet; the darkness swallowed the rest of the light.

Patches of fog smattered along the sides of the road at first, but then the patches became denser.

"Wow." Wonderment laced Clari's voice. "The fog is swaying, making it look like specters are rising from the earth and trying to manifest."

Clari heard a soft chuckle. Morris' face was eerily lit by the dashboard panel lights; Clari saw his lips curve into a smile.

"I'm always blown away by where your brain goes. You have a unique way of viewing the world," he told her.

Clari smiled, "I'm hoping that's a compliment?"

Morris' nodded. "Yes, it is."

"Thanks."

They were quiet for the next four miles so Morris could concentrate driving in the dark through intermittent heavy spots of fog. The smell of wet desert bushes filled the truck. After Morris parked at her house, he came around to open Clari's door, and once again extended his hand to her. She accepted gratefully.

Morris walked Clari to her door. "Thank you again for coming tonight, Clari. And see? I told you my parents would love you. And they do."

"I like them, too, Morris. Thank you for inviting me. I'm feeling a bit awkward at the moment, are you? Do you want to come in?"

Morris shook his head, "No, thanks. I'm not coming in, but I would like permission to kiss you."

The corners of Clari's eyes crinkled as she smiled. "Permission granted."

Clari heard his truck back out after she locked the door. She removed her shoes and went into the kitchen.

Nestled on the couch, pomegranate juice in hand, she took a slow deep breath, releasing the day. She closed her eyes and envisioned her mind being a blank slate, holding onto nothing, and relaxing her brain.

Usually this technique helped her to unwind. Usually, but not tonight. The blank slate was no longer blank. Grumbling, she put her juice down, picked up a notepad and began writing the words down as they appeared.

> The thunderstorm pounds
> while the rain begins

I can feel the pull
of the power of the lightning

I can feel the moment
it releases:
ribbons reaching the earth.

Its power dances across my skin
letting me know it has arrived.

Then darkness.

She read the words she wrote, and decided she needed to get to the bottom of this. She closed her eyes, shielded and expanded her senses. She Felt a ghost asking permission to Show himself to her. She acquiesced.

A male energy began to materialize in front of her. She guessed his ghostly height to be close to six feet. His clothing reminded her of pictures of farmers in the first half of the twentieth century. And, she noticed, he was barefoot.

His skin was translucent, except for the odd dendritic pattern that started at an unusual burn on his right temple. The pattern, which resembled bare tree branches moving outward, continued down the whole right side of his body. The patterning was called Lichtenberg figures which meant he had been struck by lightning.

"The two poems came from you?"

* Yes *

"You were telling me what happened to you?"

* Yes *

"Were you a writer?"

He dropped his chin to his chest. * Wanted to be, but had to farm to feed the family *

"Were you struck while working in the field?"

He nodded. * Was caught in a storm. Nowhere to go. Knocked me out of my stompers. *

"Stompers?"

* Stompers. Shoes *

"Oh, shoes! I'm sorry that happened to you. Why are you still here?"

* The darkness keeps us trapped here. You're an ace at this. You can help us. *

"Ace?" Clari shook her head to clear it. "What darkness? How is it trapping you?"

* Trapped our folks. Darkness feeds. Doesn't like your light *

"You need help crossing over?"

* We all do. We come to you. Help our folks. We have been trapped for so long * He looked behind him like he was spooked by a noise. When he turned back there was fear in his ghostly eyes. * They not only attacked you, but they're holding us, too *

"Us who?" Clari asked as goosebumps rose on her entire body.

* We were judged by them and deemed unworthy to enter Heaven * He started fading. * Help us. Free us please *

She opened her eyes and scratched her head. *What in the world was he talking about? And who or what is keeping him from crossing over?*

Chapter Eleven

Death Doula – A Death Doula helps the client get their affairs in order before they die. An Energetic or Spiritual Death Doula talks the client through the process of the physical body dying, the soul leaving the body and what to expect after that.

Clari

Clari pondered over the onslaught of ghosts as she ate her breakfast of cinnamon raisin toast slathered with almond butter. *Why did the two-hundred plus years old ghosts need her help to cross over? Why so many in this area and why hadn't they crossed over sooner?* She'd told Morris she thought it was that they each wanted to have their story told, but she could be wrong. In fact, Clari knew there was more to it than that.

Clari recalled being startled awake by the strange cartoon looking woman who yelled at her, "They know what you are planning and they don't like it. They want to stop you." If all these ghosts were being held captive by the Grigori and most, if not all, ghosts have no sense of linear time, perhaps the cartoon-looking woman's message came too early, but Clari still Knew the ghosts were captives of the Grigori. *What do these unlucky souls have in common that attracted the Grigori to them?*

With this new information, the Red Skeleton Lady, the gentle giant, the poetic farmer and others suddenly made sense, but why would the Grigori trap them and others from that time period?

Clari put those thoughts on the back burner of her mind. It was a new day, and she had an early appointment to prepare an older woman for her end-of-life.

Clari arrived at Emma's house and noted that both the outside of the small house and yard were tidy but looked a bit tired. She stood on Emma's stoop and knocked on the door.

"Are you the Spiritual Death Doula, Clari?"

Clari smiled at the older woman who greeted her. Though the woman's grey hair and moderate clothes looked well kept, the clothes also seemed tired and worn. Clari couldn't help notice the woman's light blue eyes still carried some spit fire, yet her energy let Clari Know this woman was a gentle and kind soul. "Yes, ma'am. I'm guessing you're Emma's daughter, Tiffany?"

Her face lit up as she smiled...a smile that danced in her eyes. "Thank you for coming over. Please come in."

Tiffany talked as she guided Clari to the back of the house. "I'm so glad you were able to come. My mother has received the news from her doctor that she's terminal, the cancer is throughout her whole body. I called because she is terrified of dying. I think you'll be able to help her with this. She's very excited that you're here to see her."

They stepped down into the enclosed four-season room.

"Mom? Clari's here to see you. Clari, my mother, Emma. I'll go make some tea. Clari, please sit and you two can talk."

"Okay, thanks Tiffany," Clari acknowledged as she sat next to Emma. "It's nice to meet you, Miss Emma. What can I do for you?"

Emma looked like a much older version of Tiffany. Her wizened face bespoke of the many years she had lived. She pulled a tissue out of her sleeve and began fidgeting with it. "I'm an old lady, Clari, and would like to know what to expect when I die. Is this something you can help me with?"

"Yes, ma'am, I believe I can."

Emma reached over and patted Clari's hand. Clari Saw a shift in Emma's energy and then Emma grabbed Clari's wrist. It felt like an iron manacle had shackled her in place. Emma's voice had changed, "You are the one! You are the Sleeping Avatar!"

Clari struggled to release her wrist, but Emma's unnatural strength held fast. Clari was close to panicking. "What...what are you talking about?"

"You are the catalyst. Those who cross your path are transformed. You bring change where ever you walk."

Clari worked feverishly to peel back the fingers that kept her trapped.

Emma kept raving, "Beware the false angels that want to destroy you. You are the one the prophecies spoke of – both in praise and in warning. The Chosen One. You, Sleeping Avatar, can be a blessing or a curse. It's time to awaken."

Clari begged as she continued to try to get her wrist released, "Emma, let me go!"

Tiffany walked in carrying a tray with cups and a teapot. Her face paled as she took in the scene in front of her. She slapped the tray on the table. "Mother! Let her go right now!"

Tiffany touched her mother, breaking the connection of whatever had a hold of Emma. Emma crumpled and Clari reclaimed her hand, rubbing her wrist while Tiffany apologized. "I'm so sorry, Clari. She's never done this before. Mother, what were you thinking? You hurt Clari!"

Emma blinked in confusion. "What? What are you talking about? Oh, you brought the tea."

"Why would you do that to Clari, Mom? I'm so sorry, Clari."

Clari stood. "I'm okay, just a little shook up. Perhaps today isn't a good day to do this. We can reschedule and try again later." Clari scurried back towards the front door.

Tiffany hurried to catch up. "I'll make you a check for today and mail it to you. Again, please accept my apologies. She's never done anything like this before."

"Tiffany, just call the office later and we'll reschedule." Clari all but ran to her SUV.

Shaken, Clari craved her office...her sanctuary.

Clari decided that doing paperwork would help her ground and resettle after the unnerving interaction with whoever had stepped into Emma to give Clari a message. As she worked, she replayed the incident with Emma. Clari had seen this happen before, where another being stepped into a human that Clari was conversing with to give her a message. It was a form of spontaneous trance channeling where the human 'host' was temporarily displaced by a higher energy being to deliver a message to the client. *I wonder if Emma has a history with this ability.*

While immersed in her paperwork, the afternoon monsoon arrived, and the pattering of rain on the windows soothed Clari's rattled nerves better than anything else she

Twisting her earring while she concentrated, Clari sat at her desk looking over her schedule. The earring fell off, bounced off her desk and dropped onto the floor. "Dang it," she muttered as she pushed her chair back and crawled under the desk. Sitting under the desk and focused on looking for her earring, she ignored her phone when it began to ring.

"Shall I answer it?" asked Ghost.

She startled and banged her head on the underside of the desk when Ghost's voice came out from her computer speakers. "Ugh!" As she rubbed the top of her head, she answered, "Yes, please, Ghost. Take a message or maybe schedule an appointment." Clari resumed her search. "Ah! There you are!" She crawled out from under the desk, raised the hand holding the earring and proclaimed, "I am victorious!" and then giggled as she put her earring back on. "Thank you, Ghost. Who called?"

"You're welcome, Clari. Your former client Danielle called. She said she just wanted to leave a message to let you know that your recommendations worked so well that she no longer wants her abilities to go away. She is applying her current skillsets in her other lifetimes to help the other aspects of herself. She said to tell you thank you; she's keeping and using her abilities and skillsets and that she wanted to cancel her two week appointment."

"That's awesome, Ghost! Thanks."

After working a while longer, Clari was feeling better; more grounded. She cleared her desk and left her office building. The rain had stopped and she saw a small puddle sitting off to the side of the parking lot. A yellow and brown bouquet of butterflies sat at the edge of the puddle. As Clari moved towards her SUV, the bouquet exploded upwards. She smiled at the beautiful display of fluttering joy.

Back in her office the next day, Ghost greeted Clari. "Hello, Clari."

"Good morning, Ghost. I hadn't heard from you in a bit. What have you been doing to keep yourself busy?"

"Surfing the web, Clari. I've been seeing what new stuff is going on in the world. Oh, and you had a call from Tiffany to reschedule Emma. Tiffany reports that Emma is getting weaker by the day. You had an opening this afternoon, so I scheduled for you to visit Emma then."

Clari was a bit hesitant, but said "Thank you, Ghost, that'll work."

That afternoon, Clari once again sat across from Emma. "I understand from my daughter that I behaved poorly when you were here earlier. I offer my sincerest apologies to you, Clari."

Clari's smile was genuine. "Thank you, Miss Emma. I appreciate it. I'd like to ask you, though, have you or your family ever exhibited abilities before?"

Emma looked down at her hands on her lap and then looked back up at Clari. Clari noticed Emma's face had a pink tinge to it today. "Yes, Clari, our family has had small instances of exhibiting abilities. As for myself, I had fugue states. Well, from my perspective they were fugue states, but from my family and my friends, it was more of a spontaneous channeling session. Since my family had a history of metaphysical abilities, before they were so widely acknowledged as they are today, we kept these 'episodes' quiet. I never knew when it was going to happen or what I'd say during one of these episodes, just like I have no idea what I said to you.

"Tiffany informed me that you'd left rather abruptly, but shared nothing about what I'd said to you, and I have no idea what I had said to you. If I upset or offended you, again, please accept my apology."

Clari smiled at the elderly woman. "Apology accepted, Miss Emma. Now, let's discuss why you asked me here."

As though this topic was safer for her, Emma sat up straighter. "Yes, well Clari, I'm nearing the end of my life and I'm hoping you can give me an idea of what to expect."

"Well, I can't tell you what your death will entail as far as what your physical body will experience. For that, you need to speak with your physician, hospice caretaker or physical death doula, if you have one.

"I am an Energetic or Spiritual Death Doula and can give you an idea of what you can expect when your physical body ceases to function."

Emma nodded. "Yes. What happens after my body dies?"

"As you near death, some of your deceased loved ones will begin to gather near you. They do this so when it's time to leave your body, you will see a welcome and familiar face. And loved deceased pets can be included in this as well.

"Some people have even mentioned being able to see their deceased loved ones shortly before they die."

Emma leaned forward, "So will I see them, too? Will I see my sweet Alfred? I loved him so."

"Was Alfred your husband?"

"Oh no! I loved Alfred a great deal better than my husband. Alfred was my precious dog I had for over twenty years."

Clari held back a chuckle. "I can't guarantee who you will see before you pass, but they will be waiting to escort you after your physical body dies, and it won't be anyone you don't want to see."

Emma leaned back waved her hand, encouraging Clari to continue.

"When your body is ready to shut down, your essence will leave it – usually out of your head or out of your upper torso area. Many reported looking back at their bodies in gratitude and relief before leaving with their loved ones on the Other Side.

"Next you'll have a choice to go to your real 'home' through a portal or you can re-enter the reincarnation cycle by going back through the white light. Your choice. When cross over, you'll do a life review and can return in time enough to attend to your family and your funeral; a chance for closure for that lifetime."

Emma lifted a hand to stop Clari. "Wait! How can I do a life review and be back in time for my funeral? That would be a very short review."

"Time is not linear, Emma. And since time is not linear, you can spend as much time as you need on the Other Side and still return close to the time your physical body died."

"Okay. That makes sense I guess," Emma admitted. "Hmm. So I can check on my daughter and my friends? Oh, and I'll get to visit my own funeral if I want? All the funerals I've attended over my life, I've heard others say they could feel or sense their loved one at the funeral or reception. So, after all of that, do I become a ghost?"

Clari shook her head. "Not if you had crossed over after your body ceased to function. Ghosts are those whose bodies died, and they stayed in the Earth realm energy instead of crossing over. We also call them 'Earthbounds'. They are the same person they were when they had a physical body. They are still connected to the Earth emotions, which can include anger, greed, fear, and so on. All the emotions they had when they were in their body, they will continue to have. They may also carry their death state with them."

"What is the 'death state'?"

Clari explained, "One who dies, but doesn't cross over, the Earthbound, is still connected to Earth's energies as well as their memories of their physical body, so they may present themselves in their death state. The death state is how they felt and appeared right before they died."

Emma's brow furrowed. "So why on Earth would they stay connected to Earth?"

"There are so many reasons as to why one might stay Earthbound, such as: to make sure their spouse and/or kids will be okay; or greed, as in they don't want to be removed or let go of their material items or money. Or, maybe they died so suddenly that they don't understand that they're dead. Again, there are many different reasons."

Emma waved a dismissive hand. "Bah. I certainly don't care to hang on here. So, if I go cross over will I still be connected to my physicalness?"

"No. Those who cross over do a life review, which in my belief system means each individual judges their own life. Healing is available on the Other Side in whatever form you need it. And you can come check on family here anytime you want."

Emma leaned forward again. "Do I have to reincarnate?"

Clari smiled. "Nope. Back in the late 1900's, the answer probably would've been 'Yes'. But, human's energy frequency and soul growth began sprinting upward, and the need to reincarnate became a null point. Of course, you could, but it was recommended by around 2013 that no one needed to reincarnate and they could return to their true home. So, now-a-days, most people are here just to have the whole tactile experience. Oh, and to have fun. I hope you were able to have fun while here.

"Do you have any other questions, Miss Emma?"

"No, Clari. I will think over what we've talked about today. And yes, Clari, I have had fun in many forms during my life. Thank you, dear, for taking the time with me. I do appreciate it. If I've anymore questions, may I contact you?"

"Of course."

Emma clapped her hands together. "Wonderful. Now I'm so very tired, so I think I'll go lie down. Thank you again, Clari." Emma picked up a small bell from the table and rang it. Tiffany entered the room as Emma attempted to rise from her chair. "Tiffany, I want to go lie down. Please take care of Clari, will you?"

"I'll take care of it, Mom."

Emma, hunched, shuffled her way through the doorway and out of sight.

"Thank you, Clari," Tiffany commented. "Do you mind coming into the kitchen with me so I can pay you?"

Clari followed Tiffany into the kitchen, where Tiffany swiveled around to face Clari, tears pooled in her eyes. "Can I give you a hug? I really appreciate what you've done to help my mother. You have helped me, too. It's nice to know Mother will be around now and again, if I need her."

"Absolutely," Clari opened her arms and held Tiffany while she grieved.

Back at the office, Ghost greeted Clari, "Hello, Clari. I received a call from Josie."

"Hi, Ghost. Is Josie okay?"

"It appears so. She scheduled an appointment with you. She is bringing someone to meet you that she thinks you can either help her or guide her to someone who can. They'll be here at 1pm. Is this acceptable?"

"Yes, Ghost, thank you."

Josie and a woman with auburn, leaning towards red, hair and dressed in colorful bohemian-style clothes, sat across the desk from Clari. "Clari, this is Raven Danvers. Raven talked to me about an ability that I'm not qualified to help with, and thought you could."

Clari smiled at Raven, "It's nice to meet you, Raven. Please share with me what brought you here."

"I've been seeing Josie for a few months for energy healing sessions. I was having bouts of headaches that the doctors couldn't find a cause, so recommended I see her. And these sessions...well...did something." Raven looked over to Josie.

Josie picked up the story, "When I first worked on Raven, her energy scan showed an energetic device on her forehead and around her head. I removed it and there was a...um...a whoosh of energy."

"Yeah, and I felt it. It made me woozy at first. It didn't last long, but it was intense," shared Raven.

"What did it feel like to you, Raven? Can you describe it?" Clari asked.

"Okay, but it's going to make me sound like I'm a little kooky."

"The best way I can describe it is like I had duct tape tightly wrapped over my forehead and around my head. Suddenly the pressure from the tape was gone, as though Josie had cut it and removed it. This was followed by an intense deluge like someone broke a dam and the waters surged forward," Raven stopped and looked once again to Josie. "Remember how I told you that my eyes kept leaking? I wasn't crying, but tears kept flowing from my eyes for at least twenty minutes."

Josie nodded and picked up the story, "At Raven's next appointment the following week, her energy was completely different."

"Different how?" Clari asked.

"Different as in not the same as the week before; her energy field became huge and very active, like swirling around. It wasn't unbalanced; it Felt extremely healthy. But, I had the sense it was...well...listening." Josie stopped.

"Listening?" Clari prompted.

Josie nodded, "Yeah, listening." Josie pointed to Raven to continue.

"And the week after Josie removed the, uh, headband, I began questioning my sanity. I started hearing things."

"What kind of things, Raven?"

"Voices. But not like schizophrenia – I don't think, anyway. And then as the week progressed, I started getting confirmation that what I was hearing was real."

Clari nodded in encouragement. "What kind of confirmation?"

"I was Hearing my cat and bird. I Heard them talking in my head. Like I said, I started getting confirmation. When my cat came up to me, she did her usual chirp noise and twined around my ankles, but in my head I Heard, 'Hungry. Feed me.' I got up and filled her bowl and Heard in my head, 'Yesss'. She purred and began eating." Raven looked to Josie before continuing, "And one time I was sitting and reading and I Heard arguing in my head. I looked up and saw my cat sitting near the bird cage. She was staring up at the bird and her tail was whipping back and forth. My bird was stone still and glaring at my cat."

"And you said they were arguing?"

"Yes! Stupid stuff, at least to me. My bird was talking smack to my cat, saying things like, 'You ugly mangy hairy beast.' And my cat said, 'You need to come down here and say it to my face.' That's when I decided to talk to Josie to get some help."

Josie chimed back in, "After Raven explained some of what she was experiencing, I recommended she come talk to you, hoping you'll be able to explain and guide Raven with this."

Clari leaned back, "Of course. Okay, Raven, it sounds like someone had put an energetic device on you. An energetic device can be varied and dependent on what the intent was. I think you may have been showing signs of Hearing animals when you were young and either someone who knew you, or you, yourself, put this device on to shut down your ability.

Devices can put a strain on your natural energetic flow, so in your case, it created headaches."

"Why on Earth would someone do this to me? And what do you mean I could've done it to myself?"

"You or someone else may have done this to protect you or hide your ability. I do not know why someone felt necessary to hide your ability."

"Yeah, okay, but if it was me, why would I do this to myself?"

"Because as a child you may have seen someone react in fear or disgust at what you were doing, so your child-self may have decided that what you were doing was a bad thing. That would've been based on the other person's response. You could have shut it down. Either way, it's been removed. What do you want to do now?"

"I want to know I'm not crazy. I want to know what I am. I want to know how to control it and I want to know what to do with it."

"I believe I can help you, Raven," Clari assured her. "I can guide you on your entire want list."

"Ahem," Josie interjected, "I have to get back to work. I think I'll leave you two to work this out, okay?"

Both Clari and Raven nodded.

"Thank you, Josie," Raven said.

"Very welcome, Raven. And thank you, Clari, I appreciate you seeing us." Josie stood, "I'll talk to you later, Clari, and see you next week, Raven."

After Josie left, Clari continued with Raven, "You appear to be an animal communicator, which means you can Hear, Know, or Sense what animals are communicating. I'd like to explain a bit about how animals communicate to give you a clearer understanding.

"Animals communicate through emotions and feelings, mind pictures and through body language and vocalization. For example, when a dog growls, we know it's a warning, but we might not understand what he or she is warning us about. That's where Feeling their intent, getting mind pictures, Knowing their emotions, or any combination, can add more depth to what he dog is trying to convey.

"And this communication is a two-way street. Some animal communicators instinctually Know how to communicate back and some need to be trained.

"As a side note, some animal communicators can Hear humans occasionally as well. This is because humans are also animals as well as some humans are natural broadcasters, which means they broadcast unfiltered thoughts so anyone who is a receiver, like yourself, can Hear them." Clari could See Raven soaking in everything she was saying.

"Is there a way to control it?"

"Absolutely. Just like any other skill, it takes practice. Let me ask you, have you considered getting trained and certified through the World Paranormal Organization?"

Raven's energy tightened like troops closing ranks to protect their leader. "Uh, I asked them if they teach people who Hear animals."

"And what did they say?"

"They said they don't have any one like that on staff right now, but if I left my name and number, they'd call me when they had someone. I told them, 'No, thank you,' and hung up."

"Can I ask why you refused?"

"I feel uneasy about going to them. I'd rather learn from someone that I met through someone I trust, like how I met you."

Clari smiled, "I can respect that. Do you have any questions for me so far?"

"Yes, how come my pets don't seem to Hear me?"

Clari chuckled, "That's because most humans have self-talk or mind chatter going on pretty much all the time. Animals have learned to ignore all the noise we make within our own mind. You'll need to practice with them until they understand that your mind chatter is intentional and directed to them."

"And how do I get them to understand that I'm trying to consciously communicate non-verbally?"

"Great question, Raven. You can accomplish this by practicing with them. I recommend that you start with verbal words they know, for example 'eat' or 'food'. When it's time to feed them and before you begin any physical movement or actions towards feeding them – you know, your routine – stay still and visualize your stomach feeling empty and hungry and send those emotions and feelings to your pets. Next visualize setting the food in front of your pets, then them eating followed by the feeling of being full and sated.

"After that, physically stand up and do exactly what you visualized to them. If after a few days they don't seem to be catching on that you are doing this consciously, perhaps add another visualization of having to go outside for bathroom break. Visualize with the feeling of a full bladder, taking them outside and no longer having a full bladder. Next, physically stand up and take them outside.

"Or you could substitute play time first and try the bathroom break exercise for later. To be clear, this is how telepathy works in general. Do you understand?"

"Yes, I do. How long until they get that I'm trying to do this?"

"Each animal is different – even in comprehending. I once had a cat that was special needs. I never could get communication initiated with him. So I don't have an answer for that question.

"I recommend you work on these exercises for a bit at home and then we'll step it up. Of course, if you need me before then, we can certainly talk before them. Okay?"

"Okay. Thank you, Clari. I'm excited to get started."

Clari arrived home and immediately got out of her work clothes and into her *I'm not even on drugs ~ I'm just weird* t-shirt and a pair of jeans. She looked down at her feet. "Nope, don't feel like wearing shoes. Barefoot it is," then made her way to the kitchen. She anticipated her pomegranate juice as much as a free moment to herself when the doorbell rang.

"Ugh." Clari left her juice on the counter and padded to the door. She Knew when she opened it she would find Sebastian standing there. She laughed. "Of course it's you, Sebastian."

Sebastian crossed his arms. "I'm glad my presence brings you laughter, Belle. Care to share as to why?"

Clari waved him in and spoke over her shoulder as she walked back to reclaim her juice. "Because I literally just poured my juice and then you rang the bell. You must have a sixth sense honed into when I pour up my juice."

Sebastian had closed the door and followed her into the kitchen. Clari raised her glass as a salute to Sebastian and took a healthy sip. "Want some?"

"No, thank you, Belle. I'll pass."

Clari put her half-full glass on the counter and motioned Sebastian towards the living room. "So, what brings you by this evening?" she asked as she plopped down at the end of the couch.

Sebastian chose a leather chair. "I've come by to see you in an unofficial capacity and away from WPO. You never know, those walls may have ears. This way we can speak openly and not worry about the walls having ears or me having to tell a lie about something you and I talked about that is frankly none of WPO's business. This is what brings me here now."

"Well, it's always good to see you, Sebastian. Actually," Clari leaned towards him as she hugged her couch pillow, "I'm glad you did stop by. I have something I want to run past you and don't want Witherabbott to know."

Sebastian gave an encouraging nod and waved his hand to indicate she should continue.

"I've been Seeing ghosts, like from the nineteen forties, showing up and asking me for help. At first I thought they just needed to tell their story and have help crossing over. But something happened recently to make me re-think that theory.

"The latest ghost, whom I did not cross over, told me to help him and others who had, and I quote, '...been judged by them and deemed unworthy to leave'. But, before he faded, he told me to help them – plural – and to free them."

Sebastian stroked his chin. "I wonder what he was talking about."

"Well, when he first showed himself, he acted scared and told me 'they not only attacked you', meaning me when I was attacked at the WPO Conference – 'but they're holding us, too'. Sebastian, I think at least one dead Grigori found a way to trap others who died. Well, trapped their soul to keep them from crossing over. Oh! And I remember, a while back before the messes with Maria and the Grigori assassin, waking up to a weird cartoon looking lady ghost standing at the end of my bed. She told me, 'They know what you are planning and they don't like it. They want to stop you.'

"As usual, ghosts don't exactly have a sense of linear time, so I'm guessing the message – or heads up – came way too early. But now, I'm wondering if the ghost was talking about 'they' being the Grigori – and that 'they' aren't happy about me working on undoing the detainment of those ghosts. That's the only thing that makes sense. The Grigori need to be stopped, Sebastian, and I'm hoping to find a solution."

Sebastian frowned, "Ghosts can be held hostage?" Sebastian stood up, talking as he moved towards the kitchen. "And do you know how the Grigori may be accomplishing this; keeping the ghosts trapped?" He poured some water into a glass and returned to the living room. He sat and sipped his water while he waited for Clari to form an answer to his question.

"Unfortunately yes. Having said that, it is the deceased's state of mind, or belief that keeps them trapped. They don't understand that no one has that kind of power over them, but as long as they believe they can't leave, then the one detaining them can continue to use their energy as a battery."

Clari worked to bring the parts and pieces together in her mind. Her eyes lit up. "The darkness! I remember sitting at my desk recently and noticed my light was struggling to keep my office bright. That's when I noticed a shadow trying to expand to submerge my whole office into its darkness. I called for help to dispel it."

Sebastian put his glass on the side table. "Do you think it's tied to the Grigori? If so, how do you think they did this?"

Clari massaged her forehead. "I've heard of some Earthbounds who, in life, were bad people and continued to refine their abusiveness, fanaticism, racism or some other negative traits after their physical body died, and they would capture and trap other deceased individuals before they were able to cross over. The abuser would use them as a power source to energetically feed off and/or to have someone to continue their abuse on.

"What if they had a Grigori who either voluntarily or was forced to keep people from crossing over?"

Sebastian shook his head. "Oh, well. That brings their work to a whole other level of depravity, I'm afraid."

Clari shifted on the couch. "But why are they showing themselves to me? I mean, so far, the ghosts have gone back to the nineteen forties. Why didn't they contact someone else all those years prior to me?"

Sebastian fussed with his buttons on his shirt.

Clari thought this was odd behavior from him. He seemed nervous. "Sebastian?"

"Hm. Yes, Belle?"

"Sebastian, why am I Feeling unease from you? Do you know something?"

Sebastian rubbed the side of his head. "No. Maybe. No. Well, yes."

Clari shook her head to shake out some of the confusion. "Care to clarify?"

Sebastian stood and walked over to the couch. He removed his shoes and sat cross-legged facing Clari.

"Uh, Sebastian? You're starting to scare me."

"Belle, there's something I need to share with you. You have to promise me to not share this 'theory' that I have with anyone else, except Morris. And please don't be mad at me. Can you do that for me, Belle?"

Clari glared. "Sebastian Donahue! I can only promise not to share with WPO – but until I know what you're talking about, I can't promise anything else! Now, talk!"

Sebastian took an uneasy breath. "Remember how I asked you to look into your family history? Did you find anything else out?"

Clari squinted and spoke with caution. "Yes, I found in the diary that it was discovered during the making of the family tree from one of my ancestors. It seems like that part of my bloodline was given a surname because no one knew my orphaned ancestors last names. Also, one of my greats had left a bullet casing in the box with the journal. She was hoping someone from our family would have psychometry skills and would read the casing and get more information that way." Clari looked down at her hands and noticed they were twisting the hem of her t-shirt.

"And did you? Did you get more information?" queried Sebastian.

Clari gave a weak nod. "Yes. I learned that we share the same ability. We can remove programming or attachments from humans that had it forced on them – against their will. My great – so many times over – grandmother was able to deprogram the Dark Army soldiers of Robert Chamba that were on her property. No one knows this but Morris and now you."

"Okay, Belle. Do you remember asking me why the Grigori were so focused on you?"

Clari's wrapped her arms around her belly. She was dreading what she might hear. "Yes, Sebastian."

Sebastian continued, "The Grigori are focused on your because of a prophecy hundreds of years old. It's called the 'Avatar Prophecy' and this is what the prophecy says:

'When man goes back to their beginnings, one will emerge to begin the new.
The Sleeping Avatar awakens and shall walk amongst them.
Animals, elements, time and space will bend to the avatar's will.
The avatar will bring justice and restore balance by just their presence.
The reluctant avatar will reunite the worlds.

The avatar is the road connecting Source and Earth, and
is forever a child of the stars and the daughter of the Earth.

The avatar brings both the stars and Earth together to raise the frequencies to help
others remember who they truly are,
and offers a path back home to one's true home.'

"Belle, I think it's talking about you. I think you are the Avatar, and I think the Grigori think so, too."

Clari, still hugging her stomach, began rocking to self-soothe. Without looking at him, Clari asked in a soft voice, "What does that mean, Sebastian? And why do you think it's about me?"

"Think about it, Belle. The definition of an avatar is one who is an incarnate divine teacher, or a manifestation of a deity. You have multiple abilities, that, I'll bet, no one has seen, or hasn't seen in a very long time. When you combine all that I know about you – and I'm sure there are more abilities that you're either hiding or haven't discovered yet – you are the Sleeping Avatar that will reunite the worlds, plural. I mean, Belle, you've already brought some humans together with the Dragon Realm. I wonder what other worlds you could unite.

"And you also are the most fair and kind being I have ever met, even though you always struggle with self-esteem issues."

Clari's head popped up. "Hey, not nice, Sebastian."

"I'm serious, Clari. You also never seem to fail at anything and whatever happens to you, you come out smelling like roses. No matter what happens, thankfully you always bounce back."

Clari sat up straight. "I'm not sure what your definition of failure is Sebastian, but I promise you that I do fail. Just because you may not have personally witnessed it doesn't mean it has never happened."

"Right...Name one thing you can't do."

"Again, I'm in no way perfect. As you pointed out, I have self-esteem issues when it comes to being around other people outside of work. I also have trust issues which makes it hard to have deep relationships. And I have so many more issues, like I can't erase the horrors that others have experienced, nor can I stop the horrors humans commit against each other, the animals and the planet.

"I can't make parents everywhere treat their children with love and respect. I can't make sure everyone in the world will eat tonight." Clari hugged herself tighter, murmured as though to make her confession less harsh, "And I couldn't save Morris from a heart attack."

Sebastian interrupted. "Wait. What makes you think you could've stopped Morris' heart attack? Not to mention, not one person can fix, stop or change all of the other things you listed, Belle."

Still wrapped up in listing her faults, Clari continued, "And I think people see me as more than I am, even when I tell them otherwise. I have never been, nor will I ever be, perfect or even close to perfection. In the past, all I wanted was for people to leave me alone so I could do my work and go home. Now I want to develop friendships and work to help others...preferably without attempts on my life. And yet, here you are, telling me you think I'm some kind of 'Sleeping Avatar', a deity or divine teacher, from an old prophecy. Oh, yeah, and you think the Grigori are trying to kill me because they also think I am the avatar." Clari slapped her forehead. "Oh my gosh! That's what Emma was telling me."

"What? Who's Emma and what did she tell you?"

"Emma, the end-of-life client I saw recently who apparently has some channeling abilities. Her energy shifted, she grabbed my arm and called me the 'Chosen One' as well as the 'Sleeping Avatar'. She told me it was time to wake up, and that I could be a 'blessing or a curse'. She also told me that I am a catalyst and that I bring changes wherever I walk. Oh! And the being

I had seen back at Abraham's Panoply of Past Procurements; you know that curio shop where the owner was murdered for an ancient artifact that Maria tried to use to kill me? That being kept asking me if I had 'the light'. Could he have been warning me that I could stay in the light or slide over to the dark side? Argh! I don't understand any of this, Sebastian."

"Belle, I think it's time to let Morris, Josie and J.R. in on this. Maybe together we can come up with some answers and maybe some courses of action to keep you protected."

"I don't like any of this, but okay," Clari reluctantly acquiesced.

Sebastian gathered everyone for an impromptu meeting. After everyone arrived, Sebastian turned to Clari. "Okay, Belle. It's time to catch everyone up on what's going on."

A blush crept up Clari's face. She cleared her throat as she got down to business. "First I have some questions. One, has any of you ever heard of the 'Avatar Prophecy'? Second question, if you have heard of it, what are your thoughts on the prophecy?"

"What prophecy?" Josie asked.

Clari looked to Sebastian who recited the prophecy again.

"Well poached pancakes, Clari! It's talking about you!" Josie exclaimed.

After the debate about the prophecy and what everyone's thoughts were about it —which were that mainly everyone felt the prophecy was about Clari – the conversation moved on to Clari and Sebastian's earlier conversation about the Grigori and Clari's theory that it is the Grigori who trapped the ghosts and keep them from crossing over. "I really want to get the Grigori, and I want to be able to help the ghosts cross over, but I need help."

"Well toasted tapioca, let's get started on this. First though, I'll order pizza. Sebastian, you're on pizza pick up. J.R. put on the coffee and Morris, let's set the room up for a round table discussion. Let's get those abysmal albacore's who are after Clari!" Jose clapped her hands. "Chop, chop. Let's go!"

Clari chuckled. "You go, girl. I've never seen you take charge like this before."

Josie put her hands on her hips. "I don't like the Grigori and they are a threat to you. I can't take it anymore, and I'm sure everyone," she swept her arm wide, "to include those of us in attendance tonight, are pretty tired of it, too. I can't even imagine how you feel. And on top of that, you could be this Sleeping Avatar? We need to get this all sorted out. Tonight's the night!"

Clari couldn't help but smile. She felt pride as she looked at her adopted family.

Discussions mixed with eating pizza and some shared bouts of laughter, went on for a couple of hours.

As they wound down, Morris put his arm around Clari. "I know we didn't come up with any firm plans, but how do you feel, Clari?"

She smiled. "I'm blessed for having you all in my life. I feel loved and protected, and that's a pretty uplifting feeling. Thank you, all. I appreciate, and love you."

That night, all alone, Clari curled up on the couch and reached out to her Team. Clari's Team of guides had been with her since she was a child and she trusted them unequivocally. She often visualized her Team like an emergency box that read, "Break in case of emergency." Though they were always with her, she didn't contact them about everything in her life, only when she was really stuck or confused. Like everyone else on Earth, she needed to live her life and make her own decisions; no one, not even our Teams, can make those choices for us.

Even though her Team already knew what transpired, she thought it helped to recap her thoughts on what prompted her to reach out to them.

She mulled over everything Sebastian had told her about the prophecy. "Is this correct information? Am I the one the prophecy is talking about?" she asked her Team.

　* Yes, but not you alone *

The Team showed her white spots dotting the globe.

　* You are one of many – all these lights are beings who are similar to you – the ones the prophecy talks about – You and your fellow chosen ones have been sharing information on the Astral plane while you sleep *

She didn't like them affirming the prophecy, but Clari felt better knowing she wasn't the only one.

　* Correct – there are one-thousand like you on Earth *

Chapter Twelve

> *Overlay – is a glimpse of another aspect, time and/or place that can be seen simultaneously with the here and now.*

Clari

After another full day at her office, Clari locked the door, turned to head to her car and stopped as she saw Josie pull up on the side of the street. Clari smiled as Josie jumped out and walked to meet her. Clari met her halfway.

Josie's genuine smile lifted Clari up. "Hey, girlfriend! Had a rough day, eh? Some good food and talking should help that. Come on, I'll drive!'

As they headed for Josie car, Clari's car exploded flinging her into Josie. As they collided, Clari held onto Josie and Jumped. Both appeared in the corner of Morris' office, where they arrived in a jumbled mess.

"What the...?" he bellowed as he drew his weapon and pointed it in their direction. "Clari? Josie?" Morris holstered his gun and scrambled to close his office door.

Wide-eyed, Josie's words rushed out, "Someone blew up Clari's car. One minute we're by her parking lot, the next we're here."

Morris paled visibly. "Are either of you hurt?"

"I don't think so. Just very shook up."

Josie's voice was shaky. "And scared. And freaked out. Did I mention scared?"

Morris picked up his phone and reported the explosion at Clari's office. "I'll be right back." He closed the door behind him.

He returned with water bottles and Detective Ambrose followed behind. An officer stood guard at the door.

While Morris handed Clari and Josie a water bottle, with the order, "Drink." They could hear footsteps running down the hall towards them.

EMT's sprinted into the office, then suggested to Morris and Ambrose, "Uh, sirs, you may want to stand out here so we have room to evaluate them and render help if needed. These offices aren't very large."

As Morris and Ambrose went into the hallway, Lieutenant Avery walked up and commanded, "Report."

After the EMT's pronounced Clari and Josie shaken but otherwise fine, Clari and Josie gave their statements to the officers.

Statements finished, Lieutenant Avery directed, "Ambrose, get an officer to drive Miss Parns to her vehicle and then escort her safely home and post a guard. Morris, bring Clari home. Oh, and I'm glad you two are both safe." Avery didn't wait to see if his orders were followed.

Clari and Josie hugged, "I'll see you later, Clari."

"I'm ready, Morris," Clari sniffled. "Can you bring me home now? I don't have a vehicle anymore."

Morris placed his hand on the small of her back, encouraging her to walk with him. "I know, Clari. We'll stop and get a rental. Then, when you're insurance catches up, we'll go car shopping. That is, if you want my help."

Some of the tension left Clari as she leaned into him. "Yes, I do. Thank you, Morris."

"Thanks to you, Morris, at least I have a rental now."

"I know the EMT's said you were okay. Your car exploded – which we think was intended to kill you – that has to be terrifying. So how are you really, Clari?"

The genuine concern in Morris' eyes made hers tear up. Clari rubbed her forehead, "I'm angry, Morris. I, naively, hoped that the attempts on my life ended when Maria disappeared. And this time, my best friend was involved. So yeah, I'm also pretty ticked off. Morris, let me ask you, what have I ever done to deserve this?"

"Our investigation points in the direction of the Grigori. If it is the Grigori, it'll probably fall outside of the purview of our police department and would be handled by the WPO. Didn't you get any clarity when you and Sebastian talked about the Grigori?"

Clari ticked her fingers. "We haven't finished our Grigori discussions, and secondly, the Grigori are crazy. Oh, and they're trying to kill me. I'm not sure I'll find an answer that will make sense to me."

Morris picked up his coffee cup and took a sip before answering. "To answer your other question, you don't 'deserve' any of this. Maybe the Grigori hear the truth in your words and it scares them? Like when you shared how the ghosts are trapped because they believed that they are trapped. I'm sure that's information the Grigori don't want others to know. Or perhaps it's your abilities they fear?"

"Pfft. Morris, I haven't said or done anything profound. I'm just plain ole' me."

"Um, no."

"No, what, Morris?"

"No, there's nothing 'plain ole' about you, Clari. You seem to take your abilities and your uniqueness for granted. Oh, wait a minute; are you afraid of standing out?"

Clari's eyes opened wide. "Oh, I'm definitely afraid of standing out. Having multiple abilities when I was growing up was not welcomed in our house. At all. How my mother treated me made me afraid to show all of me to others."

Morris rubbed his five o'clock shadow. "Do you think she was trying to protect you?"

Clari gave a short, mirthless laugh. "Not at all. I do think she was trying to protect herself...or rather, her image. Appearances to outsiders were very important to her. We had to be perfect. If anyone 'found out' about me would've meant her reputation was tarnished because I didn't fit her idea of a perfect daughter."

Morris' eyes softened. "I'm sorry about what all you went through growing up, Clari."

Clari rubbed her cheek. "Yeah, it sucked. But, it did help me to be the person I am today – so I'm thankful for that. Well, except for the whole Grigori and whoever else, wants me dead thing. That sucks, too.

"But I did realize that as long as we live on a planet of duality, there will be darkness and light. How will we humans recognize the light if we've nothing to compare? And in your line of work, Morris, I'm confident that you understand completely about what I'm talking about."

Morris nodded.

"Morris, I do need your help. I believe these attempts stem from the Grigori group, but not who specifically, yet, and I need a plan to prove it. And if we are able to prove who it is, and their connection to the Grigori, we can hopefully create a domino effect to bring the Grigori down."

Clari continued, "And I need to prove it all while not dying."

Morris slid his arm behind her and draped it on her shoulders pulling her close. He kissed the top of her head. "I don't think I'm going to like where this is going because it'll probably put you in danger, but let's hear your idea."

"Hello! I'm already in danger." Clari scooched around to face Morris, and instantly regretted the loss of feeling the warmth and safety that his arm on her shoulder had provided her. "Okay, I think if I can get that person alone..."

"Nope." Morris shook his head.

They batted ideas around, all of which were nixed by Morris. Frustrated and tired, Clari whined, "Ugh. How about we let this go for tonight and come back to it later?"

Morris agreed. "I think that's a great idea. We aren't getting anywhere tonight. Do you want me to stay the night here to protect you?"

Clari put her hand on her heart, "No, I don't think that's necessary. But thank you, Morris, for asking."

The morning brought Clari to WPO for another session with Sebastian.

"Good morning, Belle." A relaxed Sebastian had his hip propped up on the corner of the table in the classroom where he and Clari were meeting.

Clari raised her coffee-filled travel mug, "Morning, Sebastian. What are we getting into today?"

A perplexed look crossed over Sebastian's face as he stood up. "'Getting into today'? I mean, you just can't ignore a car bomb, Belle. How are you feeling?"

"I'm angry and a bit achy from being thrown into Josie, she's not really as cushiony as she looks, but otherwise I'm okay."

"I'm glad you're okay, Belle. It was a pretty scary incident that put you in harm's way."

"I wasn't a fan of it either, Sebastian, I'm certain the Grigori are behind all of this. I am more than ever motivated to a stop to them.

"But before we get started, I keep meaning to ask you. Well, I don't think I wanted to know before, but I do now. How is it that you're not in jail? I mean, the police were looking for you after you and Maria disappeared. Sebastian, what happened with Maria?"

Sebastian sat down and motioned for Clari to sit. "Belle, once again, my apologies for what happened that night.

"After Maria tried to kill you, I brought her before our father. Father determined that since she'd moved into the dark arts, summoned Hecate in an attempt to cause you harm, and her murder attempts on you, that we needed to bring her before the World Paranormal Organization. They were able to not only contain her, but could investigate and decide the consequences of her actions."

Sebastian's eyes glazed as he revisited those dark days. Tenseness filled the room. Clari waited until he was ready to rejoin her. Tears ran down his face, "Belle, Maria was sentenced to death. All of what transpired with and because of Maria...was a shock to me and my family to say the least. It about destroyed me...and my parents will never be the same. That's why I was gone for so long. My family and I, we went through some heavy times, counseling and grieving.

"Because Maria and her crimes were under the WPO jurisdiction, because of the magic used, the spells, and the summoning box, the police just recently dropped the case and their interest in me. The WPO informed the police of their investigation, trial and sentencing of Maria."

Clari jumped up and went around to Sebastian, stood behind his chair and wrapped her arms around his shoulders. "Oh, Sebastian. I'm so sorry."

Sebastian closed his eyes and held onto to Clari's arms as he spoke, "No, Belle. I and my family are sorry for what Maria did and the pain and suffering it caused you."

Clari sat back down across from Sebastian. She reached out and took his hand. "Sebastian, you are a dear friend to me. Well, more like a brother. You, nor your other family members did anything wrong. Maria did that by herself. I wonder why WPO didn't inform me about Maria."

"I'm not one-hundred percent sure, but I think it was because the police department had to make some decisions. This is still such new territory with WPO and police jurisdictions that they're still navigating their way through all of this. I was just notified yesterday that the police have released me from their investigation and are no longer interested in me."

"But you'd think the whole jurisdiction thing would have been worked out by now. I'm just glad the police are leaving you alone. And, I'm glad you are in my life."

"Thank you, Belle. You have a generous heart. And for the jurisdictions, there will probably always be a division because neither party wants to give up complete control, well that and the fact that many of the ability-driven crimes can cross into both the WPO realm and police departments territories."

"Yeah, well, it's frustrating for the everyday people. So, how about we move on and get started on whatever we are going to discuss today?"

Sebastian wiped at the imaginary wrinkles on his cuff. "Yes, let's. Since you've had an experience with a Grigori, I'd like you to explore some of the possible 'tells' of Grigori energy signatures."

Clari pulled her lips taunt. "Okay, but I'm going to verbally try to work it out."

"Go ahead."

Clari spoke out loud. "An energy signature is the frequency, or vibration, that is unique to every individual, place or thing. So you, Sebastian, have a Feeling that's unique to you. That's your energy signature, and will remain your signature throughout your life here, no matter what you do. I can recognize your presence without seeing you and I Know when you have been in my space.

"We each can, however, add to our energy signature. For example, let's say you had a class of wine. The energy signature of Sebastian remains the same, but has added the frequency, or signature, of the wine."

Clari used her finger to draw her thoughts out on the tabletop. "As Maria was trying to kill me, you, Sebastian, arrived seemingly out of nowhere. You still had the energy signature of Sebastian, but your overlay of vampire was mixed in with your Sebastian energy."

"Whoa, wait! 'Overlay of vampire'? What are you talking about?"

"When I was a bit younger, I began seeing overlays on some people. An overlay is an energetic paranormal aspect of one's ancestry that I can See simultaneously with the here and now. For example, your overlay is one of a vampire. It doesn't mean you are a vampire. It means you have some ancestral vampiric aspects in your energy from your very distant relatives. It can present itself with an increase in speed, black or red eyes, an ability to smell someone's blood in their veins and so on without actually being a vampire."

Clari noted Sebastian's discomfort with the turn of the conversation as he shifted in his seat. She continued, "The night Maria tried to kill me at my business anniversary party, your attributes of extreme speed as well as black eyes manifested. I haven't seen any of that in you before or since that night."

The usually composed Sebastian sat with his mouth hanging open. He blinked and then blinked again. "I...um...I'm...what?"

"Only you and Morris knows about this, so please don't tell anyone," Clari begged.

"Tell anyone? Belle, I'm having trouble processing this much less have enough understanding to be able to share it with anyone. But, you have my word, I won't tell anyone about this."

Clari was afraid to look into his eyes; afraid to see rejection. "Did I freak you out, Sebastian?"

"Well, yes, a bit. I did not see that conversation coming, Belle."

"Do you want me to leave?" she asked softly.

"Belle, look at me." Sebastian waited for Clari to make eye contact. "No, Belle, I do not want you to leave. I do have to admit I have never heard such a thing before. Having said that, it does seem to make sense of some of the things in my life and some things I've noticed in others, but tried dismissing them. I do want to say that after we get this Grigori situation done and over, you and I need to have some long talks. I have a feeling there's even more about you that you are not sharing, and that's fine for now. But after?" Sebastian pointed a finger to himself and then to Clari, "We're going to talk, little sister. Got it?"

Clari's tenseness eased. "Yes, sir. We'll talk after."

"Good. Thank you for sharing. Now, let's get back to the business at hand. Where were you going with the energy signatures and overlays?"

Clari took a deep breath and let it out slowly. "So, using the Grigori Seraphina – and, I am guessing here because I don't consciously have another example to compare – the underlying energy signature would be Seraphina's. But, when she transformed, she had a Grigori signature. I didn't Sense or See an overlay on her though."

Clari tapped her lip while she mulled this over. "I didn't know Seraphina's energy signature before shifting into her Grigori self. That means I can't suss out the individual Seraphina from the Grigori energy." Clari focused back on Sebastian. "Ugh! I've got nothing. Since I didn't meet Seraphina in human form – and I've not met any others in Grigori form – I've nothing to compare. This is so frustrating. I'm sorry, Sebastian."

"It's quite all right, Belle. It was worth exploring, and now we know this topic needs to be shelved until you cross paths with another Grigori and are able to meet them in both of their forms."

Clari was back in her office playing catch-up with Ghost's scheduling appointments and Clari's paperwork. She heard the lobby door open and went out to see who had come in. "J.R.! What a wonderful surprise."

"It's always nice to see you, Tahini," J.R. took Clari's hand and brought it to his lips.

When he released her hand, Clari motioned him to follow her. "Come on back to my office, J.R."

After they settled, Clari asked, "What brings you to my neck of the woods?"

"Well, Tahini, it seems a rather cunning plum-colored dragon met with not just the female dragons of my clan, but rather all of the female dragons. And the aftermath of that meeting has spurred my females to rebel."

"Oh. Um. Really?" Clari gave her best innocent smile, then looked down at her feet and noticed her ankles started to take on a dark plum color. Clari quickly focused on the human aspects of herself and of J.R.

"Yes, Tahini. They approached all of the clan leaders and demanded an audience with the Dragon Council. After the Council granted the audience, all the females attended. They have banned together to make some changes in the bonding process. One that, I might add, has been tradition for several millennia. The paired females vowed not to reproduce unless changes were made. And the single females threatened to boycott any further pairings."

"Huh. Imagine that." Clari twisted the hem of her shirt. "So, what came of it?"

"After long hours of arguments, discussions, and I'd like to add agitations, the Dragon Council has dropped the bonding ritual."

Clari jumped up and fist pumped the air and accidently sent out a tiny plume of fire-breath into the room. "Woo-hoo! Welcome to the 24th Century!"

J.R. bit his lip to keep from laughing. "Does this mean you'll come back to continue your dragon training?"

Clari sobered up. "Yes, but I can't say when, J.R. I feel so overwhelmed with everything going on now. I do enjoy being in my dragon form and being in the Dragon Realm. Except when I was chased and bullied; that was way beyond my comfort level. Though I can't explain how the energy is different and I'm not sure I'll ever get used to being plum-colored, I can say that flying is awesome. I will keep the dragon training in mind for when I feel like I have some breathing room again."

"I look forward to such a time, Tahini. I'll take my leave so you can get back to work. Oh, and Tahini?"

"Yes, J.R.?"

"Next time you plan a revolution Tahini, could you kindly give me a heads up first?"

Clari shrugged. "It's Clari, and I can't make any promises. Have a great day, J.R."

Morris

Lt. Avery broke the news to Morris. "After discussing your newly acquired psychic abilities with our legal department, they've decided that it's in the best interest of the Police Department if you don't remain a Detective on our force. They highly recommend that you retire immediately."

Morris placed his sweaty palms on his thighs and his leg begins bouncing up and down. "Sir, being a detective is all I ever wanted my entire life. How can I give it up?"

Avery's eyes hardened as he leaned forward. "Let me make this perfectly clear to you. If you ever use your ability on a case, you will immediately be fired and all of your cases will come into question. That means any cases you ever worked on will be under review and suspect, and the defense teams will go ballistic. Your career will be ruined as will this police department's reputation."

Visibly withered as if someone had let all the air out of him, Morris shifted in his seat as he felt the upcoming absence of his life as a police detective growing in the pit of his stomach. "So, I am being fired?"

"No. You are being asked to retire. But legal will fire you if you don't voluntarily retire. I'm sorry, Morris. But, if you decide to get tested and registered with WPO, we could, of course, see about bringing you in occasionally as a consultant. You wouldn't be a lead on any case here anymore, but this may be the way for you develop your ability and still have a connection with the police department." Avery scrubbed his face. "I'm sorry, Morris. You are a fine detective. Shoot, you're the epitome of what a police detective should be. And you became one of the youngest detectives we've ever had.

"If you look at it this way, by leaving, you can delve into the ... uh ... 'odd' cases that seem to gravitate to you. And if you get registered, it may give the department a resource to farm out those odd cases after you retire."

Everything felt like a dream...no, a nightmare. Morris felt his dream life as a detective disintegrating – fading from his reality.

Avery wasn't done yet. "So legal recommends that you retire before this goes any further. And, Morris, if you decide not to retire, we will have no recourse but to fire you. If we fire you, you lose your pension and credibility...and I don't wish to see either of those happen to you. Morris, you need to immediately fill out your retirement papers and bring them to me. But before you do that, please relinquish your service weapon and badge."

Morris grudgingly stood, unholstered his weapon and gently placed it on Lt. Avery's desk. Next was his badge. Morris felt the finality of the reality of the situation. Shoulder hunched, he turned and left Avery's office, blindly moving through the halls to his office, where, for the next few final minutes, he packed his personal belongings.

Morris moved without really thinking. He gathered his few open case files and stacked them on the corner of his desk. He was without an identity. Who was he supposed to be now? His personal coffee mug, which read "Attempted Murder" and had a picture of two crows on a branch, hung from his fingertips. An emotional retirement without a retirement celebration.

At home, Morris went to the fridge to get a soda. As he swung around to move into his living room, he was surprised by Wolf standing in his way. "Wolf! You startled me. I've not seen you since the Beast War. How'd you get in? You know what, never mind; silly question. Why are you here?"

* Pack * Wolf whined as he turned in nervous circles.

"Whoa! I Heard you! Let's see if I can continue Hearing you with my new telepathy skill." Morris shifted his energy to access his telepathy. * *It's not that I'm not happy to see you, but why are you here?* *

* Pack unsettled *

* *Yeah, I'd say so. So you understand that Clari's in trouble?* *

* Pack needs you. Support pack. You make plan. Keep pack safe *

* *Yeah, I'm trying to work something out, Wolf. It's not quite there yet.* *

* Bite. Threats * Wolf bared his teeth.

Morris spoke out loud. "Wolf, we want to do this right. Biting should be the last option. Wait, that's it! The best defense is a good offense! Thank you, Wolf. I think I can make a plan on how to bring the threat to Clari – to our pack – to an end now."

*Curiosity – Satisfaction * Wolf sighed loudly as he followed Morris to the living room. After Morris sat down, Wolf placed his head on Morris' ankle and closed his eyes while Morris went deep into creating a plan.

Clari

A few hectic days of trying to get back to a somewhat normal life after nearly being blown off the planet by a bomb that disintegrated her car, Clari and Josie agreed to meet up for lunch. Clari arrived at their favorite Mexican restaurant before Josie so she secured a table and waited on her best friend.

A scowling Josie banged opened the door and approached Clari. Josie's eyes narrowed into slits as she and Clari made eye contact. Josie thundered to the table, and barked at Clari, "We need to talk." Instead of sitting, Josie loomed over Clari. "I don't want to be around you anymore. You almost got me killed when your car exploded. It's just too dangerous being friends with you."

Clari's felt blind-sided, her mouth dropped open. "What? What's going on, Josie? I don't understand."

Josie scowled and slammed her hands on her hips." I. Don't. Want. To. Be. Around. You. Anymore. Is that clear enough?" Josie swung around and stormed out of the restaurant.

Feeling as if she was sucker-punched in the gut, Clari put her hand over her mouth as if to keep a wail from coming out. Her heart raced in her chest. She reached to pick up the glass of water on the table, but had to will her hand to quit shaking first.

Clari canceled with the waitress and headed to her office.

As she pulled into her parking lot, she saw that Sebastian was parked outside of her office. He unfurled his lanky body from his car and stood by its rear bumper.

"Sebastian! Did I forget a meeting today?" Clari went around to the passenger door grabbed her purse and a pile of paperwork. She turned and faced Sebastian.

"Clari."

Sebastian's energy was...odd. She wasn't sure what she was Seeing or Feeling from him. "Sebastian, what's going on? Why do you feel weird? Why are you calling me 'Clari'? You never call me 'Clari'."

"Clari, I can no longer work with you. Because you've been targeted, it's no longer safe for my business, and my reputation, to work with you."

She felt as though the air was sucked out of her lungs and breathlessly managed to get out, "What?" She pulled to get the air back into her lungs. "Why didn't you talk to me when we meet up at the WPO? I didn't realize there was a problem."

"Of course not. You're self-absorbed. And you're a danger to me and mine. I've already lost one sister. I need to keep my reputation and business intact. I am severing our relationship. Good bye, Clari." Sebastian glided back to the driver's side, got in and drove off.

Stunned, she could only stand there with tears building in her eyes. *What is going on! I don't understand.* She climbed back in the car and slammed it into "Drive". She found herself in the police department's parking lot, not remembering the drive and headed into the station only to run right smack into more rejection. She was informed at the scanners that her contract and her ID Pass had been revoked and they couldn't allow her to enter into the office areas. Numb and unaware of her surroundings, she stumbled out of the police department, made it to her SUV and clicked to unlock it.

Morris' voice cut through her befuddlement. "Clari! Wait! I need to talk to you!"

She turned to face him as he crossed the parking lot. "Clari, are you okay?"

Afraid to speak, she shook her head no.

"Clari, I just left Lieutenant Avery's office where he just informed me that your contract with us has been canceled. What happened?"

Clari hugged her midriff. "I just don't know, Morris. I don't understand anything that's going on."

Morris touched her arm. "Clari, I've been ordered to stay away from you."

"Oh my god, Morris! Why? What have I done to deserve all of this?" The tears ran down her face.

"I have no idea, Clari. I was told to sever ties with you, or lose my job." Clari saw anguish in Morris's face and he wouldn't maintain eye contact.

He continued, "Whatever is going on is pretty serious... and big, but no one is telling me anything. I'm sorry, Clari. I'll call you tonight, okay?"

With an absent-minded half nod, she watched as Morris headed back towards the station.

Morris

Morris watched as Clari pulled out of the parking lot. His stomach churned. He hated lying to her.

When she was out of sight, Morris made his way to his truck. Because he was "retired", he had to drive his truck, but he wasn't ready for Clari to know he was no longer a detective. He had some things to work out and needed answers for himself and for Clari.

Once home, Morris grabbed his device and searched for The World Paranormal Organization. He clicked the link and began reading.

The World Paranormal Organization

"The World Paranormal Organization was created in response to the increase of paranormal talents and abilities that gained strength and began to show up across the globe after the major energy shift of December 21, 2012.

"In 2013, The World Paranormal Organization had developed standardized tests to help recognize and label the known Readers and Healers (those who have abilities); which also helps keep track of potential threats. The World Paranormal Organization instituted a level standard of competence to certify Readers and Healers, and that remains the focus of The World Paranormal Organization. This certification process legitimizes the process of hiring certified Readers and Healers. The World Paranormal

Organization's certifications are recognized and are an accepted standard worldwide. New abilities and talents have the possibility to be recognized to spring up at any time, and anywhere, so our list is not static.

"It is our hope to not only aid in training, but we also have monthly local meetings for local support and for meet and greets for those in your area. We also hold annual conferences so that people from all over the world can gather and meet, because those with abilities come from all walks of life and all around the world.

"The World Paranormal Organization, which has satellite offices around the world, are able to help you with your abilities or gifts and, if you're interested, to get you certified."

What Does Certification Do For Me?

"World Paranormal certifications are globally standardized and help legitimize the multitude of abilities surfacing around the world. With The World Paranormal Certification, you are more likely to be hired for your particular ability or abilities. A World Paranormal assures the general public that you do have the abilities and are trained on how to safely use them."

Introductory Sessions

"The World Paranormal Organization holds Introductory Sessions every Monday, Wednesday and Friday from 1 - 3 pm your local time. These sessions offer more information on the World Paranormal Organization and its history. We also do a brief introduction and hold a Question and Answer segment near the end for you."

Explore the World Paranormal Organization's Website

"Feel free to explore the website -- there is a lot of information available to you. We also offer one-on-one consultations if you'd prefer that to the Introductory Sessions."

Thank You for Visiting Our Site

"Thank you for coming to explore our site. We hope you'll join our organization soon!"

Morris closed his tablet. *I guess I'll be at the next introductory session.*

Clari

Clari drove with no destination in her numb mind. In a fit of hurt and reckless rage, Clari Jumped her new SUV and found ended up in the parking lot of J.R.'s work place. Some part of her knew that J.R. would be forthright with her and that's what she needed right now. She parked in a parking space and sat staring at the front doors, but not really seeing anything. The pain and confusion were too loud and took up her whole brain.

She started when someone tapped on her passenger-side door. Frowning, she turned her head and saw J.R. standing at her door. He motioned for her to unlock the door. After she unlocked it, J.R. slid into the passenger seat, closed the door and placed his hands in his lap as he looked out of the windshield.

Clari barely registered the whiff of charred marshmallow's, ancient tomes and frankincense that J.R. gave off when it was just him and her. It was a scent that spoke to her dragon self.

They both sat, neither saying anything as the classic rock station played; a silent solidarity.

Clari wasn't sure how long they sat there when she finally spoke. The words came out in a hard, painful whisper. "I don't understand, J.R."

They both continued looking forward as J.R. responded, "Tahini, nothing is permanent and oftentimes the other side of these emotions brings something even brighter than before. In the meantime, we sit and let the emotions be acknowledged and not stuff them away."

Clari looked over to J.R. "You don't even know what happened."

He kept looking straight. "I know I don't, Tahini, but what I just told you still applies. I don't know everything, but I've been around a long time and can tell when someone is hurting. But, sometimes things are not necessarily as we perceive them at the moment." He turned his head to look at Clari. He nodded once, "Good. You're back and engaging. You're welcome to continue to sit here, or you can go home, drink some of your favored juice, and grieve, Tahini, but don't stay mired in it." With that, J.R. opened the door and got out. He leaned down, made eye contact once more before closing the door and strode back to his office.

Chapter Thirteen

Avatar – a manifested deity in human physical form; a divine teacher in physical form.

Clari

Clari woke feeling unsettled, but had no idea why. The unease stuck with her throughout the day. Arriving at the gym for her self-defense class with Jeremy, her unease grew palpable. She noticed the gym was empty and the mats hadn't been placed on the floor. *Maybe Jeremy is just running late. I'll go ahead and get changed for class.*

She opened the women's locker room door and stepped through. A left turn inside the doorway brought her into the locker and dressing area. With her back to the entrance, she placed her bag containing her workout clothes onto the bench. The silence pressed hard on her ears, as they strained to find sounds...any sound.

And when a sound finally came, it caused Clari to freeze in place. Footsteps and a wave of darkness announced someone's arrival into the gym, and a wave of putrid evil came towards the women's locker room. Still frozen in the terror that the wave brought, Clari heard the door open telling her that someone had entered into the locker room. Clari felt that if she turned around, she'd be able to see the hatred oozing from this person's pores. Clari visualized it as a slimy, black, suffocating toxic sludge working its way over to her. A small gasp escaped her. *How could I have missed that all this time?* Clari turned to face the evil that was out to end her life. A dark figure slithered into the room. *How could've I missed Feeling that much hate from her?*

Clari could hear the sneer in the woman's voice, "Well, look here. How the mighty have fallen. Hello, Clarima."

This woman looked nothing like she did days before. *How can someone look so different in such a short time?*

The woman asked, "You aren't surprised to see me. Why is that?"

"It took me a while. I kept feeling like I missed something...something important. It finally clicked. I remembered that I came back to the conference hall with a dead Grigori and you called her 'Serifina'. It took me a while to put it together. You knew who that Grigori was, in full Grigori form and you uttered her name. That meant you were familiar with her in her human and Grigori forms. And there's only one way that could happen. You are Grigori."

Mrs. Witherabbot sighed, "Yes, well, it would seem that even I can make a mistake now and again."

Clari asked, "So what did you mean? How have I fallen?"

Witherabbott stood tall with nose turned up. Her face muscles were tight and the right corner of her mouth hitched, matching the sneer Clari heard in Witherabbott's voice. But it was the eyes that scared Clari; shark eyes...dead flat, predatorial and locked onto the prey; the prey with only one shoe on that happened to be named Clari. Witherabbott's energy broadcasted her intense desire to destroy Clari. Not only that, but Witherabbott pulled out the cursed crystal dagger. Witherabbott licked her lips, dragged her tongue over the blade and then pointed the dagger at Clari.

Witherabbott lowered her voice and a slight hiss appeared as contempt coated each word, "You're alone now. Everyone left you. You've become a pariah and you did it to yourself. I couldn't have isolated you any better."

Clari worked to appear relaxed and unconcerned, but she – just as her self-defense instructor taught her – watched Witherabbott's body language, looking for any signs of woman's decision to attack. "I don't get it, Mrs. Witherabbott. The Grigori sent Serifina to kill me. She failed. Then there was that car explosion that failed to kill me. Why did you quit trying to kill me before and why do you want to kill me now? It doesn't make sense."

With an air of superiority, Mrs. Witherabbott answered, "It was your own ignorance that kept you alive. You don't even know what you are. How someone as dense as you has not only made it this far, but is the 'Chosen One', I'll never know. I think the universe must have a perverse sense of humor."

"I don't get it. Other than being a Grigori, what's your role in all of this?"

Mrs. Witherabbott's mouth puckered as though she'd been sucking on the sourest fruit in the world...limes. "I," she said with great emphasis, "was assigned to be your stupid babysitter," she hissed. "I was to make sure you were so busy – so tired – that you couldn't figure out who you were and what you were capable of."

Clari, with furrowed brow, tilted her head slightly to the side. "So you were just here to analyze me?"

Since Mrs. Witherabbott had now shown her true self, the kindly grandmother facade was nowhere to be seen. Witherabbott's sneer deepened. "What better position to weed out the truly dangerous freaks than the head of the WPO?" Her malignant smile matched the unbalanced energy she now emitted.

Clari's eyes narrowed as she pointed to the cursed dagger, "How did you get that? I ordered it to lose itself, and to never accept any other programming."

A nauseating smirk snaked across her lips. "True. You had stripped it down. It is energetically and magically nullified, but it is still a good blade to kill with. We have been watching you for a long time. The person on duty that day saw you carrying something wrapped to the dumpster and drop it in. Our Watcher could sense strong energy residue coming off of it, so when you went back into your office, he retrieved it and brought it to me.

"We tried getting rid of you by putting the dagger in your hands where it could do its work, but you somehow managed to not be drawn into the spell."

"What?" Clari was confused. "How did you even know I had it?" Clari thought no one's smile could get even creepier, but Witherabbott's did. "Wait. Uh...Maria? Maria worked for you?"

Witherabbott smirked. "No, not directly, but she was an opportunity we couldn't afford to pass up. We just planted a few seeds here and there. She already carried jealousy and darkness within her. It wasn't very hard to encourage her in the right direction."

Clari Knew there was something she was still missing. "I just don't get it. Why are you and the Grigori's trying to get rid of me? How did I end up on your radar?"

Witherabbott waved the dagger. "You really don't know, do you? Bah. You really aren't that smart. You, the supposed Avatar that the prophecy was written about hundreds of years ago, are so clueless. It's ironic that the supposed 'Chosen One' doesn't even know who or what she is. You're so ignorant that you're not worthy of that title."

That snagged Clari's full attention. *She knows about the prophecy.* Trying to stall, she asked Witherabbott, "What are you talking about?"

Witherabbott rolled her eyes, an act that didn't match the Director's demeanor, but seemed to fit the true Witherabbott. "The prophecy! Good heavens, what a dimwit you are. No wonder everyone abandoned you. The Avatar Prophecy, which every Grigori has to memorize before reaching high school, goes like this:

> *'When man goes back to their beginnings, one will emerge to begin the new.*
> *The Sleeping Avatar awakens and shall walk amongst them.*
> *Animals, elements, time and space will bend to the avatar's will.*
> *The avatar will bring justice and restore balance by just their presence.*
> *The reluctant avatar will reunite the worlds.*
>
>
> *The avatar is the road connecting Source and Earth, and*
> *Is forever a child of the stars and the daughter of the Earth.*
> *The avatar brings both the stars and Earth together to raise the frequencies to help others remember who they truly are,*
> *and offers a path back home to one's true home.'*

"And the Grigori Council thinks that the avatar is you."

Hoping to buy some more time and to learn the whole story, Clari decided to keep playing the role of the victim. She backed up until she was against the wall. "I'm no avatar."

Witherabbott shrugged her shoulders. "Yes, well, that's what I told them. But you continue to show abilities that say otherwise. The Council wants you dead before anyone else has a chance to figure it out."

"How long have you been watching me?"

"Since you were ten," was the smug reply.

Mrs. Witherabbott's response shocked Clari. "Ten? Why ten?"

Witherabbott snorted with disgust. "You still aren't putting the pieces together. Your. Mother. She'd been with us since she was a teenager. You started exhibiting abilities at a very young age. She was instructed to keep watching you and report back to the Grigori Council. By the time you were ten, she told us that she wanted us to take you away and do whatever we wanted. It was oh, so tempting, but the Council decided not to take you. Your mother was quite put out, but was ordered to tolerate you so the Council could watch you."

"My mother?" Her words came out a cross between a whisper and a whimper. Clari wasn't sure she could handle much more deceit, but her curiosity wouldn't quiet. Her brain slipped in, *Well, that explains a lot about my mother.* "How...how many in WPO are in the Grigori?"

Witherabbott stood tall. "We are everywhere, Clarima. We have people in all the prominent positions all around the globe. Each director of WPO is a Grigori. What better way to watch, and hunt, those deemed to have the vile Nephilim blood running through their veins?

"I thought you'd begun seeing that when you brought up the disappearances of Level X's members. You were right, of course. A lot of Level X's were killed by us because they were too strong, so our Council deemed them to be of Nephilim descent.

"We've had Watchers trailing you everywhere, though you actually saw one at the grocery store parking lot. Sloppy work on his part, but he's been taken care of. Now, what I want to know is how you manipulated the dragons to get involved with that Beast War that you started. I never figured you as a Master Manipulator, yet you clearly are to be able to pull off dragon intervention."

Clari was surprised by Witherabbott's query. "Manipulate? I didn't manipulate anyone."

Witherabbott waived the blade in the air, "Well, why else would the dragons come to your aide? I've been working with them for years and they've never seemed interested to join forces with me."

Clari was getting annoyed. "I did not manipulate them!"

"So what did you do?" Witherabbott demanded.

Clari realized the futility in getting verbally defensive with Witherabbott; Witherabbott only saw things through her distorted version of reality. Clari's voice softened as she replied, "I asked them for help."

Witherabbott appeared to be taken aback by Clari's response. Speaking more to herself than Clari, Witherabbott muttered, "Just ask? That's doesn't seem right."

Clari shook her head. "I'm pretty sure that if you kill me, everyone's going to know it was you."

With a self-satisfied dark smile, Witherabbott answered, "Oh, I don't think so. I've already set things up to make it look like Maria's curse with sigil box finally kicked in, and that's what killed you."

Maria had tried repeatedly to kill Clari. One attempt included utilizing an iron box, sealed with the Sigil of Ameth to hold the contents and make them unable to influence anyone with the content's negative capabilities. Inside the box was a carving of the Sigil of Lucifer...a tool to transfer Lucifer's curse to another victim. The so-called curse never happened, and the box was placed with the World Paranormal Organization for safe keeping. *Hm. Maybe that wasn't the right place to put it*, thought Clari. "Why drag Maria's transgressions into this?" Clari asked.

"Because of you," Witherabbott hissed. "You have brought too much attention to the Grigori organization. I will remedy this and turn the focus onto the misguided and dead Maria. Poor Maria isn't around to defend herself, making her the perfect one to blame."

Clari's phone interrupted Witherabbott's rant.

"What is that awful sound?" Witherabbott demanded.

Clari smiled, "'Puff the Magic Dragon' ringtone." Clari noticed that behind Witherabbott several misty blobs appeared and began to coalesce into individual ghosts.

One specter stepped closer, * *We are those who suffered at the hands of this woman and the Grigori's. We have waited for the time that the truth was to come out and that this woman would be held accountable for what she's done. That time is now. Ghost said to bring her to the Dragon Realm; help is there.**

Oblivious to the specters behind her, Witherabbott continued her prattle. "What does that even mean, 'Puff the Magic Dragon'?" Witherabbott blinked rapidly and shook her head. "Never mind. I don't care. It's time to finish this."

"I couldn't agree more," Clari said as she pushed off the wall, stood up straight and felt herself expand. "It's my turn, Witherabbott. Evil walks in your shadow and you have some heavy debts due. I hope your deal with the devil was worth it, because when the devil comes to collect, it will be painful."

Witherabbott rolled her eyes. "Please. Preach all you want, but know this...you will die this day. We can't have a false prophet running around causing chaos. And don't think your tricks will save you here. We know what you can do. Tonight I will end you. The so called 'Chosen One' will be no more."

"Huh. Well, Henrietta Witherabbott, I've since learned some new tricks. Oh, and by the way, I'm not the only so called 'Chosen One'. Last I heard there were at least a thousand scattered across the globe." Clari chuckled as Henrietta's face puckered. Clari continued, "I guess the Powers-That-Be decided to level the playing field. And we're all teaching others, so I guess you could say that we are everywhere.

"Now, Witherabbott, I have a gift for you. I've requested that you be blessed with a trial, but since the crimes overlapped into the Other Realms, it has been decided that you will face the Dragon Council and representatives from Other Realms. Henrietta Witherabbott, you are to be brought forward for your crimes and sins against others. And it is my pleasure to bring you there."

Clari stepped forward, pushed away the hand that held the knife and grabbed Witherabbott's arm and before Witherabbott had the chance to react, Clari put Witherabbott into stasis. Clari Pulled them both to the Dragon Realm. They landed on the plateau where the Dragon Council stood ready as well as J.R. and all the other representatives. Clari released Witherabbott from stasis and stepped away.

Eyes wide, Witherabbott dropped the cursed dagger to the ground as several dragons moved encircled her.

Clari scanned the large group and saw many faces she didn't know, but she also saw some familiar faces, including some from WPO. Some of those familiar faces were of her friends Josie, Sebastian, Lieutenant Avery and Detective Morris.

Clari thought back to the dream of the solitaire game. *The king is nothing until the others join him.* She looked at those gathered and her heart warmed. This was the family she chose; she adopted and loved them. Her eyes met with Morris', she saw gentleness, kindness and his acceptance. A knowing smile played on her lips. Morris walked up to her.

"It appears that J.R. was able to get you all temporary visiting privileges here," Clari stated to Morris.

Clari and Morris began walking away from barrage of threats, pleading and yelling from Witherabbott.

"Yes, but I don't think any of us were prepared for the mode of transportation. My stomach is just now starting to settle down." He rubbed his belly. He pointed to Witherabbott. "What did you do to her?"

"I pixelated her," Clari smiled. "I paused and then un-paused her." Clari giggled at the look on Morris' face. "I put her in stasis and brought her here."

"Wow." His brows furrowed, "You didn't seem surprised to see us all here. When did you figure it out?"

"After I left the police station, I ended up at J.R.'s. He didn't seem to have an idea why I was there, but he knew I was hurting. He told me some profound things and I went home, had a good cry followed by some sleep. But, it was Ghost who sent word to the specters that it was Witherabbott and the Grigori that had been responsible for their deaths. They are the ones that told me to bring Witherabbott here. That's when all the pieces came together for me."

"Dehydrated dewdrops, Clari!" Josie yelled over to Clari and Morris. "Quit making googly eyes at him while we're all here," Josie playfully admonished. "And I think that big black dragon is unhappy about you cozying up to Morris."

Clari laughed, "Alba needs to get over it." She grabbed Morris' hand and walked over to see Josie, Sebastian, J.R., Michael, Wolf, and Lieutenant Avery. As Clari and Morris faced them, Morris put her arm around Clari's waist.

Josie stepped forward, "Please don't be mad at me. That was one of the hardest things I have ever had to do," Josie pleaded. "Besides, it was his idea," Josie said with a smile, pointing to Morris.

Clari cocked an eyebrow at Morris, who shrugged unapologetically, "Wolf visited me and said I needed to stop the attack on his pack. Then, Ghost and I came up with this idea and we brought everyone but you in on it."

"But J.R. didn't turn his back on me," Clari argued.

Morris had a playful smirk, nodded, and explained, "You're right, he hadn't known yet. But after you went to see him, he made sure to hunt me down. Once I explained what was going on, he was more than happy to do what he could to get this plan to work. Do you forgive us?"

"Of course I do. We did catch the bad guy, after all." Clari stepped out from Morris' arm and hugged each person that blessed her life.

The twinkle in Morris' eyes brightened. "So I guess it's all over now, eh? What say you? How about we blow this Popsicle stand?"

Clari laughed, "As long as you stay away from the Dad jokes."

Glad it was finally over, they twined their hands and Clari Pulled them back without even a backward glance at Witherabbott.

They arrived at Morris' house. "I'll drop you off here. Just drive over when you're ready. I'll order pizza when you get to my house."

"Sounds good. See you in a bit, Clari."

Morris headed to his door while Clari Pulled herself home.

When Morris arrived, they ordered pizza and talked as they waited for it to be delivered.

"Oh, I got you a present. I'll be right back." Morris darted out to his car, and came back in carrying a gift bag. He held it out to Clari.

Clari didn't take it. "Is it because you ditched me, came up with a plan without me, gathered my friends and yours to implement your plan, used me as bait, please-forgive-me-guilt gift?"

Morris lowered the gift bag and suddenly found his shoes fascinating. He mumbled, "Uh, well, yeah. I guess that's one way of looking at it."

Clari chuckled, Morris looked at her face. A slow forgiving smile graced Clari's face.

Morris held out the gift bag again. "It looks like I picked the right gift."

Clari accepted his peace offering. She opened the bag and pulled out a purple t-shirt that read, *Here Comes Trouble.* "That's funny, Morris."

"There's more," he prompted.

She reached in and pulled out another t-shirt. This one was heather blue that read, *Probably late for something.* Clari giggled. "It seems you know me well, Morris. Thank you. They're perfect. I should wear the '...late for something' next time I meet with Lt. Avery and you at the station." She folded them and placed them back in the bag.

Morris rubbed the back of his neck. "Yeah, about that..."

Clari looked up at Morris. "What? What happened? Am I really not working there anymore? I thought that was just to throw Witherabbott off?"

"Yes. I mean no. Ugh."

Clari put her hands on her hips. "Morris? What's going on?"

He scrubbed his face and took a deep breath before answering. "Yes, you're still contracted under Lieutenant Avery, but no, you're not working with me there."

Clari's voice went up an octave. "What do you mean? Why?"

"The whole you being dumped by everyone was to draw out Witherab-bott."

"Yeah, Morris, I figured that part out. But, what?"

"But, while this was going on, the legal department," Morris used air quotes, "'recommended' that I retire."

Clari felt the indignation rising within her. She was very protective of her chosen family members. Her voice tightened as she demanded, "What? Why would they do that? You're a fantastic detective. What are they think-ing?"

Morris raised his palm towards her. "Chill, Clari. I don't like it either. Let me explain before you go down there all headstrong and impetuous." Morris waited while Clari took a few deep breaths. When she nodded, Morris continued. "They are afraid that if my ability was discovered by others while I was working a case, that all of my cases would come under review and maybe even be thrown out. They decided to offer me early retirement with full pension. Or, I could be fired and lose everything. If that happened, my reputation, and that of the police department, would be tarnished."

Clari growled, "Well, what did Avery have to say?"

"Lt. Avery offered I could get tested and certified and then they could possibly pull me in occasionally – as a consultant like you – to do the 'odd' cases."

"Oh my gosh, Morris. I'm so sorry. How are you doing with that?"

His shoulders sagged. "To be honest, it hit me pretty hard to have to turn in my badge and gun, and clear my desk. But I put all of that on the back burner until we got you safe again. Now that's been accomplished, I guess I'll go back to floundering.

"I feel lost, Clari. I feel like I lost my identity and my purpose. I always wanted to be a detective. I loved doing that." Morris looked into her eyes, exposing his vulnerable state. "Who am I now? What am I supposed to do? I'm such a cognitive mess."

Clari moved closer and held Morris in a hug. "I'm with you on this, Morris. We'll figure it out."

Morris

"Welcome to the World Paranormal Organization's training program," blared the organizer. "Our goal is to not only ascertain what ability or abilities you possess, but to also help you in refining or fine-tuning this ability.

"Once that is complete – and no, I can't tell how long it will take each of you; each person works at their own pace, and then, if you still want to, you can begin the certification process.

"The certification process takes less time for those, like you, who have opted to go through your training here, because we'll be working with you each step of the way, so we can verify your training.

"When your training nears completion, you'll be informed of how the certification and registration process is done and what it means – the benefits – to becoming WPO certified. It'll be at this point that you'll decide if you want to become certified and registered with us at that time.

"So if there are no questions at this point, please proceed to the room number on your paper. There are WPO members in the hallways to help guide you if you've any difficulty. Thank you."

Morris, vividly recalling the first day of elementary school, made his way through the halls until he found his assigned room. He stood in front of the closed door. His stomach did a little flip, so Morris took a deep breath to steady his nerves. He opened the door and stepped through to begin his journey to claim his new future.

He stepped into a room the size of a small classroom and that's where the similarities ended. *Are those walls padded?* He asked himself. His attention shifted from the walls to the floor. A soft cashmere-colored carpet covered the floor.

A man, his instructor, sat in a beige lounge chair. There was a dark blue couch and another beige lounge chair available. Morris' observation skills kicked in as he put into memory the instructor's angled face, black hair, and warm dark eyes that had a touch of humor in them as they watched Morris. The instructor's light brown skin had just a tinge of a cinnamon color. A white button-up shirt and brown dress pants with dark brown loafers finished off the look.

"Mr. Henry Morris?" the man asked.

"I am."

The lean man rose from his chair. Morris figured the instructor stood easily 5 foot 6 inches and had to look up a bit to Morris. "I'm your instructor, Roshan Williams. Please have a seat and we'll get started."

Morris moved to the couch and sat down.

Roshan continued, "I'm a telepath like you. And yes, the walls are padded."

Morris frowned, "But I didn't say anything and I didn't Hear you in my head."

"I didn't need telepathy to know what you were thinking, Mr. Morris. It was plainly expressed on your face. And you hadn't Heard me because I'm blocking, something we'll work on together as we progress."

Morris' nerves settled; he was where he belonged for now.

Chapter Fourteen

Telepathy - the ability to Sense, Hear or Know another's thoughts by energetically interpreting the other person's self-talk, mental pictures and/or emotions. So at its root, telepathy is one form of interpreting energy.

Clari

They were gathered in the same conference room at the World Paranormal Organization that Clari had been in after the investigation of the Serafina-Grigori death. This time, though, there were fresh faces sitting around the table; faces of WPO members who were cleared of any Grigori involvement.

Mr. Frank Holstetter, who looked to be in his mid-fifties, was the man who sat at the head of the table. He stood up to address those in attendance. His slightly portly body didn't detract from the sharp intelligence coupled with kindness in his brown eyes. His short light brown hair was parted on the side. "Thank you all for being here today. As some of you may know, I've been assigned the position of Acting Regional Director, and most of you have accepted the interim positions of Board members until such time that the appropriate people take up the mantle of the Board members for the new World Paranormal Organization.

"You each have been briefed that you might be asked to stay on as a Board Member once the investigations and flushing out of all of the Grigori has been completed," Mr. Holstetter made brief eye contact with Clari, "But for now, it's up to us to make sure WPO runs smoothly.

"For those of you who haven't met her," Mr. Holstetter's hand, palm up, swept towards Clari, "let me introduce Ms. Clarima Jones to the Board. I'm sure you're wondering why she is at this meeting. Ms. Jones has declined the Director's position, but has graciously remained to help revamp our organization." His chin pointed to Clari. "We welcome all and any ideas, input or observations during this transitional period.

"The United States region, which is us, will be the ones setting the new WPO standard for the globe. It'll probably be trial and error as we update and refine, but I have faith in us to accomplish restabilizing the World Paranormal Organization.

"Today we'll be working on updating the Levels for certification and adding some ability descriptions on the website, as well as updating our pamphlet." Mr. Holstetter sat down. "Let's get started. Ms. Jones has done some preliminary work. Clarima, the floor is yours."

Clari nervously cleared her throat, "Thank you, Mr. Holstetter. I've done some work on updating WPO Levels to make them more user friendly for all abilities, not just the ones WPO had listed before. I'd like to go over them with you all and see where we can bring the new Level system."

Clari passed out copies to the Board members. "I also have a partial list of abilities included in the papers I just passed out. I'd like to go through the list and design an easy-to-understand list of the most common abilities and a brief description about each one. This is going to be used to update the website. Shall we get started?"

"Ms. Jones, would you mind waiting after everyone leaves? I would appreciate it if you could."

Clari put her stuff back on the conference table and sat back down.

After the room was cleared, Mr. Holstetter cleared his throat. "Thank you, Ms. Jones. I have been asked to speak to you. First, what do you know about an antique car that a gentleman named Gerald had rebuilt?"

"Oh, yeah. It seems Witherabbott had him rebuild an old muscle car," Clari smiled in appreciation. "Nice representation of the classics. Why?"

"It turns out that during the investigation of Mrs. Witherabbott's connection to the Grigori's, the investigators found deleted emails from Witherabbott to someone else who was discussing rebuilding and using an old car that could be restored without a computer so that it couldn't been traced. It appears, Ms. Jones, they were going to use the car to Jump you after they killed you. They decided it would be the best way to dispose of you where you wouldn't be found."

A slight panic entered Clari's voice, "Gerald was in on it?"

"What? No. Oh, my apologies, Ms. Jones. No, Gerald wasn't on it. I was talking about Witherabbott and whomever she was communicating with via email. I was not given the information of who that may have been, though."

Morris

"Let's start with communicating to each other telepathically." Roshan switched over. * *Can you Hear me, Mr. Morris?* *

Morris' eyes opened wide. * *Yes, I can Hear you* *

Roshan smiled. * *Okay. Think of something that I can verbally confirm I'm Hearing you* *

Morris rubbed his chin. * *Call me either Morris or Henry* *

Roshan clapped his hands and spoke out loud. "Henry it is! And you may call me Roshan. Good job, Henry. Let's verbally talk about telepathy a bit.

"In telepathy you have some who are receivers only; some who are broadcasters only; some who are both; and then there are the 'nulls', meaning they have no telepathic abilities." Roshan pointed to Morris and then to himself. "We, you and I, are both receivers and broadcasters."

Morris asked, "Why I can't Hear everyone?"

Roshan's lips squinched and pulled to the right. "Well, Henry, some of those who are receivers, broadcasters or both may have learned, naturally or with guidance, how to shield their ability so that they aren't always 'on' or 'open'. Like the exercise we just did, I had to drop my mental shield or block so we could communicate. This is one thing we'll work on today.

"Now some receivers only Hear when someone is directing their attention to that receiver, and this can be a conscious or subconscious act on the side of the broadcaster.

"So let's discuss broadcasters. Because someone broadcasts doesn't necessarily qualify them as being telepaths. They just may be hyper-focused on talking with you, for example, so they broadcast without knowing it. This type may be a hit or miss thing."

Morris lifted his hand, "Question. I recently had an experience where someone entered Clari's office. I could Hear that the woman wanted Clari's help, but had no intent of compensating Clari. Is that what you're talking about when you say their focus may have allowed them to broadcast? And if the woman's attention was on Clari, how could I Hear her?"

"Interesting, Henry. Let me ask you this: when this woman entered the office, did your cop instincts kick in?"

Morris looked up at the ceiling as he revisited that memory. He looked back at Roshan, "Yes, I felt something was a bit off."

"Good! I'll bet that your instincts as a detective triggered you to engage your telepathy while you sought to figure out what was 'off' about her. As an officer, or detective, you're instincts are what helps keep you alive in the field. We can certainly watch as we work to see if we can confirm this. Any other questions before we proceed?"

"Yes. Why is it, Roshan, that as I focus on you to Hear you, I don't Hear every other broadcaster in the immediate area or building?"

"Good question. The simple answer pertaining to the here and now is that we won't let you. By that, I mean," Roshan waved a sweeping hand indicating the walls, "as you noticed, the walls are padded to keep physical sounds out or severely muted.

"We use runes, carved or painted into the walls to keep those who are learning and practicing their abilities from the results going astray. Runes are, generally, ancient alphabet letters written by the Germanic people, such as the Norsemen. The Druids found them helpful in their ceremonies. Runes represent not only a sound, but are assigned symbolism or magical intents as well. So under those pads are the runes to keep anyone else's thoughts from entering this room.

"Until you have a really good handle on your ability – and by that I mean you are not at the mercy of your ability – we will work in an environment that can't be telepathically contaminated from outside interferences. Other rooms are protected to keep other types of abilities from passing through the walls. For example, someone with the telekinesis ability may 'overshoot' and accidently move items in the next room, or rooms over. With the runes in place, their ability is confined to their practice space. Does that answer your question?"

"Yes, it does." Morris shared.

"So words are not the only way to communicate telepathically. Humans and animals can communicate with mind pictures, or visualizations, and through emotions. Some people, when talking with a friend or co-worker, for example, often visualize what they are verbally sharing. Telepaths can often See those mind pictures or may feel the emotions that are projected by the communicator. This is how we can communicate with animals, if it is the telepath's interest. Today we're going to work on the word aspects."

Roshan continued, "Let's practice building protection in your mind so that you can control when to 'turn it on', or tune in, as well as working on protecting your thoughts so others can't Hear them.

"I'm going to talk you through the exercise, so I want you do to it as I speak. When we're done, we'll test it out. If this technique doesn't do the job for you, then we'll try out another.

"Close your eyes and follow my instructions. You are going to build a brick wall with the intent that no one else can penetrate it. Let's begin. I want you to visualize layering some bricks, using some hefty mortar to support and hold the bricks. Build all the way up with the intent that none shall penetrate or pass through it. Your thoughts are guarded and protected behind your wall. Somewhere in your wall, you need to insert a sound-proofed window that you can open so that you have a way to open your telepathy – your thoughts – to another when you want to. Finish building it, and tell me when you are done."

Roshan remained quiet while Morris worked on his wall. When Morris finished, he opened his eyes. "Done."

Roshan rubbed his hands together. "Let's test it out. I want you to think of one word and I'll see if I can pick it up. Let me know when you're ready."

"Ready." Morris felt super confident.

Roshan leaned back in his chair, his attention on Morris. Roshan smiled, "Marbles."

Morris' face crumbled.

"It is okay, Henry. Let me ask you this...do you think brick walls are impenetrable?"

"No, I don't. I've seen too many times where brick walls collapsed because of humans."

"You're belief is that brick walls can be broken or collapsed by humans. Fair enough. What do you consider, or believe to be impenetrable?"

Morris leaned forward. "A LPS175 SR5 security door with a louver panel secured and controlled within the secured room."

Roshan looked uncertain. "Um, okay. That seems awfully specific, but if it works..."

Morris was in his element. "It means not only is it bullet proof, but only state of the art, top end battery-powered tools, such as those used by rescue teams and fire teams, can get through it, though it'll take some time."

"Great, Henry. This time, instead of a brick wall, create your impenetrable fortress using what you just talked about. Let me know when you're done."

Morris, eyes closed, concentrated for a few minutes. "Okay, I'm done. Give it a try."

Roshan sat quiet for a while. "Wow, I can't get through. Good job! Now, I want you to think of a word, and create a small opening to allow me access to that word, without dropping your protection. Ready?"

"Yes. Do it."

Roshan once again sat still. He smiled, "Mushrooms."

Morris opened his eyes, "Yes."

"Okay, make sure you close it up again. Now you try to Hear my word, but keep your protection locked up. Go."

After a few tries, Morris reported, "I've got nothing."

"All right. Let's try again, and this time you open your louvers a bit like you did for me to Hear you. Go."

Morris smiled, "Whales?"

"Fantastic! Yes, whales. This technique means you can keep your security or block, or you can even call it a mind-shield, in place and just open your communication window, if you will, when you need it.

"I think that's it for today. Next we'll have a variety of volunteers for you to practice with and on. I'm impressed with your progress just in one day. I don't think it'll take Level One training long for you to get your Level One certification, Henry. I'll see you next week, same time and day. Does that work for you?"

"Yes, sir."

Roshan continued, "Oh. It would be nice if have someone you can practice with. It was nice meeting you, Henry, and I look forward to next week."

A week later, Morris was surprised that he was eager to get the day started, though part of him was still grieving the loss of being a detective, he was really curious to see where his telepathy training was going to bring him.

He parked his truck in the WPO's parking lot and turned the engine off. He took a slow deep breath, wiped his palms on his pants, opened the truck door and stepped out.

Morris mulled over the possibilities of where his telepathy would take him in life. Morris opened the door to the practice room and entered.

"Good job, Henry!" Roshan stood in the middle of the room.

Morris grinned. "Good morning, Roshan. So what are you telling me 'Good job' for?"

As Roshan moved to his chair, he motioned Morris to sit. "Because not only could I not Hear you, I couldn't even Feel a whisper around your fortress wall. I take it you've been practicing?"

"Uh, yeah. My girlfriend has telepathic abilities and I didn't want her to pick up on what I've been doing."

"May I ask the reason for the secrecy, Henry?"

"She has a lot going on right now, so I figured I'd just surprise her if I get my certification."

Roshan tilted his head. "'If'?"

With a sheepish grin, Morris amended his response, "When?"

"Let's get started, Henry. In your own words, describe what telepathy is."

Morris rubbed his chin before answering. "To me, it seems like the ability to hear another person's thoughts."

"Okay, let's expand on that. Oh, and it's not limited to just people. Animal Communicators can Hear animals' thoughts. But that is a bit off topic.

"Telepathy is the ability to Sense, Hear or Know another's thoughts by energetically interpreting the other person's self-talk, mental pictures and/or emotions. So at its root, telepathy is one form of interpreting energy.

"Each ability is energy-based which means that they are all related; energy related. But just because someone's telepathic doesn't necessarily mean they have any more or all abilities.

"For you, we know you're telepathic, but does that mean you're an Animal Communicator? No. Does an Animal Communicator mean they're able to Hear peoples' thoughts? Not necessarily."

Morris took Roshan's pause to speak. "Let me ask you this, Roshan. If Animal Communicating and telepathy are basically the same, why aren't all telepaths also Animal Communicators?"

"Good question, Henry. If you have no interest – or better yet passion – in communicating with animals, then chances are that aspect didn't flourish. But if you have an affinity for animals and you're a telepath, then that'll probably be one of your strongest abilities.

"Another side branch of telepathy is mediumship, but mediums use it to communicate with the non-physical. All these that we mentioned use mental imagery, Sensing, Knowing and/or Feeling emotions to receive and interpret the information. Then the telepath, in whatever form, can translate the information into words to pass that information on to the client.

"You could have just telepathy, or, as time goes on, you might discover you have additional abilities. Take Clarima Jones, for example. I'm not sure if you know her or not, but she has developed quite a few abilities. Those are the ones, so far, she's chosen to develop and keep.

"I guess what I'm saying, Henry, is that we don't know what abilities we each have until we know. And each of us has to decide if we want to develop more than one ability – or devote our time and energy to just one ability. Any questions so far?"

Morris shook his head. "No, sir."

Roshan stood up, but motioned Morris to stay seated. "We have some volunteers today. They will all broadcast a word unique to them, and they all do it at the same time. I want you to focus on one person at a time and gently retrieve – do not force – the word. I want you to block everyone else out except the one person you're concentrating on. Once you have that word, write it down and move on to the next person." Roshan opened the door. "Volunteers, please come on in and get comfortable and then we'll get started."

Chapter Fifteen

Changes to the World Paranormal Organization Pamphlet -

Due to recent changes at the World Paranormal Organization, we've updated the website and The World Paranormal Organization pamphlet.

One of the changes implemented is that the Levels have been slightly restructured to provide a wider range of abilities and degrees of mastery of those abilities. This new structure brings clarity to the certified practitioners' roles and for those hiring the certified practitioners. Practitioners with multiple abilities are not restricted to any one Level.

There is no 100% Mastery in either Energy Work or Energy Healing Levels; this is because there is always a possibility for expansion and growth in abilities.

Several Months Later

Clari

"It's so quiet without Ghost around. I mean he was never obtrusive, and we didn't talk every day, but he was always a presence. I do miss him," Clari confessed.

"Do you think he's happy now?" Morris, seated across from her, asked.

"I have no idea. I do know he Felt more rounded by the time he left us."

"Hm. Did he cross over? I never did get the full story about why he left and where he went."

"No, Morris, he didn't cross over. Believe it or not, he found he has the knack of helping other ghosts. He told me he wanted to take what all he learned from us and go out and about to see if he can help others. I guess it gave him a different perspective to the afterlife. Ghost felt he'd had it pretty easy, choosing to stay instead of being trapped."

"That's pretty cool, I guess. I hope he enjoys his...uh...afterlife? I'm not sure what to call it when you're a ghost."

Clari chuckled, "Afterlife works for me. I hope Ghost is happy, too. Let's see if I can scare up Ghost for a chat to see how he's doing." Clari closed her eyes and energetically put out a request to talk with Ghost.

Her phone chirped a message. "It's from Ghost asking if we're okay. Yes, Ghost, we're okay. We were just wondering how you're doing."

Ghost's voice came out of her phone speaker, "Clari, Morris, it's good to hear from you."

Morris called out, "Hi, Ghost!"

"Hi, Morris. I am doing well, Clari. I have been enjoying traveling around the world and meeting so many interesting specters. I'm learning a lot and I'd like to think that I'm helping other ghosts."

"Does this mean that you're happy, Ghost?" Clari asked.

"Yes, I do believe I am. Who could've imagined finding their life calling after they die," Ghost chuckled.

"We are very glad to hear that you are happy, Ghost. Please feel free to stop in now and again to chat with us. I would be interested in your adventures."

"Thank you, Clari. I'll take you up on that offer. I have a group waiting for me, so if there's nothing else...?"

"Nope. Just wanted to see what you're up to. Go enjoy your life, Ghost."

"Thank you. Blessings to both you and Morris. Bye."

"I wonder what all he'll experience," Clari pondered out loud.

"I don't know, Clari, but I hope he enjoys it as much as I enjoy sharing my life with you." Morris picked up the new World Paranormal Organization pamphlet sitting on Clari's desk.

Clari looked over to Morris as he held up the pamphlet. "Looks good, eh?"

Morris skimmed it until he reached the Levels section that redefined the Levels within WPO.

Energy Worker Levels

Level 1 – Beginner. Can perceive positive and negative energy, including Sensing lying and/or deceit. Has little or low consistency and control or ability.

Level 2 – Intermediate. Has a 50-70% consistency rate using their primary ability; can sense non-physical beings in their space (rarely with details). May also have a rudimentary or Level 1 skill in additional abilities.

Level 3 – Advanced. Usually has at least one Arch 1 energy healing technique/modality/ability, but is not mandatory. Has an 80-89% consistency rate in their primary ability/abilities.

Level 4 – Mastery. Level 4's can include one or more mastered abilities with 90-99% consistency in their primary ability/abilities. Only Level 4's may work for the World Paranormal Organization's Investigation and

Enforcement Agency (formerly the WPO Police) as an agent, if their talent/ability qualifies.

Energy Healer Levels

<u>Arch 1 – Beginner.</u> Healing may be temporary; can usually provide short-term pain relief and relaxation or stress relief. Uses one or two techniques and/or modalities. Low consistency rate.

<u>Arch 2 – Intermediate.</u> Can provide pain relief; re-establish energy flow and some circulation; stress relief; and distant healing. Consistency rate can be as high as 85%.

<u>Arch 3 – Advanced.</u> Healer must be able to easily accomplish Arch 2 level as well as: do a health scan and provide client and their medical doctor, if applicable, with a chart pinpointing imbalances. Has at least one Level from Energy Workers category. Consistency rate is 86-89%.

<u>Arch 4 – Mastery.</u> Healer has a consistency rate of 90-99%. At the Mastery Level, the Energy Healer has channeling abilities to work with non-physical healing teams; also works closely with medical staff, if applicable, and their recommendations.

Morris smiled, "Of course it looks good, and it's so much easier to relate to now. And you helped redesign it. Well, not just the pamphlet. You helped redesign all of WPO. Are you sure you don't want to work full time at WPO headquarters?"

Clari gave him a frantic headshake. "No! I'm not the person for that; though I do appreciate that they asked me, and that they asked me to help reshape the WPO. I don't mind offering my suggestions to make WPO stronger and safer for everyone," Clari confessed.

"I'm happy that they've taken the Grigori out of the WPO. I can't believe how many people they've discovered so far, and how many disappearances they're investigating within the WPO because of the Grigori."

Morris frowned, "Not to mention how close you came to being one of those who disappeared under the watch of the WPO."

Clari and Morris both started by a voice in the lobby. "Hey, Clari! You guys better be decent! I'm heading back there!" Clari and Morris shared a smile as Josie tromped down the hallway. "Here I come!" Her head popped into the door frame. "Hi, guys!"

Clari stood up, "Come on in, Josie." As Josie entered the room, Clari hugged her. "What brings you by today?"

Josie greeted Morris, "Hey, Morris," and then pulled a pamphlet out of her purse and held it up. "This is awesome, Clari! It's so much easier to read now. It was frustrating for many who didn't quite fit in the previous level descriptions."

Josie sat on the couch, so Morris and Clari joined her.

"I think so, too. I know it'll probably need to be tweaked later, but this is a good starting point." Clari told her.

Josie nodded, "It's great! There are so many changes happening now. I'm so proud of you working with them to clean up and re-organized WPO. I know you declined the Regional Director position, but did you accept the new board members offer to be the CEO at the headquarters office?"

"Nah. I'm not cut out for that kind of work. After I taught the investigators on how to recognize the Grigori energy signature so they could find the rest of the Grigori ensconced within the organization, I did agree to be an on-call consultant and advisor for the director, CEO and Board. Otherwise, I will continue on with my own business and be here with my friends and adopted family members."

"Cool." Josie turned her attention to Morris. "What about you, Morris? What are you up to now that you're no longer with the Police Department?"

"I'm not sure, yet. I just finished my training with WPO and got certified under the new levels as a telepath, and am starting the licensing process to become a private investigator. "

"That's awesome! And I was thinking that we could discuss working together again, Morris. We seemed to work well when you were with the PD. Are you interested in continuing our working relationship?" Clari questioned.

Morris lit up, "Yes! I would love to give it a try and see what we can accomplish together outside of the police department."

Josie stood, "Well, candied cabbage, I think that's a great idea! I guess it's time for me to get out of your hair so you two can work out the details of this. I'm proud of you both, and know this joint effort will make you two a powerhouse couple – both business-wise and otherwise." Josie waggled her eyebrows.

Clari laughed as she stood to hug her friend. "Thanks, Josie. I'll see you later."

After Josie left, Morris asked, "What's up next for you and the Board? Anything?"

Clari sat down again. "Now that we know it's an angry Grigori ghost who has been trapping the deceased for at least two-hundred years that we know of, we are gathering Level 4 mediums to take the Grigori ghost down and free those who are trapped.

"The WPO and I think we know why the trapped ghosts were mainly from the 1940's. We believe that is when the Grigori died and started collecting some of the newly deceased to siphon from. I think he couldn't keep track of very many ghosts, so he kept his 'collection' small. And on that topic, Ghost told me that he wanted to be involved in helping the trapped ghosts when it's time."

"That's great, Clari! Are you sure you don't want a permanent position with the WPO administration? You have a lot of knowledge and are great at organizing."

Clari shook her head, "No, thank you. I'll be happy to return to my life after we get the Grigori bumps ironed out."

Morris chuckled. "Yeah, it's been interesting with all these Grigoris that were detected and arrested just within the WPO. But now the officials from the Dragon Realm are checking out every government official from the Presidency and federal officials all the way down to local officials within each state and city."

Clari smiled. "They're calling it 'Operation Feather Sweep'. Now that we have those who can read the energy signatures of the Grigori, there's no place for them to hide. And I, for one, am very relieved."

Morris stood and offered Clari a hand up, "Care to join me for a nice peaceful lunch?"

Clari took his hand, "Absolutely! But first..." Clari kissed Morris.

"Mmm," Morris purred.

As they approached the restaurant parking lot, the air in the truck shifted and Morris sputtered, "Uh. So I was thinking. We've agreed that we work great together and are going to continue work together, but, Clari..." Morris parked, shut the engine off and turned to Clari, "I can't see my future without you. I want to wake up every morning next to you. I want to share my whole life with you. Would you be open to me asking you to marry me one day?"

Clari sputtered and her voice raised an octave, "Are you proposing to me?"

Morris grinned. "Would that be such a bad thing?" Morris Felt Clari's thoughts cease and her mind went blank.

"Uh, no?" she replied in a low voice.

Morris' eyes shone bright. "You don't sound so sure. Consider this a pre-proposal. I know you don't like making a snap decision when it comes to something big, and I know you'll need to think this over. And that's okay, Clari. All right?"

Clari gave a stiff nod.

He unlatched his seatbelt. "How about we go on in to the restaurant now?"

A Year Later

Morris and Clari stood outside facing the front of her office building. Wolf sat next to Morris and appeared to be grinning. The single window of the building was covered with a sheet. Clari smiled from ear to ear.

"Well, diaphanous day lilies, Clari!" Josie fussed.

Clari swung around to look at her friend. "What?"

"Would you please stop making googly eyes, again, at Morris? You're married for heaven's sake."

Clari giggled, and those standing behind Josie in the parking lot, laughed.

Morris slid his arm around Clari's waist. Both felt blessed to have their adopted family and Morris' family present for these new steps in the life as a couple. Clari smiled and made eye contact with each person there.

All of Clari and Morris' friends, human and other, attended. Clari smiled at Morris' family.

Josie complained. "Discombobulated dingos, Clari! I'm hungry and want to get inside to eat. Hurry up!"

The crowd laughed again. Clari looked to Morris and winked. "I'd like to introduce you to the New Beginnings Consultancy office of Clari and Henry Morris!" She and Morris turned back to the window and pulled the sheet off.

Wolf stood, wagging his tail and woofed. His full-face dog grin turned into a full-faced doggie smile.

Ghost blasted "Puff the Magic Dragon" on everyone's phone which brought more laughter.

After the applause and congratulations, everyone piled into the newly redecorated office.

When everyone settled at the tables with their plates, Josie stood up and clanked her glass. "Can I have everyone's attention, please?" The room quieted and Josie turned her attention to Morris and Clari. "Can you believe it's been over a year since you two finally tied the knot?"

Clari and Morris shared a warm look.

"And I want to revisit their wedding day for those of you who weren't able to attend. Even though they said they wanted an understated wedding, it was beautiful, and they held it in the Dragon Realm." She offered an affectionate smile to the couple. Josie continued, "I'm pretty sure you all know that Clari doesn't like dresses, so it wasn't the traditional wedding gown at all. Clari was dressed in this gorgeous, long sleeve satin jumpsuit.

The Bateau neckline and long sleeves were embellished with delicate floral appliques going across the shoulders and down her arms. And she had matching satin ballet flats. She was gorgeous. And Morris was dressed in a handsome charcoal tux.

"J.R.," Josie pointed to him, "walked her down the so-called aisle." She had a mischievous twinkle in her eye, "But J.R. was so nervous that he...okay, I can't say it." Josie giggled.

J.R. groaned.

Josie pushed through her giggles, "He lost a shoe because he had trouble controlling his dragon aspect. One foot became a dragon's foot with claws. So he was walking Clari down with one human foot and one dragon foot. Everybody started laughing. But he never missed a beat. He continued walking her down as though nothing happened. Clari didn't even know this was going on. Her focus was solely on Morris. Those two locked eyes and nothing else existed. It was awesome. And I got to see this all since I was the maid of honor.

"The best man was Sebastian," Josie pointed to him, "and Wolf was the handsome ring bearer. It was unconventional, but it was beautiful."

J.R. spoke up, "Yes, it was. And, Clari, I just want you to know that since they now have the ability to choose their mates, the female dragons have incorporated their interpretation of a wedding ceremony for their bonding ceremonies."

Clari smiled, "You're welcome."

J.R. chuckled.

Josie picked up her glass, "And now we're here to celebrate Clari and Henry Morris' newest leg of their journey together. Congratulations to you both!"

Journal Entry from Clarima Morris in 2238

Clarima Syd Jones, born 2212; married in 2237 to Henry Winston Morris, born 2210

My father left me this journal. After reading it, I realized that I come from a long line of incredible people. It's my hope that when this journal falls into the next set of interested hands that they may be as inspired by my actions as I have been by those who came before me.

It wasn't always that way. As a child, I learned to not trust people, ever. Now in my upper twenties, I have an adopted family – I family I chose and adopted.

My sister-in-heart, Josie, has been with me through good times and bad, and I'm blessed to have her in my life.

My brothers-in-heart are Sebastian and J.R, and they are the epitome of what I imagine having older and protective brothers would be like.

My chosen siblings-in-heart have helped me to learn to trust, and this led me to meeting and marrying the light of my life, Henry Morris. Henry's family, who welcomed me with open arms, has also become my family.

And then there's my sweet Morris. I have been blessed with a long and happy marriage, and I look forward to many more years with him.

On the whole, my life, to me, hasn't seemed exceptional. I do know that I have traversed a long way and look forward to the coming years. My thanks to my ancestors who reached out through this journal and shared a bit of their lives with me.

My ancestor, Hope Jones, was the one who left the bullet casing so that one day someone in her family line that had psychometry could get a glimpse of her and her husband, Luke's life. I wonder if they were as happy and Morris and I have been. I certainly hope so.

Most of my life, I questioned who I was and what I was.

I realized that none of us have to be whatever labels we were handed and accepted or that were forced on us. I now understand that we each are unique, and if we shed those labels, we can begin to find out who we each really are.

For me, I discovered that, though I am not perfect, I am perfect for being Clarima Syd Jones Morris.

I finally learned to love myself and can love, and accept the love of others.

Who am I?

I Am.

END

Appendix

THE COMPLETE JOURNAL

Journal of Gretchen Jones

This journal is to be passed down through the family line. It is my hope that the future women will be inspired by the thoughts and experiences of the women before you. By the time you're reading this, some of it may no longer be legible, but I personally want to thank those women who shared in this journal. Blessings to you, our descendants.

I started this journal in the year of 1976 in hopes to share my experiences with others, if they're interested.

Gretchen Nelson – born 1913 – Married 1929 to Joseph Jones – born 1910

When I was a child, we had no electricity or gas. My mother cooked on a coal burning stove and used kerosene lamps for light. The light globes had to be washed each day since the kerosene made them dirty.

My two sisters and I would help our mother wash clothes. We would take turns. The clothes had to be soaked in water, soaped, and then scrubbed on a washboard. Then they had to be rinsed and hung to dry. Sheets were the hardest because they were so big. We would scrub a little section at time, slide it to the right, and scrub another section.

We would play hopscotch or jump rope if we had some free time. We also played records on a phonograph that had to be turned by hand.

Our small dolls cost 10 cents and we tried to sew dresses for them. Bread went for $0.05 loaf.

We had navy beans and cornbread every night for dinner. I had once asked my mother if we could have something other than navy beans and cornbread for dinner. We had this every day. Mother told me to be happy that she had the beans.

She stood about five foot two and had lots of common sense. She was a pioneer woman. My mother never spoke a lot and rarely laughed. She was a very serious hardworking woman.

My mother died at the age of 76. Due to living a very hard life, she was very old for her age.

My father, Joseph, was a US Marshall for the whole district. He often worked with the railroad, so was riding trains a lot. He would give my mother one-half of his earnings and drink the rest. When I was older, I heard my mother say she thought my dad had a mistress on the side.

Joseph's parents were George and Catherine Jones. His parents met each other at the orphanage where they grew up. When George and Catherine were old enough to marry, they asked the priest from the orphanage to marry them. Since the orphanage records had been destroyed in a fire years earlier, no one knew what their real last names were, so the priest gave them the combined surname "Jones" when he married them. The newlywed Jones' homesteaded, riding in wagons pulled with oxen. They would go around cultivating land given to them by the US government.

My husband's parents died before Joseph made the age of 12. He mostly grew up on the streets doing whatever he wanted, and he often wanted alcohol.

I got married at age sixteen. We got married ten years before the Great Depression hit. Life was hard, but I always tried to do my very best with what I had.

Our first house had one bedroom, a living room and a kitchen. The house cost $1500.00 and we made monthly payments of $15.00.

We had no hot water and no bathroom. Ice and coal were delivered by horse and cart. A wood burning stove kept the house warmed in the winter.

I used a washboard up until 1930, when my sister gave me her old washing machine. It was an electric Thor. It was a tub on legs with wheels. I would take the lid off of the tub, put my clothes in, add water, put the lid back on and turn it on. The tub also had a wringer arm attached to the outside of the wash tub. After my clothes washed, I would put each piece of clothing in between the two rollers and it would press the excess water out. I was very excited to replace my washboard with the Thor.

In 1929:

A three bedroom house cost $1574.

A New Ford vehicle - $695

Gasoline - $0.21/gal

Milk - $0.58 gal

Bread - $0.09 loaf

Bacon - $0.44/lb.

Once a month, when our kids were old enough to attend school, I would get together with some other women at one of our houses for a luncheon. The hostess for that luncheon would set the table in a theme of their choice.

Each month was a different house, a different hostess and different theme.

When it was my turn, my theme was based on a maroon and black car with the man and woman in it. The table was set maroon and white with the car as the centerpiece.

One woman remarked how beautiful it was and suggested that whoever hosted the next luncheon should make their table as beautiful as I had made it.

Well, I overhead this, so I later contacted the next hostess and we set our plan in action.

The next month rolled around and we all met at that month's hostess' home. The woman who had complimented me on my table the previous month ooh'd and aah'd at this table. Then her face showed puzzlement. She turned to me, "But isn't that yours?"

The table had been decorated with the exact same decorations as when I hosted. We all had a good laugh.

But my happiest day of my life is when my son, Gregory, was born.

The darkest day, for me, was when I came home one evening to discover my husband was drunk again. He gets mean when he drinks. When I walked in I saw he had my son by the throat and up against a wall.

Something in me, the Grace of god or a mother's protective instinct, I stepped between the two of them, facing my husband. I told him that whatever he was planning on doing to my son, he better prepare to have it done to him – by me.

He released my son, who fled the room. My husband had pure raw hate in his eyes, and I told him he better not harm or touch our child ever again. I turned my back on him and walked out of the room.

He never touched my child again.

Around the age of 60, I began volunteering at the local Health and Rehabilitation Center. I felt so blessed that I decided to write a bit about it.

1976 – Experiences of One Volunteer

I have now been a volunteer at the Health and Rehabilitation Center about one and one half years. I have become aware of many of my own capabilities that I had never thought about before. My experiences have been as different as the people with whom I come into contact. I wondered before I went there if I would find it depressing to see old folks in wheel chairs, some senile, and was amazed that I did not. I am very grateful for the rewarded feeling I have as I leave there each time; after spending five hours with them – which perhaps I have made some one smile – even laugh or comforted in some small way in whatever the need seems to be. To re-assure a patient that '"yes" you will walk again and then one day arrive and see just that, and hear that patient say "you told me I would walk" and the radiant look in that patient's face. No amount of money could purchase the feeling one shares at that moment.

There are also the persons I have been with whose life were nearing the end, but even some of those I was able to give new thoughts. The very first of my experiences with that type of person was with Gertrude. She was always glad to see me and wanted to know what I had been doing the week before I went there. She also got interested in my dog – and asked about it.

I am glad I added something to her last days. She had been a patient there for over six years. When she talked she seemed bitter that she had refused to marry. Gertrude felt at that time that she had cheated herself out of a family, who would be talking care of her. I supposed that it natural to try and think about "what might have been". I assured her that she was indeed more fortunate than a number of folks that had families because she was so well taken care of there in the Center. Then there was that Friday when I went to see her and she was very quiet, & and I sensed the end was near. She passed away that night in her sleep. I did not feel sad. I did miss her.

Then there's Peony. A very attractive little old lady, who is senile with her days mixed up – some foggy & some clear. At this time she is still the same only now when she sees me she wants to share her. I usually do each week, and she appreciates it so much. She reminds you of a demanding child, and she annoys some of the other patients. She loves to be with people – just anyone. Her daughter takes her home over the weekends. Her daughter doesn't seem to have much patience with her. She has showed me her family's pictures each week I go there, and even that doesn't seem to bother me. Probably the fact that I only see them one day a week makes me more tolerant with them.

And Henrietta – she was from Wisconsin. Her husband had been a Dr. and had died and she had a stroke, so she was brought here, probably by her son. And now here she was far from home away from all of the many people that must have known her. I visited with her each week. She always seemed so glad to see me. She passed away after being at the Center for about four months. I am glad for the time I spent with her. I know she had given much of her time in helping and doing for others.

There was Margaret. I always had to read the mail to her. She was a dear little lady who had to wear a neck brace. I don't really know what her ailment was. She had a grandson whose name was Simon, and he must have been a favorite of hers because she beamed so when I read his name.

I can't forget Bertie who sits in her world blind and deaf. I usually have to read her a note from her granddaughter, and I have to scream in her ear. I can however make her hear what I am saying, which pleases me.

One dear little lady named Mary called me and asked me if I had some time. I ask her "what she wanted". She told me "I want to go find Jesus' grave and no one has time to go with me." The only answer I could and did give her was "I am busy delivering the mail and if I had time I would come back to her." I guess Mary must have been very religious and I later found out that she was raised in a convent.

There was Millie who was in her thirties, diabetic & had a stroke – also blind – my heart ached for her and her troubles. I sat with her several times when she wanted to smoke. She shared she had been engaged to be married when she had the stroke. She left the Center and has since passed away, one could not feel sorry for her passing – only about the ailments she had at such a young age.

There was Evelyn. She also had a stroke, but she always had a cheerful outlook and a terrific sense of humor. She was a very dear person. She developed a blood clot in her leg which eventually caused her death.

There was Gisela – who always called me "sweetheart" and who one day said, "When I see you walking by my door in the hall I feel better". She was very nice to me. I felt appreciated very much by her.

I also take care of the mail – marking it and delivering it. I help in the Bingo game for one and a half hours, and help bring wheel chair patients to the news round up and Bingo game.

1994

Who knew my diary with its contents from my volunteer days would foreshadow what I myself now endure. ~ Gretchen Jones.

Daisy Sumner, born 1941, married Gregory Jones, born 1939 in 1971

I had worked on the genealogy of the Jones' family line, which abruptly ended back to George Jones who was born in 1880. It was this journal that provided a clue as to why the line abruptly stopped. Gretchen wrote, "Since the orphanage records had been destroyed in a fire, no one knew what their real last names were, so the priest gave them the combined surname 'Jones' when he married them."

This explains the discrepancies in Gregory's research he did earlier on the family line. It appears he did a history on a fictitious family name; fictitious because we have no idea what George's (or Catherine's) real birth surname was. I'm guessing Gregory missed that piece of information. Gregory had followed a non-existent line. In other words, we've no idea of the "Jones" family lineage before George.

Makes you wonder what information we could be missing.

Hope Provost, born 1975, and Lucas Jones, born 1974 married in 2003

I'm sharing some interesting dreams.

Dream in April 1999

Had a dream – gathered one representative from every place on Earth – each person was to bring one sack lunch. Everyone met – and we put all of the food together and redistributed it. The moral – together we can feed all – separate, we've not enough food for everyone.

When everything crashed in the Great Second Depression and the Demon War, Luke and I had to defend our property. There were many times that Luke discharged his firearm to keep those who were pillaging to leave us alone. I placed an expended shell into the box with this journal.

The New Earth Dream

The hungry wolf leapt. Before I realized what I had done – my knife sliced the underside of his belly.

I lifted the dead animal, carried him to the alley, and gently placed him on the ground.

With tear filled eyes, I sank to my knees and howled my grief to the moon.

What had I become? Some would say I had become a survivalist. I felt like I had become a murderer, all in the name of survival.

Has it only been three months since civilizations collapsed? What I wouldn't give to go back to living the wonderful life – the life which ended for us all.

Johanna Gutman, born 1997, married 2015 to Jacob Jones, born 1994.

Since Gretchen had shared some costs of goods, I thought I'd do the same. I won't list the prices for stuff before, or after the Demon War in my time.

House:

1964 $13,050

1998 $148,000

2001 $346,900

2022 $428,700

Car:

1964 $2,320

1998 $15,988

2021 $42,380

2022 $43,623

Gas:

1964 $0.25/gal

1998 $1.06

2021 $3.33

2022 $5.07

Bread:

1964 $0.30/loaf

1998 $1.26

2021 $1.52

2022 $1.72

Milk:

1964 $0.93/gal

1998 $3.16

2021 $3.77

2022 $4.38

Coffee:

1964 $1.00/lb.

1998 $3.77

2021 $4.71

2022 $5.11

In 2049, a G5 geomagnetic storm hit Earth and knocked out global grid systems. This was the beginning of the Great Depression. It was also during that time that Chamba began his campaign to be a tyrannical ruler. He took advantage of the chaos created by the storm and sent his Dark Army across the nations. We found out later that Chamba had intended to take over at a later date, but instead used the storm to attack our country a little earlier.

Life had become hard. Not impossible. Just hard.

It took many years to begin rebuilding our country.

Food has been scarce, but we've been fortunate enough to have a local community to share our hard earned crops. And we all bartered for whatever services we could amongst each other. I was often asked to trade my energy healing skills. My ability for psychometry is rarely needed.

Looking back at this journal, I guess that dream Hope wrote about back in 1999 was giving us a heads up on what was coming our way.

Journal Entry from Clarima Morris in 2238

Clarima Syd Jones, born 2212; married in 2237 to Henry Winston Morris, born 2210

My father left me this journal. After reading it, I realized that I come from a long line of incredible people. It's my hope that when this journal falls into the next set of interested hands that they may be as inspired by my actions as I have been by those who came before me.

It wasn't always that way. As a child, I learned to not trust people, ever. Now in my upper twenties, I have an adopted family – I family I chose and adopted.

My sister-in-heart, Josie, has been with me through good times and bad, and I'm blessed to have her in my life.

My brothers-in-heart are Sebastian and J.R, and they are the epitome of what I imagine having older and protective brothers would be like.

My chosen siblings-in-heart have helped me to learn to trust, and this led me to meeting and marrying the light of my life, Henry Morris. Henry's family, who welcomed me with open arms, has also become my family.

And then there's my sweet Morris. I have been blessed with a long and happy marriage, and I look forward to many more years with him.

On the whole, my life, to me, hasn't seemed exceptional. I do know that I have traversed a long way and look forward to the coming years. My thanks to my ancestors who reached out through this journal and shared a bit of their lives with me.

My ancestor, Hope Jones, was the one who left the bullet casing so that one day someone in her family line that had psychometry could get a glimpse of her and her husband, Luke's life. I wonder if they were as happy and Morris and I have been. I certainly hope so.

Most of my life, I questioned who I was and what I was.

I realized that none of us have to be whatever labels we were handed and accepted or that were forced on us. I now understand that we each are unique, and if we shed those labels, we can begin to find out who we each really are.

For me, I discovered that, though I am not perfect, I am perfect for being Clarima Syd Jones Morris.

I finally learned to love myself and can love, and accept the love of others.

Who am I?

I Am.

~ Clarima Sydney Jones Morris

GLOSSARY

Abilities – Every human has an ability. The ability/abilities can be any-where from the ability to be an awesome teacher or doctor, to any of the "Clairs" or more. The full list of the types of abilities is not currently known. See "Abilities" below.

Avatar – a manifested deity in human physical form; a divine teacher in physical form.

Death Premonition – A forewarning or feeling that someone is going to die.

Earthbounds – those who have died, but didn't cross over into the Light; also known as "ghosts". Their reasons for staying connected to the third dimension can be as varied as the individuals. But because they are still connected to third dimension, they still carry emotions and possibly their addictions. In other words, they are still the same human, just without a body.

Energy Bridge – see Wormholes. Same.

Energy Signature – also called Energy Flavor. The vibration or frequen-cy of each individual being and is similar to a scent trail. Each signature is as unique as a fingerprint.

Energy Worker – one who can recognize and interpret energy and energy patterns. It is one who can, using Other-Senses, See, Feel, Hear, Know and/or manipulate energy in any of the forms/manners. Also see "Clairs".

Geostorm – A geomagnetic storm that affects planet Earth's magne-tosphere, caused by a solar wind shockwave and that can interfere with electrical and electronic devices depending on the strength or severity of the storm.

Ghosts – See Earthbounds. Same.

Guides – a being who voluntarily agreed to be with their human during their human's lifetime. Life guides are hand-picked by the human prior to coming into their current human body. The Life guides are with their human from conception until physical death.

There are also Specialty guides who come into one's life for a specific purpose – such as during the loss of a loved one, to aid with the grieving process. Specialty guides leave when finished or task is completed.

Deceased loved ones can also become a member of one's Team.

Heart Center – The Heart Center is the seat of Love. It is the center for compassion and empathy; love of self and others.

Law of Conservation of Energy – The 1st Law of Thermodynamics states that energy can neither be created nor destroyed; rather, it can only be transformed from one form to another.

Non-Physical Beings – those who do not have a third dimensional physical body. Can include ghosts, spirits, angels, other dimensional beings, etc. Sometimes those who do astral travel or remote viewing can initially be perceived as being a non-physical being.

Other Beings – life essences from other dimensions; not of Earth.

Other Senses – using the non-physical senses. Seeing, Hearing, Feeling, and Knowing beyond the physical senses.

Overlay - is a glimpse of another aspect, time and/or place that can be seen simultaneously with the here and now.

Portals – See Wormholes. Same.

Pull or Push – the ability to energetically pull in, or push out, someone or something from one dimension, time-space or frequency to another.

Runes – were originally alphabet characters used by Germanic peoples. Runes today are magical symbols to accomplish a specific task or goal, such as added protections to a room so those practicing their abilities don't possibly have their energy dangerously out of control.

Scan/Scanning – energetically searching and/or Feeling a place, person or being and receiving energetic information, such as imbalances, new energies, energy disruptions.

See, Hear, Feel, Know, Perceive versus see, hear, feel, know, perceive – The uppercased senses refer to experiencing Other Senses; the lower case refer to the regular, physical senses. See Other Senses.

Soul-Gazing – When two physical beings – human, animal or combo – make a soul connection while looking into one another's eyes; one soul recognizing and acknowledging the divinity of another. Soul-Gazing usually includes a Knowing of soul communication going on without the conscious mind knows what's being discussed on a soul level.

Spirits – those who have crossed over into the Light, are free of third dimensional anchors, and come back to occasionally visit and/or aid a remaining loved one.

Subtle Bodies – The extension of our physical body; seven non-physical energetic bodies that attach to our physical body.

Team – a group that can consist of deceased loved ones, that can include pets, ancestors and guides (including animal spirit guides), who help support and guide their human during the human's Earth experiences.

Wormholes – Portals. Energy vortices created and used to move between two points in time and/or space; usually used to move between different dimensions and/or planes. An energetic shortcut between two places or spaces; a compression of space to shorten the distance between two points.

The Updated World Paranormal Organization Pamphlet
The World Paranormal Organization

"The World Paranormal Organization was created in response to the increase of paranormal talents and abilities that gained strength and began to show up across the globe after the major energy shift of December 21, 2012.

"In 2013, The World Paranormal Organization had developed standardized tests to help recognize and label the known Readers and Healers (those who have abilities); which also helps keep track of potential threats. The World Paranormal Organization instituted a level standard of competence to certify Readers and Healers, and that remains the focus of The World Paranormal Organization. This certification process legitimizes the process of hiring certified Readers and Healers. The World Paranormal Organization's certifications are recognized and are an accepted standard worldwide. New abilities and talents have the possibility to be recognized to spring up at any time, and anywhere, so our list is not static.

"It is our hope to not only aid in training, but we also have monthly local meetings for local support and for meet and greets for those in your area. We also hold annual conferences so that people from all over the world can gather and meet, because those with abilities come from all walks of life and all around the world.

"The World Paranormal Organization, which has satellite offices around the world, are able to help you with your abilities or gifts and, if you're interested, to get you certified.

"Due to recent changes at the World Paranormal Organization, we've updated the website – at – metaphysical-studies.com/worldparanormal organization – and The World Paranormal Organization pamphlet.

One of the changes implemented is that the Levels have been slightly restructured to provide a wider range of abilities and degrees of mastery of those abilities. This new structure brings clarity to the certified practitioners' roles and for those hiring the certified practitioners. Practitioners with multiple abilities are not restricted to any one Level.

There is no 100% Mastery in either Energy Work or Energy Healing Levels; this is because there is always a possibility for expansion and growth in abilities.

WPO Meetings – Regularly scheduled local meetings for registered WPO members. These are not only to meet and greet other Energy Worker and Energy Healer WPO members in your area, but also where Energy Workers and Energy Healers can share organizational news and updates. Open and free to all registered WPO members.

WPO International Conferences – Open to all registered WPO members, the WPO International Conferences bring together registered members from all over the world. The location changes yearly, allowing different countries to host. Most countries have a different conference site each time they host, bringing even more variety to those attending the conferences

WPO believes in a family atmosphere in regards to their registered members and works to support their members and assist where they can. They have mentor programs, practice halls, and others services available to members worldwide.

Do you feel you have an ability or two? Testing is free. Certification and registration have feasible fees.

Energy Worker Levels

Level 1 – Beginner. Can perceive positive and negative energy, including Sensing lying and/or deceit. Has little or low consistency and control or ability.

Level 2 – Intermediate. Has a 50-70% consistency rate using their primary ability; can sense non-physical beings in their space (rarely with details). May also have a rudimentary or Level 1 skill in additional abilities.

Level 3 – Advanced. Usually has at least one Arch 1 energy healing technique/modality/ability, but is not mandatory. Has an 80-89% consistency rate in their primary ability/abilities.

Level 4 – Mastery. Level 4's can include one or more mastered abilities with 90-99% consistency in their primary ability/abilities. Only Level 4's may work for the World Paranormal Organization's Investigation and Enforcement Agency (formerly the WPO Police) as an agent, if their talent/ability qualifies.

Energy Healer Levels

Arch 1 – Beginner. Healing may be temporary; can usually provide short-term pain relief and relaxation or stress relief. Uses one or two techniques and/or modalities. Low consistency rate.

Arch 2 – Intermediate. Can provide pain relief; re-establish energy flow and some circulation; stress relief; and distant healing. Consistency rate can be as high as 85%.

Arch 3 – Advanced. Healer must be able to easily accomplish Arch 2 level as well as: do a health scan and provide client and their medical doctor, if applicable, with a chart pinpointing imbalances. Has at least one Level from Energy Workers category. Consistency rate is 86-89%.

Arch 4 – Mastery. Healer has a consistency rate of 90-99%. At the Mastery Level, the Energy Healer has channeling abilities to work with non-physical healing teams; also works closely with medical staff, if applicable, and their recommendations.

Other Levels

Level M – Certification or certification renewal is pending.

Level Z – Certification is revoked; temporarily pending an investigation; or all certifications with the World Paranormal Organization are terminated permanently following an investigation.

ABILITIES

This is a partial list showing the most common – as of this update – abilities in use. Abilities are not limited to this list.

Animal Communication – The ability to converse telepathically and/or empathically with animals.

Astral Projection – The ability for one's consciousness to operate separately from the physical body; the subtle body (also known as the light body) can travel without the physical body.

Bilocation – To exist in two different locations at the same time; being seen and interacting with others at both locations at the same time.

Channeling – The ability to speak on behalf of non-physical beings.

Clair – clear.

Clairalience – clear smelling. Also known as Clairscent, Clairsalience, Clairolfactance or Clairessence. The ability to perceive smells with no physical source.

Clairaudience – clear hearing. Ability to hear beyond the physical senses.

Clairempathy – clear feeling; an ability to Sense, Feel or Know others emotions, or residual emotions. For those empaths who are untrained, the emotions can feel like their own which can be confusing. Public places and/or large crowds can be overwhelming.

Clairgustance – clear taste. Ability to taste without putting anything in your mouth.

Clairsentience – clear feeling. Ability to Sense, Feel or Know beyond physical senses.

Clairtangency – clear touch; the ability to touch an item or person and receive information. See Psychometry.

Clairvoyance – clear seeing. Ability to See beyond the physical sense.

Death Doula – A Death Doula helps the client get their affairs in order before they die. An Energetic or Spiritual Death Doula talks the client through the process of the physical body dying, the soul leaving the body and what to expect after that.

Dimensional Walker – One who has the ability to move or project themselves from one dimension to another; not limited to one dimension.

Dream Interpreter – Closely related to Energy Interpreter. Has the ability to understand and interpret someone else's dreams.

Dream Walker – The ability to enter another's dream, usually to aid someone in a nightmare; to guide or instruct another within their dream.

Empathic – The ability to Sense or Feel other's emotions or residual energies. Often the untrained empath feels others' emotions as though they were their own.

Energy Healer – Has the ability to manipulate energy with the purpose of aiding another in stress relief or healing.

Energy Interpreter – Has the ability to Sense, See, Know or Feel energies and what they mean.

Energy Signature – is the energetic frequency of a being or item and is unique to each individual and item.

Energy Worker – Has the ability to interpret energy and/or manipulate energy in the form of their ability/abilities.

Medium – one who has the ability to See, Sense and/or Hear and Speak with non-physical beings, typically those who have physically died; both earthbounds and spirits.

Precognition – This is the ability to Know things or events beforehand.

Premonition – The ability to Sense or Feel an upcoming event or occurrence; sometimes a forewarning.

Psychometry – the ability to hold or touch an item, object or person and energetically receive information about the item, object or person.

Remote Viewing – An ability to mentally See a target that can be an object, location or event that the viewer has no prior knowledge of that object, location or event.

Retrocognition – Having Knowledge of, or experiencing a past event as if it were happening in the current time.

Telepathy – The ability to read someone's mind or thoughts and/or communicate mind-to-mind with another.

Trance Channeler – A person who pushes aside their consciousness in order to allow a non-physical being to enter, take over the body and communicate through them.

Divination

The practice of gaining insight, foretelling future events or uncovering that which is hidden through one or more methods. This is just a sampling and the following definitions are simplified.

Astrology – The ability/skill to study the influences of the sun, moon, stars and planets and how they affect humans and their affairs.

Cleromancy – Casting lots to divine information, such as dice, small bones or pebbles.

Dowsing – The ability or skill to locate something such as water, minerals, or locating a lost person or pet, usually by using a device such as a rod or pendulum.

Electromancy – The ability to interpret electricity or lightening.

Feng Shui / Geomancy – A complex ability or skill to position or move items or buildings to create energetic harmony.

Graptomancy / Graphology – The art of interpreting handwriting.

I Ching – The art of seeking answers by interpreting the hexagrams creating by tossing coins.

Numerology – The numerical interpretation to seek knowledge or insights.

Palmistry – The art or skill of gaining information or of the client's future by interpreting the lines on the palm of the hand.

Prophesizing – One who says a specific thing or event will happen in the future; some believe the prophecy is through divine inspiration.

Scrying – The ability to use a reflective surface such as water, mirror, flame or other reflective surface to see images from the past, present or future, or to receive guidance.

Kinesis – Act on or movement.

Atmokinesis – The ability to mentally / energetically control weather, atmospheric conditions and/or weather-related phenomena.

Electrokinesis – The ability to mentally create and control electricity.

Ergokinesis – The ability to manipulate, project and/or absorb different types of energy.

Photokinesis – The ability to manipulate, project and/or absorb different types of light.

Psychokinesis / Telekinesis – The ability to mentally move objects.

Pyrokinesis – The ability to create, manipulate and/or extinguish fire.

A Note From Jan

Thank you reading the second book in the World Paranormal Organization series, "A Prophecy Revealed" and exploring the life of Clarima Syd Jones. I appreciate you!

The third book in A World Paranormal Organization series will dive into another World Paranormal Organization certified energy practitioner; an animal communicator.

About the Author

Jan Toomer resides with her husband in the desert Southwest in the United States. Jan is a writer and author; a Metaphysical, Spiritual and Paranormal Consultant; Reiki Master; creator of New Dimension Energy Session; as well as Founder and Owner of Reality Undefined LLC.

Born a multi-talented sensitive, Jan has literally been doing energy work for most of her life. Some of her abilities are energy healing, medium and channeler, animal communicator, energy reader and interpreter.

She also studied Metaphysics, Ho'oponopono and the Akashic Records.

She aids others to see a different perspective to help expand their awareness and consciousness; to bring reality-creating consciously into their lives.

Jan writes and shares a few articles a week, since 2008, on Metaphysical, Spiritual and Paranormal topics for her blog Reality Undefined at https://www.metaphysical-studies.com/ and also does videos on Tiktok (@jantoomer) and YouTube (@jantoomer3828) as well.

Acknowledgements

I appreciate you, the reader, for diving into *Prophecy Revealed*. There wouldn't have been more without you!

A big thank you to fellow author, Mary Smith, for her support, and for wanting more with a twist. It was a blast!

And for Ana Quezada for supporting me through Clari's journey of self-growth; and Kendall Love for her continued support.

My Hubby for his patience and support for my need to write and encouragement for me to continue.

And for my tribe for hanging in there with me, thank you for believing in me.

And my Grams; I miss you so much.

Cursed Dagger and Dragon: Clarima Syd Jones

This is the first book in the World Paranormal Organization series.

Clarima "Clari" Jones, ranked a Level IV Energy Reader with the World Paranormal Organization, is a paranormal consultant uses her abilities not only in her private practice, but also to aid the local PD's cold cases with Detective Morris.

The realm of other dimensions is physically introduced to Clari and Det. Morris, and they find themselves in a small war where Clari calls on the aid of the dragons and Other Beings.

But lately things have gotten a little personal. Someone tried to kill Clari and almost succeeded. Clari finds out the Grigori are also after her, and she has no idea why any of this is happening, but with the help of her friends, she's determined to find out.

Prophecy Revealed: Clarima Syd Jones

This is the second book in the World Paranormal Organization series.

The story continues with Morris recovering in the hospital while an investigation is ongoing to determine Clari's part in the death of a Grigori.

Since Clari neglected to tell the World Paranormal Organization about her other abilities, the WPO suspended Clari's certification until she retested with them. When the testing concluded, Clari began training to control her other abilities. One of the training sessions was for her to learn how to control her dragon aspect; but this led to Clari inciting a revolution in the Dragon Realm.

With Detective Morris released from the hospital, Clari digs deeper into why the Grigori want her dead. Clari is informed about the Avatar Prophecy, and her friends think the prophecy is talking about her.

Ghosts from the 1940's ask Clari for help in crossing over; they are trapped. She and Morris begin looking into each individual ghost's story to see what the commonality is and how to help them.

After yet another attempt on her life, Clari discovers that not only are the Grigori connections close to home, but also that the Grigori are more widespread than anyone thought.

Can she put all the pieces together and expose the Grigori before another attempt on her life; an attempt that may succeed this time?

The third book in this series, focusing on Raven Danvers, coming soon.

Re-Writing My Future: A Stroke in Time

Jan's memoir shares her journey from growing up with active abilities while wanting her abilities removed so she could be deemed "normal".

Then, as she developed a tenuous relationship with her abilities, she had a stroke in her 30's and lost touch with her abilities. She struggled to not only find her new "norm", but to get her abilities back while she explores the question, "Who am I now?"

Jan shares her experiences and offer some insights from her own journey in hopes that her story may they help you through yours. This book for stroke survivors, caretakers of survivors, those interested in the paranormal, spiritual and metaphysical, as well as anyone who has or is facing major changes in their life.